"What if I roughed up my image a little?

"Mixed with some cowhands, cowgirls? Learned some of their everyday tasks? Did some chores?"

"Sophie, that's not a good idea."

Sophie jabbed a finger at Gabe's chest. "Put your money where your mouth is, mister. What's wrong with Sweetheart Ranch?" Which, of course, would mean being near Gabe. She hadn't considered that. She'd already made the suggestion, though, and couldn't, or wouldn't, take it back.

His gaze had shuttered. "Doing what there?"

Sophie shrugged. "What I said. I don't know. Cleaning stalls—"

"Mucking." His mouth looked tight.

"Word gets around. Everyone in town would hear about a different side of me, the local side."

And since he'd be there, too, Sophie would have an up close view of Gabe. She didn't need to act on her secret attraction to him, but why not indulge her hopeless fantasy while she worked?

That sounded safe enough. It wasn't as if she'd ever need to trust him with her heart...

Dear Reader,

I grew up in an Ohio town a bit larger than the fictional setting for my Kansas Cowboys series. Like the residents of Barren, Kansas, my real family was very close-knit. My brother and I and all our cousins knew to stay on the right path. If we didn't, word would surely get back to someone and we'd hear about it. Just like people in Barren do.

During high school, I worked as a page at the local library, an iconic redbrick Carnegie building. In the children's department, I checked out books and "read" shelves, keeping fiction titles in alphabetical order and nonfiction titles lined up according to the Dewey decimal system. To this day I can't help myself—I straighten the books in any library. So it seemed natural to make my newest heroine a librarian. Sophie Crane has had her share of romantic troubles, but she's most at home among the books in her hometown.

Gabe Morgan, not so much. He's my Runaway Rancher. But we do have our similarities. I spent my teenage summers not on a ranch but a small farm, an idyllic place where I helped tend the livestock— pigs, chickens (don't ask me to fetch another egg from an occupied nest!), cows (I once saw a calf born)—and rode horses. I may be an amateur "rancher," but my Gabe's a real cowboy who has a mysterious past that needs to be looked into.

I hope you enjoy Gabe and Sophie as much as I enjoyed writing about them.

Happy reading!

Leigh

HEARTWARMING

The Runaway Rancher

—

Leigh Riker

HARLEQUIN®
HEARTWARMING™

ISBN-13: 978-1-335-42681-9

The Runaway Rancher

Copyright © 2022 by Leigh Riker

For questions and comments about the quality of this book,
please contact us at CustomerService@Harlequin.com.

Harlequin Enterprises ULC
22 Adelaide St. West, 41st Floor
Toronto, Ontario M5H 4E3, Canada
www.Harlequin.com

Printed in U.S.A.

Leigh Riker, like so many dedicated readers, grew up with her nose in a book, and weekly trips to the local library for a new stack of stories were a favorite thing to do. This award-winning *USA TODAY* bestselling author still can't imagine a better way to spend her time than to curl up with a good romance novel—unless it is to write one! She is a member of the Authors Guild, Novelists, Inc. and Romance Writers of America. When not at the computer, she's out on the patio tending flowers, watching hummingbirds, spending time with family and friends, or, perhaps, traveling (for research purposes, of course). She loves to hear from readers. You can find Leigh on her website, leighriker.com, on Facebook at leighrikerauthor and on Twitter, @lbrwriter.

Books by Leigh Riker

Harlequin Heartwarming

Kansas Cowboys

The Reluctant Rancher
Last Chance Cowboy
Cowboy on Call
Her Cowboy Sheriff
The Rancher's Second Chance
Twins Under the Tree
The Cowboy's Secret Baby
Mistletoe Cowboy
A Cowboy's Homecoming

Visit the Author Profile page
at Harlequin.com for more titles.

To Lauri Hensley

My dear friend—who reads even more than I do

CHAPTER ONE

THE BARREN LIBRARY was hopping, and Sophie Crane had a headache. In the far corner of the large, high-ceilinged main room, one of the after-school pages was reading a book to a group of five-year-olds at Story Time, half of whom were talking and giggling among themselves. One boy poked another, then jumped up to run around the room, his arms flapping like a bird. The kids' parents sat at nearby tables, perusing cell phones, iPads or clicking away on laptop computers. All typical activities Sophie, as head librarian, might observe any day.

All she needed to do was get through the rest of the afternoon and then go home, take a Tylenol, and rest until supper with a cold cloth on her forehead, but that wasn't to be.

The main doors opened and a woman in a stylish dress stepped inside. Sophie nearly groaned aloud. Claudia Monroe could only mean trouble. She spied Sophie immediately. "That is a stunning suit," she said, her brown gaze sweeping Sophie from her throbbing head, along her charcoal gray pin-striped jacket and skirt, to the peep toes of her navy patent leather heels. "And those shoes must have cost a fortune. You are the only person in this town who dresses well."

From experience, Sophie knew the compliment had sharp teeth. "Except you, Claudia."

"I told Bernice the other day—"

Sophie stopped listening. Her temple pulsed with pain. Claudia and her friend Bernice Caldwell were the biggest gossips in town, and what one didn't know about Barren, Kansas, the other did. Not long ago, in fact, Claudia had made her own daughter's life miserable, publicly taking the side of Lizzie's now ex-husband who'd cheated on her, shaming Lizzie in front of the whole town. She was sure Claudia's assessment, her seeming approval of Sophie now, hid another agenda. Claudia deposited a Martha Stewart volume on home entertaining on the front desk, then patted her brown hair, which had gold highlights. "There are those in town, of course, who wouldn't agree with me. Your predecessor, Miss Bramley, was, shall we say, not as beautifully turned out, but she looked the part of a head librarian." Claudia sniffed. "Some say you won't stay long in this job, that you'll soon get a better offer again—that you're not one of us anymore." She paused. "Silly, I know, I'm not one of them—"

Meaning she was.

"Claudia, I'm home to stay."

"Well, there is our upcoming sesquicentennial celebration to consider. Your involvement could go a long way to help how people see you, to reestablish your local reputation, your credibility."

"I'll keep that in mind." Sophie's headache worsened. This wasn't the first time she'd heard similar comments. Never mind that she'd been born in Barren, spent most of her life here. Her absence for a few years to work at Wichita's university library, another in Oklahoma, and finally Kansas City until she'd come home again last year, brokenhearted, had altered the locals' opinion of her. Just because she dressed up for work, which helped her professional image, didn't mean she wasn't still a small-town girl at heart. Instead, many now viewed her as "big-city." "In the meantime, I see nothing wrong," she said, "in maintaining a few standards."

Claudia's smile didn't reach her eyes. "Far be it from me to criticize anyone for having high standards when so few these days seem to care."

Sophie thanked her for what seemed to be an insincere compliment before Claudia turned and headed for the doors again, having returned her books without choosing to borrow new ones. At the desk Sophie's assistant, Rachel Whittaker, raised an eyebrow at the woman's retreating back.

Feeling a bit deflated, Sophie surveyed her domain again. Despite people like Claudia, she loved her hometown, which this summer would indeed celebrate its one-hundred-fiftieth year of existence—talk about having roots! And already much excitement about the various events was in the air. But *how* could Sophie ever feel accepted once more?

She was pondering how to change people's minds about her when Gabe Morgan swept through the doors, and her heart skipped a beat. My, the library really was Barren central today. Tall and lean, handsome as the day is long, Gabe had dark brown hair of the richest shade, like mink, and brown eyes with glints of amber.

"Hey," he said. "Glad you're still here."

"I'm always here until five o'clock. Except on Saturday when we close at noon. Although

I usually stay later," she rushed on, "to tidy up and shelve books. People always leave them lying out everywhere. I don't really mind," she babbled. "I know better where things go—"

"I'm sure you do." Gabe was grinning, which only added to his usual magnificence. Sophie had had a hopeless crush on him since the day her brother—she prayed Max didn't know about her feelings for Gabe—had first brought him home. "Soph," he said now, using his customary nickname for her. "I already know you're Barren's most solid citizen. A pillar of the community in Stewart County, a paragon of virtue." He paused before adding, "And one mighty fine librarian."

"Are you making fun of me?" She was never sure about Gabe's dry humor, and Claudia's remarks were still fresh in her mind.

"Wouldn't think of it."

Sophie wasn't convinced. She'd misread people in the past and was now slow to trust. She also envied—not an appealing trait—Gabe, who was more laid-back, while she tended to take life too seriously. And yet, there was something else, something deeper, about him and even mysterious that made her want to tell him everything would be all right, when she was no longer sure about that herself.

"I didn't expect to see you here today," she said. "May I help you with something?"

"I'm running an errand for Kate." His boss, a widow and single mom, owned Sweetheart Ranch where Gabe was foreman. "She says you're holding some books for Teddie." Kate's little boy was literally a genius. He certainly kept Sophie on her toes.

"Oh. Yes—right over here." She practically dove back behind the front desk. On a shelf under the counter, she'd stashed several books about mineralogy, Teddie's latest interest. Sophie had selected this week's pile, most of them from the adult section, with great care. She set them on the counter. "These are the best we have on the subject. If Kate wishes, I can order others from the branch in Farrier."

"I'll tell her. Thanks." As easily as if the heavy books were feathers, Gabe scooped them up in his strong arms. "See you tomorrow, Soph."

"Tomorrow?"

His gaze faltered. "Didn't Max tell you? He invited me to dinner, but if that's not convenient—"

"Of course it is." No, her brother hadn't mentioned that. As busy as he was with his veterinary practice, Max often neglected to clue her in. He could be frustratingly dense, and even as a boy his head had often been in some cloud. "You're always welcome."

"But I know Max takes you for granted."

Sophie sighed. "He doesn't mean to. He's just preoccupied at times."

"That's an understatement." Gabe was frowning. "You want me to talk to him?"

"That's not necessary."

"You're sure? I mean, there's no guarantee Max will remember asking. He's as likely to spend the night in some barn delivering a foal—"

"Please. Come to dinner." But there it was again, that little chink in Gabe's armor, because that was what it was. Some tiny break in his easygoing facade, as if he didn't expect to be welcome anywhere. Sophie certainly knew that feeling. Having felt the same way moments ago with Claudia, she wondered why Gabe did, too, which made her sad. Maybe no one else saw it, but Sophie did.

"See you, then," he said. "And take care of that headache."

How had he known about that? Rubbing her temples, she watched him stride across the tile floor to the main doors where he raised a tanned index finger in salute, then clambered down the steps outside.

Sophie couldn't look away. The very sight of him always touched her foolish heart.

SOMETIMES GABE PRETENDED Sweetheart Ranch was his, although he was only Kate Lancaster's foreman, temporarily at that. But his daydream was a pretty one, had been for the year-plus he'd worked here and, as he surveyed the pancake-flat acreage, one foot propped on the bottom rail of the paddock fence, this sweet late afternoon in May stirred his very soul. The perfect hiding place.

Kate and her son, Teddie, had become a sur-rogate family of sorts, yet like a reminder that Gabe didn't really belong here, Noah Bodine, her new fiancé, came around the corner of the barn. Tall and solid, with dark blond hair, the part-time rancher, part-time CEO of a grow-ing cybersecurity firm, looked right at home on the ranch. Besides helping Kate when he was needed, Noah owned a large stake in his family's huge, adjoining WB Ranch.

Noah's happiness lit his hazel eyes. That had become his normal expression since he and Kate had gotten engaged. "Big news around town," he began.

"I heard all about the sesquicentennial earlier today." People hadn't talked about anything else. Well, except for Sophie Crane at the library. She'd seemed more intent on chattering about her job, which charmed Gabe and made him smile to himself. He had a soft spot in his heart for Sophie, and he'd still been distracted, thinking of her on his way back to the ranch.

His mind drifted again. He liked Sophie. He liked her clear blue eyes and the way she piled all that pale, silky hair into a loose bun on her head most days, liked her obvious competence and pride in her job, not to mention her straightforward approach to life while he tried to stay in the shadows. Yet Gabe saw much more in her. If he could stay here, if she wasn't the sister of his best friend, he might…

Noah waved a hand in front of Gabe's face. "Anybody home in there? I just talked to Finn Donovan." Finn was the new mayor of Barren, having exchanged his sheriff's cruiser for a town-issued gray sedan. "The council is over-the-top about this celebration—planning a parade, bringing in a carnival with midway games, holding the usual chili cook-off…even a closing-night banquet. With fireworks afterward."

Gabe didn't particularly like large social

events or the attention they included. He wasn't one for chitchat or, especially, probing questions. At such times he walked a tightrope of sorts between wanting to be part of things while he was here and keeping a low profile so as to not have the truth exposed.

Noah said, "If you don't want to get involved, keep your head down. Kate and her friends are collaring people to help."

Gabe gave Noah a vague answer. "I'll help wherever I can."

Noah clapped him on the shoulder. "Then you're on my list, too, buddy."

Noah had started for the house and was halfway across the yard when Kate, her dark hair swinging, came out of the barn. "Thanks for getting Teddie's books, Gabe. He's already read two of them."

"It was no trouble. You're welcome."

Gabe liked Teddie, too. Behind his black-framed glasses, her little boy's brain chewed up information as if it were popcorn. At four, he'd recently been enrolled in a gifted school program to better challenge his uber-bright mind, and he knew Sophie was having a hard time supplying the kid with books on every subject under the sun.

But Gabe sensed it wasn't her son Kate wanted to talk about, which put him on alert.

"I've just looked at Critter," she began.

"Yeah, I think we'll need to call the vet." Gabe's roan gelding had gone lame, and he'd doctored him long enough to know he couldn't handle the problem himself. "Might ask Max about the colt, too."

Kate's smile switched off like a light bulb. "What's wrong with him?"

"Not a thing," he quickly assured her, taking his foot off the fence rail. The premature foal had given them all some bad moments last winter, but the infection that could have killed him was gone now and he was thriving. "He's growing like a bean stalk, but he's developed a nasty tendency to kick."

"I noticed that, too." She frowned. "Do you think this is a bad sign about his nature?"

"Just feeling his oats, probably." Gabe dug the toe of his boot into the dirt. "Can't hurt to get Max's opinion."

Kate, small and fine-boned, studied him for a moment. "Oh, while you were in town, you had a phone call here at the barn," she said. So, was that what she really wanted to talk about?

He swallowed. It shouldn't surprise him that his dad had resorted to calling the barn's landline. His father had left several messages on Gabe's cell that he had yet to return, mostly because he was stalling. "I'll take care of it." Just not right now.

"You know," Kate said idly, her gray gaze sharp, "when my aunt was living here—well, she's actually my cousin, though I've always called her aunt since we were kids—she conned me into answering whenever her ex-husband phoned. Why do I get the impression you're avoiding someone, too?"

"Not avoiding. I was in Barren when my dad called, getting those books for Teddie, picking up supplies at the ag store and Earl's Hardware. Before that, I ate lunch at the café."

"Not a man," Kate said. "It was a woman."

Gabe groaned inwardly. He should have guessed the real caller instead. Now Kate looked more suspicious.

"I didn't ask for an alibi—" she half smiled "—or a complete rundown, but I have to wonder. You never talk about yourself, Gabe. We all know you're from Texas—"

"Odessa," he supplied as if that lie, close enough to the truth, would settle the matter.

"But that's all we know. And that your father is in the oil business?"

"Yeah, kind of." Gabe didn't like to lie

any more than he already had, so he merely shrugged.

Kate tilted her head. "If there's something bothering you, I'm happy to listen."

"Nah," he said, "thanks but I'm good." Gabe forced a grin. "Except, of course, that I'm still smarting over that same cousin's rejection, not that she ever gave me any encouragement."

Gabe didn't do unrequited love well—or, in that case, brief attraction—but he'd bounced back from rejection almost as soon as Meg, Kate's said aunt/cousin, who wasn't much older than Kate, had disappeared down the drive with her ex. Gabe didn't know any other woman who'd married the same man twice. He silently apologized for using her to change the subject.

Kate was frowning a bit. "You sure you're okay?"

"More than," he said. "Just real busy. This has been the spring to top all springs, you ask me." As if he'd always been here, always would be. "I'd better get back to work."

But he didn't belong, Gabe reminded himself. If he sometimes wished that Sweetheart Ranch was his, or one like it, he also yearned for the kind of family he'd never known, a woman of his own to love as Noah did Kate.

After she left to have lunch at the house with Noah and Teddie, Gabe drifted back into the barn. For now, he'd made a new life for himself.

He would stay on Sweetheart Ranch as long as he could. If someone learned his secret, it would no longer be his home.

CHAPTER TWO

STILL FIGHTING HER HEADACHE, Sophie dropped her bag on the hallway table next to the day's mail, then called out. "Max? You home?"

There was no answer. Her brother had probably been called to see a patient in some local barn. He often worked long hours—unlike Sophie's nine-to-five schedule at the library—even in the middle of the night. A vet's work, he said, was never done. She didn't think Gabe had been quite fair about his taking her for granted.

Sophie worried about Max. He didn't eat well, too often resorting to fast food on the run, and, although he must be one of Barren's most eligible bachelors, he was already thirty-four with no wife and children to balance his life. But then, Sophie was in the same position. Living with your brother when you were thirty years old didn't seem like a mark of achievement, either, especially when she'd once lived on her own. She didn't regret sharing their family's frame house on Cattle Track Lane, yet...

Sophie wouldn't think of Gabe Morgan, whom she'd seen earlier at the library.

On the refrigerator door, under a magnet in the shape of a Hereford cow, she found a note from Max scrawled on a scrap of paper.

Won't be home for dinner. Strangulating lipoma in old horse. Emergency surgery.

Well. Poor thing. She felt sorry for his patient, but that problem was only one of many her brother dealt with every day of the year. Unlike Sophie, Max had never left town to "find himself," as he'd termed her foray into the outer world, which, to put it mildly, had backfired on her.

She was rummaging in the fridge for something to cook for dinner when her phone rang. "Have you read today's mail?" her friend Kate asked.

"Why? I glanced at it on my way in—the usual bills, a few home-improvement flyers, maybe what appears to be an invitation, but..."

"Look again."

"How would you know what's in my mail?"

"I talked to Annabelle Donovan this afternoon. She tells me you should expect a letter from Finn—the mayor's office." Annabelle, another friend, was married to the ex-sheriff.

Sophie's next thought was *What have I done*? A traffic or parking ticket she'd neglected to pay? But she often walked to work, counting steps on her fitness tracker, talking to people she knew along the way. Saving gas, which meant fewer trips to the local Brynne Energy station. "I can't imagine why," she began, then, "Oh. That must be about the sesquicentennial."

Every committee was looking for volunteers. Sophie kept sticking up her hand, in part to make people see that she meant to stay and be part of this town again, but perhaps she could handle one more commitment.

"Yes," Kate agreed, sounding more excited than another volunteer request should warrant.

"Hold on, I'll go check." Sophie drifted back into the front hall. She riffled through the stack of mail, discarding most of it, the pieces plopping into the wicker wastebasket under the entry table. "Here it is," she said, slitting open the envelope from Finn's office. The letter inside made her jaw drop.

"Told you," Kate crowed, obviously having heard her gasp.

"You know what it says?"

"Annabelle showed me. Finn wanted to be

sure of his wording, so she did a bit of editing before the letters went out. I wanted to be the first to congratulate you. The mayoral committee notified all the candidates today. Annabelle hand-delivered them, that one right to your box."

"Tampering with US mail," Sophie murmured, "is a federal crime," but her pulse was thumping, and she couldn't seem to make sense of the words in front of her. She reread the letter.

"Well? What do you think?" Kate asked. "Big news, huh?"

"Obviously, there's been some mistake. This can't be true."

"This isn't one person, Sophie. The nominating committee is a representation of the whole town."

"But one person would have had to give my name before the others voted on the slate of nominees, right? Who could that be?" Sophie wasn't exactly winning any popularity contest in this town.

"Maybe there are more people in your corner than you believe."

Remembering Claudia Monroe, Sophie doubted that. She read the letter a third time, aloud now so Kate could hear—as if Sophie needed a witness to confirm what it said.

She could barely take in what this meant.

Yet there it was in plain English. Sophie stared at the words that could truly make her a favorite daughter of Barren again, not simply the librarian of the town—a *former* resident who'd sought her future elsewhere. And failed, at least in matters of the heart. Her confidence had been badly shaken by twin betrayals, and she'd come home feeling humiliated. But she remembered what Gabe had said. *Pillar of the community.* Then she laughed a little as a first bit of joy streaked through her. Huge news, all right.

"Kate, I'm a candidate for Barren's Citizen of the Year!"

AT THE BUNKHOUSE Gabe prepared his dinner. Sometimes he ate with Kate's family, but not often. He doubted Noah, who had recently moved into the house after his engagement to Kate was announced, wanted Gabe there. Like a fifth wheel. Not that he'd said as much.

And about today at the library, and Sophie… If he wasn't…hiding out here until the heat was off in Midland—not Odessa, as he'd told Kate and other people—he'd be interested in her for sure when, for the past few years, he'd avoided most women. His hands-off attitude with Sophie wasn't only because he and Max were friends or because Gabe wouldn't stay forever.

He was moving a pair of burgers onto a plate when his cell rang.

He glanced at the name on the display and thought of not answering, but she'd only call again as she had earlier. "Hey," he said, juggling his plate and the phone. "I'm about to eat. What's on your mind?"

The familiar female voice could scold like nobody's business. "Gabriel Morgan Wyatt. If you were here—which of course you aren't—I'd send you to your room."

Gabe grinned. "Sorry, didn't mean to sound rude. Hi, Jilly." Then he tensed. She'd used his real last name. "How are things in Midland?"

"Your father hasn't heard from you in weeks. That's how they are."

He flinched. Leave it to her to come straight to the point. He could almost see her face pinched in disapproval, her hair, brown sprinkled with silver, mussed from running her hands through it. "I know. I mean to call but something always intervenes."

"Then don't let me keep you now."

"Hey," he said again, noting her frosty tone

and fearing she'd hang up, "I always like to hear from you." She'd been one of the most influential people in his life.

"More to the point, *he* would like to hear from you."

Gabe wondered about that, but the woman who had mostly raised him knew how to make him feel guilty. A look, a word, reduced him to the little boy he'd once been. For an instant he could envision the house where he'd grown up, feel the somber and lonely atmosphere pervading the cavernous space that should have been a happy home.

Sometimes he wondered if he'd grown up or if, inside, he was still that small boy, yearning for some scrap of attention from his hardworking dad who'd been so often absent that Gabe rarely saw him. His beautiful, elegant mother had seemed gradually to go missing, too, until she wasn't there at all. Now Jilly, his childhood nanny, his adult friend, who'd cared for Gabe after his mom died, had taken him to task again.

"I'll call," he said. "I promise." Just not right now.

He should have known that wouldn't satisfy Jilly.

Gabe pushed his plate away. He and his dad

might not be best buddies, and they disagreed about Gabe living in Kansas instead of Texas. He didn't want to feel even more guilty for leaving his father in the lurch than he already did, even when that had been for his dad's ultimate protection. Why couldn't he and Jilly see that?

Years ago, during one of the many booms in West Texas, Gabe's father had taken a huge risk, bet everything he had on finding oil on his share of the vast, rich Permian Basin—and struck black gold. Over time, he'd built Brynne Energy, his fledgling business, into a megacorporation with branches all over the world. He'd been on top of the heap until one dark night eighteen months ago, when something had gone very wrong. And Gabe knew what that was.

"There's a new Senate investigation," Jilly informed him, the words dropping like stones. He could hear the sour note in her voice. "You'd think there'd never been an oil spill in the Gulf before. That's terrible, I know, and I'm horrified, concerned about the damage done and lives lost, but ever since this started they haven't stopped looking for more dirt. He was in Washington all week."

"The BP spill took tons of time to resolve,"

Gabe pointed out. "More than sixty thousand barrels a day were leaking into the sea back then. This spill has been close to that."

Unfortunately, the comparisons, in part deserved, were being made now with Brynne Energy, and Gabe had stopped watching TV to avoid the nightly anchors spewing vitriol about his dad's apparent mismanagement as CEO, his alleged indifference to the workers on the rigs who'd died or been injured because of him. That wasn't true, yet there seemed no way to refute the narrative unless this investigation turned up evidence to exonerate him and the company, which wasn't likely to happen. Gabe's involvement could only make things worse.

Jilly sighed. "I'm not making excuses for Brynne. I once worked there, remember, in a high-level job. Mistakes were made—you didn't hear that from me, Gabe."

"What would you have me do?" No, scratch that, but he'd spoken too quickly.

"I'd have you get on a plane—come home. Or would you rather keep pretending you're a cowboy? I'm sure that's safer."

"I am a cowboy." And he also felt like a heel. But if he went back…

"Gabriel, you're not some drifter who wound

up as foreman on that woman's ranch. You could buy and sell that spread a thousand times over. You could own that whole town. Instead, you're mucking stalls, chasing cows and living in a bunkhouse. Don't think I don't know why."

"Stop right there," he said. "I'm not a kid now and what I choose to do—where I live and how I work—shouldn't concern you." Ouch, that had sounded harsh.

"It wouldn't," she said, "if I didn't love you."

"Aw, Jilly. I didn't mean that, either. Don't you think I'd be there if I could?"

"Your support—standing beside him through this—would mean even more to him than your staying to take over the reins when he retires. Which you should also be doing."

Another sore point between them. "The reason I left was to keep my father from possibly ending up in federal prison. I *know* things, Jilly. I know who the guilty parties are. I left—granted, against his wishes—to prevent another disaster. I appreciate the heads-up," he said, "but I'm staying where I am. I won't be the one to ruin him and a lot of other people. Let me know when the investigation ends."

"I'm sure you'll see that on TV." She hesitated. "And he'll be standing there alone."

No, he wouldn't, except in the emotional sense, which triggered another spasm of guilt. His father had a battery of high-powered, high-priced lawyers—one of whom had suggested *sotto voce* to Gabe eighteen months ago that he might want to take an extended vacation to avoid being interrogated by one of those committees. And he wasn't the only one, which Gabe wouldn't mention to Jilly. So far, his friend Aaron had remained silent. If he ever stepped forward, he could put Gabe in the crosshairs, too.

"Enough about Brynne, Jilly. How are you doing?" he asked, hoping to salvage the conversation. "Maybe you should take a plane instead. Come visit. I'd love to see you."

"I'm fine—as you said, yourself—right where I am." She still lived in the mansion in her own suite of rooms. Jilly took care of his father now and Gabe knew she genuinely worried about him. So did Gabe, even though they weren't close. Yet the best thing was for him to keep hiding. And hope Aaron kept quiet, too. Or the huge potential fines, the crushing cost of cleanup over time, the environmental carnage that never should have happened wouldn't be the only fallout. Along with the company, his father could be destroyed.

"Keep me posted, okay? Jilly, I—"

"Go eat your dinner," she said, then ended the call.

Gabe's burgers were cold. He slapped them back in the frying pan, ramped up the gas on the burner and stood there watching them sizzle.

Not even the thought of Sophie Crane could make him smile now.

Instead, he kept hearing Jilly's words.

Don't think I don't know why.

But Gabe didn't intend to be the whistleblower on his own father.

CHAPTER THREE

SOPHIE DIDN'T YET know quite what to make of the letter from Finn's office. Still, it was not only an honor to even be nominated; the award could be her means to regain acceptance in Barren. Citizen of the Year!

The next night, expecting Gabe to arrive any minute, she fussed over dinner. Max's casual invitation to Gabe hadn't included supplying the meal himself. This happened several times a month, which meant she'd had to cook tonight. Sophie loved her brother but, ever immersed in his vet practice, he tended to overlook the rest of his life, leaving any details to Sophie.

Sometimes she wondered how he'd managed when she was in Kansas City.

As usual, he was "running late."

She blew a wisp of hair off her face and checked the one-pot Southwestern-style casserole that had been simmering in the Crock-Pot all day. At work she'd been too busy to think about it. The new library budget numbers were due soon, and she'd had to juggle those depressing figures while, with her assistant taking a personal day, she tended to the front desk and tried to keep up with the many demands for research assistance from a class of seventh graders doing a project. All this while she tried to take in what her shocking nomination for the award meant. There would be campaigning next, of course, which she didn't look forward to, then a vote by all the citizens of Barren.

The front bell rang, two quick bursts of sound, short-circuiting her thoughts before Gabe walked in. Hearing his footsteps in the hall, Sophie felt her heart again pick up speed. He followed his nose into the kitchen, sniffing at the rich aromas. "Smells good in here, Soph."

"We aim to please." Which had sounded less than welcoming.

Gabe's expression fell. "Is this a bad night?"

"I told you. There's never a bad night to feed you. Dinner's almost done. Grab a beer from the fridge and, if you would, open that bottle of wine from the top shelf."

If they both kept moving, maybe Sophie wouldn't feel tempted to stare at him. Gabe had dressed for the occasion in the cowboy's version of formal wear—crisply creased dark jeans and a snow-white shirt. It was obvious he'd polished his boots. More often, he and Max slouched in the living room in grungy work clothes, feet up on the living room coffee table, to munch on pork rinds and watch sports.

Gabe opened the middle drawer in the kitchen island and rummaged around for the corkscrew. "Got it." Deftly, he pulled the cork, then poured a glass.

"Set it on the table," she said as he went to hand it to her. "I need to dish up."

"Where's Max?"

"Stuck at the clinic." This had certainly happened before when Gabe ate with them. "He was closing up when Blossom Hunter came in with her daughter. Apparently, their new kitten has an eye infection, which Max is treating. He should be home soon. I hope." No, prayed. Being alone with Gabe rattled her.

"Let's wait for him, then."

She rolled her eyes. "Let's not. I never know when he'll show up to eat. It's as if the word gets out that he's about to close, and everyone in town appears with a multitude of vet issues.

Honestly, at times I'm tempted to study the apartment ads in the *Barren Journal*."

Gabe's face clouded. "You'd move out?"

"No, but I do think about it. Of course, I never follow up."

"You did once," he pointed out.

Yes, and she was still picking up the pieces of her shattered self-esteem. If only in KC she hadn't trusted her boyfriend or her best friend. "And look where I ended up. Right back where I started."

"Is that bad?" Gabe asked.

"No, just…why are we having this conversation? You didn't stay in Texas."

"True," was all he said. Gabe never revealed much about his background. Maybe he was ashamed of where he'd come from, so Sophie didn't press him, even when she wanted to.

He took a sip of his beer. "But if you really want a different life—"

"I don't." She wanted to be right here, but to belong, without the prospect of another heartache. Her job, her shared home with Max, and feeling accepted again, would be enough. "Barren, the people here, are important to me. They always have been. Just because I spread my wings for a while elsewhere doesn't mean I'm not one of them still. I came back, didn't I?"

"And yet—I'm guessing—you feel a bit… disconnected, even lonely."

"You sound as if you know about that, too."

But Gabe didn't answer.

"Or maybe it's just me," she said.

"Sophie, I do understand. And Max has mentioned your ex-boyfriend to me."

"Ew." Apparently, her brother had told him at least part of her sad story. If he hadn't, someone else in town would have. She picked at a piece of nonexistent lint on her sweater. She'd changed after work and hitched her hair into a ponytail. She didn't want Gabe to think she'd dressed up for him. "I mean, how many girls get a selfie from Las Vegas starring their BFF and their own boyfriend? He and I had even started talking about buying a place." She'd thought Will had been as serious about their relationship as she was.

Gabe stared. "They ran off together?"

"Eloped to Vegas. The picture was taken in one of those wedding chapels."

"You didn't suspect anything was going on beforehand?"

"No, I thought he was about to propose to *me*. How could I have been such a fool?"

"I think he was the fool."

"In my mind I was already planning our

summer wedding, and don't you dare feel sorry for me now." Sophie recognized the expression on his face. "I'm here again, and I'm staying even if some people in Barren doubt that."

Gabe studied her. "That must have been hard, though, getting blindsided…"

As if he'd had a similar experience. "Funny thing, I actually met Will through Bess. They worked for the same software company. When they left for Nevada, I believed they were attending a conference. Turned out there wasn't one."

"Kind of blew your trust, huh? I can see why, after that experience, coming home and being considered part of Barren again is so important to you." He made a sweeping gesture as if toward a dustpan. "Don't give those two another thought. You're a far better person, Soph." He picked at the damp label on his beer bottle. "And I hear you're Barren's new celebrity."

"You mean the award nomination? Me and a number of other people."

"Kate told me."

"I never thought she was one of the town criers, but I can give her a pass. I think she's more excited than I am."

"You'd like to win, though, right?" She tried

a shrug, but Gabe didn't buy that. "Of course, you would. And you should."

"It's no big deal. I have enough to handle. I'm on some of the planning committees for the sesquicentennial—and isn't that a mouthful?—so whatever happens with the award, happens."

"Soph."

"Because, really, how important is that?"

"Pretty important," he drawled, "considering how hard you're trying to convince yourself—and me—that this is 'no big deal.'" Gabe leaned against the kitchen's center island, his boots crossed. "Come on, you want it. You want it bad." As if he also knew that feeling.

Sophie flushed. He'd seen right through her. "So now you're an expert on my innermost wishes?" Gosh, she hoped not. One of them concerned Gabe.

"Seems obvious." He took another swallow of his beer, but he didn't look as relaxed as he must want her to believe. "You deserve recognition in this town for all you do."

"I'm head librarian, yes, but obviously to some I'm also an outsider." Sophie backpedaled, not wanting to confess any further that she didn't feel accepted in Barren as she had once before. "Anyway. I should focus on next year's budget. We need more money for the library, more books, more staff, and rather than an increase, the mayor wants to cut." She peeked again at the casserole. It was beginning to stick to the bottom of the pot. What was keeping Max so long? "I wouldn't call that worthy of acceptance or recognition. It's just my job."

"You do it well along with half a dozen committees, the church auxiliary—"

"I like to contribute," she admitted. "I'm proud or would be…to be part of Barren."

A mental image of Claudia Monroe flashed in her mind as Gabe turned her slightly to frame her face in his hands, the first time in memory that he'd deliberately touched her. The heat in her cheeks flamed hotter. Sophie tried to draw away, but Gabe lightly held on.

"Never mind what people think. Don't underestimate yourself," he said. "Being nominated is huge."

His steady gaze on hers threatened to turn Sophie into a puddle on the tile floor. He couldn't be interested in her—not that way. He was just being…nice to his best friend's kid sister. She would die on the spot if he ever guessed how she felt about him. He was right, though. "In Kansas City I felt sure of myself until Will and Bess shattered that confidence. Now I'm trying to claw my way back."

"That's what it takes."

"Gabe, several of the candidates are people who've won before. So the voters—the community—might not lean toward them, but another man, a prominent attorney who recently won a high-profile case, at least Barren's version, will surely have an edge, and that one other woman on the list has everything going for her. Lauren Anderson's byline appears in the *Barren Journal* every week, showcasing her talents. Talk about good PR. She's bold, a standout."

"Super-aggressive," Gabe agreed. "Most reporters are, but you can beat her, too."

"You really think so?"

"Sure. Hands down."

The first shock of learning about the nomination was slowly wearing off, and Gabe's belief in her seemed contagious. Sophie grinned. "I admit, I went to bed last night smiling to myself."

Gabe was about to answer when they heard Max's truck in the drive.

"Ah. He's finally here." She drew away from Gabe's touch, his penetrating gaze, and turned off the Crock-Pot. But he wasn't finished.

"I can't imagine anyone else winning," she heard him say. "I'll help however I can."

THEY WERE HALFWAY through dinner before Max seemed to notice how quiet Gabe and Sophie were. For Gabe's part, he was pondering her reaction to the nomination, that slow shift from self-doubt to the realization that she could, indeed, win. Also, he couldn't get Jilly's call last night out of his mind. As they ate Sophie's oh-so-excellent casserole, Max talked about the new receptionist he'd hired six months ago and regaled them with a blow-by-blow account of the Hunters' kitten and its eye infection.

"Max, could we hear about something else?" Sophie said, her fork poised in midair.

"Oh. Too graphic? Sorry, I forget I'm not with a bunch of other vets." He helped himself to a second serving of the ground beef, rice, beans, corn and tomato concoction richly blended with cheese. "So. What's new, Gabe?"

"Spring has us going at the ranch. Lots of new calves, crops in, but you're busy, too."

Max raised an eyebrow. "My clinic hours posted on the door are only a suggestion. I'm spending even more time in the field." Without a pause, he added, "I hear Kate and Noah are engaged now."

"You should see those two. Quite the love-birds."

"Big wedding plans?"

"A simple ceremony at Sweetheart, but we'll see. Noah's mother has other ideas, which should come as no surprise."

They both laughed—Jean Bodine, the family matriarch, was a force to be reckoned with—but Sophie's gaze remained on her plate, and Gabe wondered if she was still ruminating about the award. Or was she upset because he'd touched her? She'd looked so vulnerable then, clearly wanting the award yet doubting she could win. Gabe did understand how she felt. He too was an outsider looking in.

Max launched into another saga about a cow that had needed a Cesarean earlier that day. His dark eyes lit up and he seemed oblivious that Sophie had asked him to change the subject. She pushed her plate aside. "Dessert," she announced, springing up from her chair.

After she'd disappeared into the kitchen, Gabe leveled a look at her brother.

"What is wrong with you?"

"Huh?" Max looked blank.

"All that talk about scalpels, stitches…

You're ruining Sophie's dinner, and while we're on this topic, you invited me. She did not. Yet Sophie had to cook after a long day at the library. You're not the only one with a demanding job."

Max blinked. "Sophie doesn't mind cooking. She likes having people over."

"Did she say that? Or do you assume she does?"

Max ran a hand over his dark hair, which had a serious cowlick that made his appearance seem boyish. "Are you calling me a selfish jerk?"

Gabe shook his head. Max was one of the best guys he'd ever known, a good friend, but he had a real blind spot about his sister. "I've watched all this for over a year now. Your sister puts up with your changeable hours, reheats your dinner when you're late, cleans this house, even manages the bills so you don't have to bother." This must be his night for defending Sophie. "Sometimes I think you don't see her. Have you even congratulated her about the award?"

"What award?"

"My point." Gabe shouldn't have said anything, but Max reminded him of his own father, his frequent absences, his preoccupation and seeming indifference to his son. After Gabe's mother died, his dad had become even more distant, leaving Jilly, who'd originally come to take care of his mom during her chronic illness, to raise Gabe. Jilly had given up her lucrative job at Brynne Energy to do so. From the kitchen he heard Sophie banging around, perhaps overhearing them and wishing Gabe would stop. "Citizen of the Year," he said through gritted teeth.

"Citizen of the Year," Max repeated. "Sophie? Huh. How about that. She didn't tell me. I got in late last night, left early this morning. We didn't see each other."

Sophie came through the swinging door from the kitchen, a plate in one hand, a stack of dessert bowls in the other. She appeared carefully unaware of what she'd missed. "Berry pie. There's vanilla ice cream if you want it."

"Pie's plenty," Gabe muttered, taking the dishes from her.

Max might not be the best brother at times, but then Gabe—considering his rocky relationship with his father—wasn't the best son, either.

And in the back of his mind, along with the memory of his latest conversation with Jilly, was another issue. All his life Gabe had wondered if people really liked him for himself or because his dad was filthy rich. Even his former fiancée—the reason Gabe avoided relationships these days—had turned out to be just another gold digger with no interest in creating the loving marriage and family Gabe still wanted. Here in Barren, and on Sweetheart Ranch where no one knew who he really was, or what he was, for a while longer he could be just a cowboy.

He was a good one, as Sophie was a great librarian.

But what if someone learned the truth about him, about his reason for being here?

And the lies he had told?

CHAPTER FOUR

SOPHIE HAD MADE herself a promise. She would never be lied to again.

Two people in her life had already betrayed her. Will and Bess had lulled her into thinking they each cared about her until it became abruptly obvious that they didn't. She hadn't exchanged a word with either of them since she'd left Kansas City. It was a good thing Gabe had no interest in her beyond their casual relationship, mainly because of his and Max's friendship. Despite his unexpected support of her—never mind her inconvenient crush on him—she wouldn't be able to trust Gabe, either. Will had damaged her to the core, and she sometimes had the feeling Gabe was hiding something, too.

So, what had last night been about? That long, penetrating look and his kind words about the award? His fleeting touch? His belief in her?

Sophie marched into the old brick building

on Main Street that housed the *Barren Journal* offices. Lauren Anderson stood at the front desk, riffling through some papers. The reporter's sleek, dark bob swung perfectly at her shoulders. She glanced up, blue eyes as sharp as glass, gave Sophie's suit of the day a quick once-over, then coldly smiled. "Congratulations on your nomination."

"And to you."

Lauren barely paused before saying, "Of course, there's no real competition…" She trailed off as if further explanation wasn't necessary. Had she meant Sophie?

She refused to take offense. "We're not the only nominees," Sophie reminded her. "What about the others?"

"Bob Murphy? He's not even a good lawyer. He probably pleaded that big case, then walked off with a huge fee. We're doing a story on him next week. Murphy doesn't have a chance to win the award."

"Cooper Ransom's also on the list."

Lauren folded her hands on the paper stack. "He's too tied up at the NLS ranch with Nell and their baby to even campaign."

"Campaign?" Sophie hadn't dealt with that aspect yet. She wasn't a fan of public speaking.

"How else can the good citizens of Barren

make a choice?" Lauren sent Sophie another look that said, *Just how dense can you be?* "My position here at the paper gives me an edge. People already know me."

Yes, but what opinion did they have of Lauren? She had confidence, Sophie had to admit, which might normally equal her own, but at the moment Sophie took second place there. "Edge?" she echoed.

Suddenly Lauren grinned. Her gaze had shifted to the door behind Sophie, who didn't need to turn around. She always sensed Gabe before she saw him, as if some disturbance in the air had announced his arrival. He stepped inside, then shut the door. "Lauren," he said with a tip of his Stetson. "Hey, Soph. What brings you here?"

"I'm placing an ad."

Gabe held her gaze. "Looking for an apartment?"

"No," she said, remembering their conversation last night. "For committee volunteers. The town celebration seems to be growing by the day."

"A hundred and fifty years is something to celebrate."

"We have a lot of slots to fill." She rummaged in her bag for the ad she'd written, then slapped the copy on the desk. "Lauren and I were just talking about the award. She seems sure Bob Murphy or anyone else but her won't win."

Lauren waved one well-manicured hand. "Sophie's upset because she knows she's not even in the running. I wonder who put her name in the hopper."

Sophie wondered, too. "Obviously, for now that's privileged information."

Gabe jumped in. "Barren is a small town and I know you're not from here, Lauren—"

"Neither are you," she pointed out.

He leaned against the counter. "So you may not know how things work."

Lauren seemed to realize she wasn't winning any points with Gabe, either. Quickly, she backtracked. "You can tell me later. Actually, I want to ask you something. Alone."

She glanced at Sophie, who pushed the ad copy toward her. "I hope this can run—prominently placed—in the next edition. You can bill me."

Sophie shoved past Gabe and then out the door.

As soon as it closed, it opened again. "Soph."

Her eyes must have been snapping with temper. "I can't abide that woman. Ever since she came to Barren, she's been nothing but trouble." And like Gabe, Lauren Anderson had an aura of mystery about her. What was behind those sharp eyes and that mean smile? Sophie suspected there was some underlying story. "But don't mind me. You should go back inside, see what she wants from you."

"She trashed you before I got here, didn't she?"

"She tried," Sophie muttered.

"Is there any way I can help?"

"You mean like last night? I overheard you talking to Max." She took a breath. None of this was Gabe's fault. She should thank him for riding to her rescue then, not that she couldn't take care of herself, which was as important to Sophie now as it was to not trust the wrong people. "If you really want to help as you said, pick a committee."

"Which one are you on?" Gabe tensed, as if he wished he hadn't spoken so quickly.

Sophie gave him a cheeky smile. "I doubt you'd enjoy the library women's book sale committee."

"I'd be outnumbered."

"Bake sale, then? Chili cook-off?"

Gabe was frowning, probably wishing he hadn't offered to help. He made a clear-as-glass attempt to smooth out his handsome features. "What else have you got?"

"Well, there is my finance committee." She wrinkled her nose. Why was she encouraging him? Did she really want to sit in a room at the community center with Gabe?

He paused again, then said, "Sign me up."

AT THE VET CLINIC Averill McCafferty stared into the medicine cabinet, having forgotten what she was looking for. She'd been working with Maxwell Crane, DVM, for six months, and she had to admire his devotion to his work, which at the same time protected him from a whole bunch of other stuff. Like having a personal life of his own.

Recently, he'd confided in her during an after-hours conversation. "Years ago, like Sophie, I wanted to leave this town, too, but then our parents were killed—"

"Max, I didn't know. How terrible."

He'd let out a shaky breath. "They were hit by an unlicensed driver going down the highway near Farrier in the wrong direction. Sophie was still a kid, sixteen then, and I was commuting to college. I'd wanted to transfer out of state, live on campus, but what choice did I have then but to stay?"

"We always have choices." And Averill had made some bad ones.

"By the time Sophie left home after college, it didn't seem like the right time to relocate. My practice was just getting off the ground here. Then last year, Sophie quit her job in KC and came home, heartbroken. She needed me again."

"Sophie's a grown woman."

"She was in pieces, Averill. I mean, her almost-fiancé and her best friend? Who does that? Send a picture of their cheesy wedding in Vegas? I don't think she'd survive another setback. If anyone ever—*ever*—feels tempted to break her heart again, I won't be responsible for my actions."

"I understand, but how can you prevent that? It's not as if you're even home that much." Averill kept track of his appointments, answered the ever-ringing telephone at the clinic, dealt with the people who rushed in to invade his space at all hours of the day or called him out at night. "Sophie has to heal herself. Get her mojo back. You've already given up another year of your life since that happened." Averill didn't want to think about Max moving somewhere else, though. She liked this job. She liked him. Understatement.

"It's not a sacrifice to be here for my sister," he'd said. "As much as I can."

Averill had half smiled. "You do a good job of appearing not to hover."

He hadn't answered that. Max often seemed oblivious to the world around him, which only endeared him to her.

From the first moment she'd laid eyes on him, and to her own growing frustration now, Averill wanted more from Maxwell Crane than a job. Or the trust in her that had allowed him to confide in her about Sophie. Still, she hadn't come here to fall for someone, a reminder that didn't change anything for Averill. What would she do if he felt the same way? Or if these new, unfamiliar feelings threatened the temporary haven she'd found in Barren? Max deserved someone better than her.

"Averill," he called out now, his voice full of impatience.

"Coming." She set aside the memory of their conversation, stopped daydreaming and shut the glass-fronted door of the medicine cabinet. With the vial she'd been searching for in hand, she strode into the adjoining exam room. "We're low on this but the expiry date is still okay. I'll order more before we run out."

"Thanks." He didn't look at her, just held out

his hand for the medication, then returned his attention to the patient, a gangly Great Dane with a nasty gash on its side that needed stitching.

She lingered for a moment, sending the dog's pet parent a sympathetic look, her heart melting at Max's intense concentration. "Do you need me?" She hoped he did, just as her stomach rumbled. The clinic's vet tech had gone home at five o'clock. It was now seven thirty.

"Nah, you can leave."

"You're sure? I can stay."

"Go." He held a syringe up to the light, tapped it to dispel any air bubbles in the anesthetic, then bent over the table to jab the needle into the injured animal in his care.

Averill admired his loyalty—but that wasn't a life. One day Max might wake up to realize he was ready to retire, as if he ever would be, and that he'd forgotten to marry...and be loved.

Averill had once dreamed of a family and marriage for herself. But until she learned to deal with the guilt of her past, there was no way that would ever happen.

She shouldn't worry about Max. She should try, when that wasn't possible, to fix herself.

CHAPTER FIVE

THE MONDAY NIGHT meeting of the finance committee—Gabe's first—was in session. Sophie, its chairperson, stared down at the papers in front of her on the long table in the community center that was part of the municipal complex, not that Gabe would call Barren a true municipality.

He caught her eye. "What's the word, Soph?"

"Not good, but it's early days yet," she said, glancing up at the other members of the committee, some of whom Gabe didn't know. She'd been avoiding his eyes since their talk on Friday outside the *Barren Journal* office.

Gabe especially liked the town mayor. According to Sophie, Finn Donovan, the ex-sheriff, whose keen hazel eyes studied each member of the committee, had rarely worn a uniform then, preferring to be more approachable. Now, like most other committee members, he was in jeans and a T-shirt. His dark hair was cut in a neat, no-nonsense style that suited his former occupation in law enforcement. He leaned back in his chair. "Once we start fundraising, we should be fine, Sophie. The people of this town will come together."

"Turning into a real politician here, Finn," drawled Hadley Smith, a local rancher with dark hair and deep blue eyes. "That's a nice speech but this isn't a rich town. In spring people are occupied with planting, calving… Their money, if they have any, is tied up. We're short on millionaires."

Gabe squirmed in his seat, tempted to raise his hand, say he'd be glad to write a check for whatever amount they needed. Which, of course, he couldn't do. That would risk exposing his lies.

"Thanks, Hadley. I know that." Finn's voice held sarcasm. "More to the point, we need to nail down some specific ways to get the money we'll require. I talked to the carnival group this morning, and they'll want a deposit up front. Right now, the bank balance on our account is anemic. That right, Sophie?"

"Yes."

"We'll need to hustle."

"Then why are we planning such a huge celebration?" Cooper Ransom, another of the award nominees, said. "You want my opinion, we should scale back."

The woman at the end of the table stiffened. "Exactly which events would you eliminate?"

"Well, for one—do we need the annual chili cook-off?" Cooper paused. "The same guy wins every time." He sent his wife, Nell, seated beside him, a meaningful look.

"Ned Sutherland has the magic recipe," someone else said and people laughed.

Sophie leaned toward Gabe. "Ned is Nell's grandfather. He does make a mean pot of chili."

An older woman with corkscrew curls waved a hand for attention. "We don't need to get rid of the cook-off. We need more competition."

The meeting droned on. Gabe was having trouble paying attention. In Texas, he'd attended his share of such meetings at Brynne during his brief tenure. This seemed to be more productive than the usual corporate slog, but he wished he hadn't been as quick to volunteer, mainly to please Sophie. And frankly, he was more worried about her recent inability to look him in the eye, which made him feel oddly guilty. At the *Barren Journal* office, after Sophie left, Lauren had surprised him too. "Are you free for dinner some night?" she'd asked.

"You mean a date?" Gabe wasn't interested.

"Let's call it a chance to get acquainted instead. We're both strangers here—as you pointed out." She'd sent him a winning smile. "We can share notes about how to cope." He hadn't said no. He'd decided, as a precaution, to find out if Lauren might be looking into his past. If so, he'd put a stop to that.

"Gabe." Sophie was speaking now.

"Sorry, wasn't listening." He blinked. "What did I miss?"

He wasn't the only one whose eyes had glazed over. Gabe had noted the yawns around the table. He straightened in his metal chair. The hard back had been digging into his spine, which should have kept him alert.

Her tone was taut. "I asked if you would be willing to spearhead our first fundraiser?"

"Uh, sure. Why not? As long as I can juggle my work at Sweetheart."

"We decided last meeting on a silent auction," Sophie said, taking in the other members. "Then that's one issue resolved. I think we'll need a door-to-door campaign for donations to the general fund for other events. It will give us a personal link with the community. I'll buttonhole as many as I can at the library."

"I'll coordinate," Nell put in. "I can make a spreadsheet. If everyone involved in the fundraiser keeps me updated as to those people you've seen, the pledges they've made, we won't be approaching anyone twice."

"I'll knock on doors," Gabe said.

After the meeting finally ended, Sophie stayed behind to talk with Finn as the last committee members dispersed. In the hallway, Gabe could hear engines firing up outside, horns tooting, people pulling away from the community center to head home. He waited until she came out of the room.

"Soph, got a minute?"

Her footsteps faltered. "Please don't tell me you're going to resign from the committee. I didn't mean to trap you in there."

"I should have been paying better attention. I don't mind asking people to donate items for the auction." He paused. "I'm concerned about you."

She pushed out the door and started walking toward her car. "Why?"

Gabe fell into step beside her. "Should I have kept quiet with Max? I know you heard us, but

I really don't like the way he treated you that night at dinner."

"Then you don't understand him. It's not that he doesn't care about me. He does, maybe too much at times."

"Or does he care more about his next patient, whether that's at nine in the morning or after midnight?"

"That's his job."

"Yeah, but not his life, a personal one—"

"Well," she said, looking down at her feet. "That's where, I'm sure, you're different."

Uh-oh. He'd been wrong about the reason her eyes evaded his. This wasn't about Max. "Meaning?"

Sophie hesitated. "I hear you're having dinner with Lauren Anderson."

"I would have told you but—" He hadn't seen her again until tonight.

"No need." Her voice brightened. "I shouldn't have mentioned it." She hurried to her car, stuck the key in the lock, opened the door. "*Your* personal life is your personal life. There's no reason you shouldn't have a good time. I only wish Max would."

"Sophie."

"Good night, Gabe."

She slipped into the car, put it in gear and pulled away, leaving him to stare after her.

To wonder.

Why did Sophie care—as she apparently did, despite the disclaimer—about who he saw on his own time?

He wouldn't dare act on his attraction to her.

But Sophie's reaction was something to think about.

WHAT HAD SHE been thinking?

Last night, in a burst of jealousy, Sophie had all but let Gabe know how she felt about him when her secret—her guilty pleasure, really—had to remain hidden. Not only because of Gabe's friendship with Max or his likely temporary status in Barren but because she couldn't risk her heart—or give her trust—again, as if she needed that reminder. Bernice Caldwell had told her right before the committee meeting about Gabe's date with Lauren.

She regretted that she hadn't been quite able to hide her feelings from Gabe. Maybe, focused on his dinner date, he hadn't noticed. Working with him on the finance committee would be hard enough. Then, when no one else volunteered, she'd asked him to head the silent auction but never imagined he would agree to help with donations, too.

This morning she'd been unable to concentrate on the library budget, which Finn expected on his desk later. The library, the celebration. Money problems everywhere. How much more could she pare from the ever-growing expenses here? What was she prepared to sacrifice?

"I've already cut what I can without compromising our operation," she told her assistant, keeping her voice low so other patrons wouldn't overhear.

"What about Story Time?" Rachel Whittaker asked, her gray-green eyes keen. "We already have trouble getting our pages to read to the kids. When they don't, we have to do that."

Briefly, Sophie considered eliminating Story Time or even letting their pages go. Still, they were a big help and were paid a pittance, like interns, to gain experience. That wouldn't save much money. She smoothed a hand over her peacock blue suit with silver buttons. "But people do rely on us to provide that time for their children. One mother tells me every week that we're a lifesaver. Otherwise, she can't get any work done on her laptop here. This is the one break she has in her week."

"I'll read stories if you need me to, but, honestly, Sophie, we shouldn't be the town's babysitting service."

Rachel, a widow in her thirties, already worked more hours than Sophie's current budget could afford, but Sophie sensed that Rachel needed her time here even more than the library needed her.

Sophie studied the latest version of her budget, then sighed. "The only place left to cut then—I'll have to stop ordering so many books." Another taboo pleasure. "We'll have to rely more on Farrier to borrow from their larger, better-funded collection." She thought of Kate's son, whose insatiable curiosity already made her task harder. "Right now, I have another pile of books waiting for Teddie. Half are from their library."

Rachel smiled. "What's this week's passion?"

"Chemistry."

"Farrier is the most practical solution, though."

"I know," Sophie said with a sigh. The main doors opened, and Max's receptionist walked in to plunk her latest borrowed books on the counter. In the past half year, she'd become a regular visitor to the library. "Hey, Averill. How was the Grisham?"

"Excellent, as always. He's one of my go-to authors."

"His next will be out soon. I'll put you on the list."

"Please do, thanks." She nodded at Rachel. "Sorry to interrupt. I can see you're both busy. I'll just browse a bit."

"Take your time."

She watched Averill cross the room but not into the fiction stacks. Sophie turned back to Rachel. "I'm going to disappear for a few minutes, make some adjustment to the budget— again—then send it off to Finn."

"I know how painful this is for you. I'll handle the front desk. We're not that busy this morning."

Sophie walked into her small office and kicked off her gray snakeskin heels, which had begun to pinch. She sat at her desk, head in her hands before she finally straightened to key in a lower number in the budget. Somehow, the library would survive.

But the budget wasn't her only concern this morning.

In the future she vowed to be more careful with Gabe. She wasn't about to make a fool of herself again, this time with him rather than Will.

By the time she emerged from her office, shoulders squared and head high, Sophie had convinced herself that both decisions were right, and necessary.

At the front desk she relieved Rachel who went to shelve the books that had been deposited in their overnight drop. Sophie chatted with Averill while she checked out her books. An older title of Grisham's that she wanted to reread, a couple of cookbooks, and *The Principles of Veterinary Practice*. "Taking your job seriously," Sophie said.

"I need to learn more of the terms."

"What's it like, working for my brother?"

"No complaints."

Sophie laughed. "Wow, you must be a saint."

"Hardly," Averill said, her face averted. She slid the books into a big canvas bag, then hurried toward the main doors.

Rachel wheeled the cart they used to shelve things back to the desk, looking after Averill who quickly disappeared down the outside steps. "Strange," she said.

"Averill? She's an avid reader, my favorite type of person, if not much of a talker."

"No," Rachel replied, "but I watched her. Sophie, she just stole a book."

Sophie couldn't believe that. "You must be seeing things. She borrowed a few novels, a vet overview…"

"Yes, and another from nonfiction, but not from the animal section. And she didn't bother to check that one out."

GABE HAD GIVEN out the daily assignments to the other cowhands at Sweetheart, including Kate's newest hire, a sandy-haired kid named Johnny. Gabe wasn't sure the boy would stick around, and he wasn't that good with horses, but time would tell. Then, hoping to drum up interest in the silent auction, Gabe set out to get donations of items from some area ranchers. His first stop was the WB adjacent to Kate's spread, where he found Zach Bodine, Noah's brother, hosing down a large black horse in the sunlit barnyard. Steam rose off its hide. "Hey, there, Gabe."

"How's it going?"

"Great." He sent Gabe a smile as bright as the sun that glinted off his dark blond hair.

"Marriage agrees with you."

Zach rolled his eyes. "Well, we still have our second, summer wedding to get through." He and Cass had eloped while in the Bahamas last winter, and his mother, the WB's matriarch, hadn't been pleased to miss the event. She'd also balked at their having a home ceremony soon afterward, insisting that with the experience she'd gained planning her daughter's recent wedding, she could handle Cass and Zach's repeat vows but needed more time. "I'm avoiding the house this morning. My mom and Cass are deep into their plans. I'd kill for another cup of coffee, but it's better to keep out of their way. I told them to just let me know if I need to rent a tux and where I should be on the big day."

"Seems the plans have gotten more elaborate." Which would be true twice over since Zach's brother and Kate were getting married, too. Gabe doubted that would happen after all at Sweetheart. The bells were certainly ringing at the WB.

"I don't think a simple wedding is in my mom's DNA. Cass was only too happy to go along."

"I don't know much about weddings." Gabe shifted his weight from one dusty boot to the other. He'd mucked stalls before he left Sweetheart. "But I'm in pretty deep myself with this sesquicentennial thing."

Zach turned off the hose. "My brother already talked to me," he said. "I'm on Noah's rodeo committee. We held one a few summers ago that was successful. You, too?"

"I'll probably enter, but I'm on the finance committee in charge of our first fundraiser. A silent auction. Asking people for goods we can raffle off. You got anything you'd want to contribute?"

Zach drew a scraper along the horse's wet hide, flinging water everywhere. "What sort of stuff?"

"Horse-related items are probably a sure thing for people around Barren, but we'd like variety." He paused. "A group of the women are already making a quilt. Somebody else will give jars of home-canned fruits and vegetables. Sam Hunter has an ancient John Deere he restored, complete with a fresh paint job, and you know how pricey old tractors have become."

"Nobody except the dealers knows how to repair the newer ones with all that fancy tech. When my dad was ranching, he could fix anything. Now that kind of vintage equipment can sell at auction for many thousands. Still, cheaper than a new one, and people like to get their hands dirty. Who wants to wait a week for the dealer's repairman to come out?"

"We should get good money then for Sam's tractor."

Zach ran a hand down the stallion's nose, and the horse pushed his face into Zach's stomach like a kitten might. "Tell you what. I have a calf this spring out of Sam's best bull and my prize-winning Hereford cow. The calf's yours for the auction. Might make a good 4-H project for some kid. Come in the barn. I'll introduce you to him."

Gabe felt his insides begin to unwind. On a ranch he always felt at home, the mess in Texas with Brynne far away. He was reminded of Jilly's call. He still hadn't phoned his father.

In the dim light of the cooler barn, Gabe was impressed with the calf, but he soon noticed Zach looking at him instead.

"What?"

"I probably shouldn't say, but I had breakfast in town earlier—left those wedding planners to their task here—and people were buzzing about you and Lauren Anderson."

Gabe groaned. "She invited me out to dinner. That's all."

"Is it?" Zach raised an eyebrow. "She usually gets what she wants."

He scoffed. "That won't be me." Gabe meant to make that clear to Lauren. He had a different reason for going to dinner with her—self-protection.

"She's not the woman on your mind?"

Gabe's gut tightened. "There is no woman."

"Why not? You're, what, around thirty?"

"And a few more. Thirty-two."

"Settling down was a pretty effective way for me to get my mother off my back. Plus, I'm totally in love with Cass. Now Mom's hoping for a first grandchild from us." He cocked his head. "I'm not trying to tell you your own business, but if Lauren doesn't appeal to you there are other women in town."

Gabe shook his head. "I'm gun-shy. I was engaged a few years back. We were three days from the wedding when I realized I was about to marry the wrong woman."

He should have known sooner than he did. He and Iris had had more than one conversation about their future together, including Gabe's hope to buy a ranch in the area and run some cattle, but she'd kept her own wishes to herself until close to their wedding. "Cows? When you're in line to become Brynne's next CEO? I don't see myself with a bunch of livestock, living in a log house that some people find so attractive in the middle of nowhere. I like my life here in the city—and a social scene—near all our friends. When your father retires, he might even give us that beautiful big house." Not that she'd planned to fill it with children.

But he wasn't about to give Zach any details about Iris that might lead to Gabe being exposed. He wouldn't mention Texas's best high-end caterer from Dallas, either, or the huge reception hall that had been booked; tons of flowers ordered for the church; a long stretch limousine; Iris's wedding gown with its ten-thousand-dollar price tag. Along with the humiliation of having their daughter practically left at the altar, and the blow to their social standing, Iris's parents had lost a lot of money. Many people in Midland still didn't speak to him.

"Sorry to hear that, Gabe. Still, what about Sophie Crane."

Gabe began to sweat. Talking about his ex-fiancée was one thing. Sophie was another. Her reaction the last time he'd seen her had intrigued Gabe. Was their attraction mutual? But how could that matter? He wouldn't let it. He'd made up his mind. Hands off, and not only because of Max. If she ever found out about Brynne and the lies he'd had to tell, she would despise him.

Zach looked thoughtful. "Sophie spent a few years away from here, making it in the big city where a couple of relationships ended badly. You like her, don't you?"

Way too much.

"Sure," he said. "We're friends, but that doesn't mean we're a match."

Zach clapped him on the shoulder. "Sometimes it's not apparent at first. I should know. Cass and I gave each other the runaround for years before we finally saw how good we are for each other. I'd marry her more than twice if that's what she wanted."

They both laughed, but after making the arrangements for Zach to deliver the calf, Gabe headed for his truck, his thoughts in turmoil.

Because of what Sophie had told him about her ex and her best friend, he had even more reason not to get involved. She didn't deserve to be hurt again. And surely Gabe would hurt her.

CHAPTER SIX

THE OBVIOUS CHOICE for dinner with Lauren Anderson was the Bon Appetit, Barren's version of a Michelin-starred restaurant. Gabe wasn't looking forward to tonight. He suspected this wasn't simply a way for "two strangers in town" to "get acquainted," as Lauren had said. But he hadn't wanted her to think he had anything to hide. So, if necessary, he would make a preemptive strike to keep her from looking into his background. As he pulled out her chair at their corner table, nevertheless he wished he could have said no.

His neck felt so tight he could imagine it suddenly snapping like a broken spring. Gabe shook out his napkin, then looked around. "Have you met Jack Hancock?" The restaurant's owner and executive chef.

"I've seen him around town, but no. Not yet."

"I'll introduce you," he said, but as it turned out, Jack was not on duty tonight and it was the sous-chef who sent a complimentary shrimp ceviche to the table.

Gabe studied the menu and then the wine list. He chose a decent bottle of red, which Lauren said she preferred to white.

"What would you like to order?"

She glanced up from her menu with a mega-watt smile. "The coq au vin sounds good."

"The best in town." He tried a feeble grin. The Bon Appetit was the only French place in Barren.

"Then that's what I'll have." When their orders had been taken, and the wine poured, she raised her glass. "To...us."

"Lauren—"

"I should have said to *you*," she murmured.

He feared he might choke to death here in the Bon Appetit on the steak with pommes frites he'd picked for his meal. He wished he'd spent tonight watching baseball with Max.

She looked at him for a long moment, eyes sparkling. Trying too hard. "Gabe, you're blushing."

"Must be the wine. I'm usually a beer man."

"Still, I imagine this little burg is not your usual milieu, either."

"Ah, now we're speaking French to go with the ambience."

"Am I wrong?"

He cleared his throat, remembering she was a reporter. "Not exactly."

"I saw immediately that we're kindred spirits. Both Westerners. You're a Texan, right?"

"Yeah. I was."

"Dallas-Fort Worth?"

"West Texas."

"And you like it here?"

"I do. No plans to leave." Not unless his friend Aaron decided to talk, and someone made the connection with Gabe to Brynne. Or his father's demands for him to come home finally succeeded. "Don't you intend to stay?"

"For now." She paused. "You do have that cowboy thing going for you."

Gabe had worn his usual outfit for such occasions—a white shirt with pressed jeans and boots polished to a mirrored shine—similar clothes to those he'd worn to dinner at Max and Sophie's.

"Fortunately, Sweetheart Ranch agrees. Which is good enough for me."

"What's your hometown?"

His pulse leaped. Like Kate, she was obviously probing for information. The true reason for tonight's dinner? If so, his suspicions had been right. "Uh, Odessa," he lied. "Bigger than here." And, like Midland, where oil rigs dotted the dry landscape. Then there was the big house where he'd grown up. No way would he mention that.

"The seat of Ector County?" Lauren knew her geography. He hoped that was all it was.

"Yeah. A small portion of the city spills over into the next county." Gabe's neck tightened even more. "I was glad to escape," he said, which was the truth. But one day he'd have to go back.

"Me, too. I'm from just outside of Santa Fe."

"Tell me more."

"I'd rather talk about you."

Gabe began to feel trapped. "Lauren, what are you doing, writing a story? I didn't realize this was going to be an interview."

She leaned back in her chair. "As I said, I'd like to get to know you better, that's all. Find out what makes you tick. I admit, that's a habit of mine. Goes with my chosen field."

After that, he resorted to abrupt, mostly one-word answers that didn't tell her anything. When their food finally arrived, Gabe dug in, praying there would be no more probing questions. That lasted through the meal, with only a bit of small talk, until dessert.

"Where did you learn to be a cowboy?" she asked.

That much he could tell her. "When I was a kid, my dad instilled a strong work ethic in me. Every summer from the time I was twelve until I left for college, I mucked stalls and watered horses at a local ranch. In that area there are mostly Herefords—Barren seems to prefer Angus—and eventually I learned more. Rode fence, herded cattle...the usual stuff."

All true, but he realized that he hadn't learned a thing about Lauren except a vague reference to where she was from. And that she was obviously trying to flirt—perhaps to get under his guard? Those long eyelashes of hers led a very active life but had little effect on Gabe. He was too busy dodging her questions and trying not to think of Sophie. He'd rather be having dinner with her. That thought, without his saying a word, seemed to bring up the award for Citizen of the Year.

"I should wish my competitors well," Lauren said idly, "but I intend to win. I hope I have your vote."

"You didn't have to ask me to dinner for that."

"Ah, but I wouldn't have missed this for the world."

Time to set her straight. "I haven't decided on my vote." He knew he would end up marking his ballot for Sophie but wasn't about to let Lauren know that. Plus, he had to protect himself from her prying questions. As for Sophie, he already liked her too much for his own good. And hers.

Lauren said, "I'll need to convince you, then."

Gabe didn't answer, and as they finished their crème brûlée Lauren returned to what seemed to be her favorite topic tonight.

"Odessa. Oil, right?"

His pulse thumped, hard. "Lots of it in the Permian Basin." That fact wouldn't tell her much.

She tilted her head to study him. "Were you one of those daring wildcatters? Hoping for a gusher? Or, when you weren't chasing cows, an oil rig worker?"

Gabe took a deep breath. "Not me." Now she was getting too close to home. Odessa was roughneck country; Midland was corporate oil. "I don't like heights—or oil, except in my truck." True enough.

And then, finally, she said it. "Your dad's in the business?"

"Yeah. Sort of." His standard answer. Most

people didn't pursue that. For years, he and his father had been at odds over Gabe taking control at Brynne. He'd briefly gone to work for the company after college to test his own conviction that he didn't belong there.

Lauren finished her dessert. "Nothing more?"

"Nope. Unless you want to reciprocate." That was probably a bad idea.

"Not tonight, which is about you." She held his gaze. "You're a mystery, Gabe Morgan. One I intend to solve."

"Hey, I'm an open book," he lied again. "What you see is what you get."

"All right, cowboy." Clearly, she didn't believe him.

Gabe signaled for the check. She'd invited him, but he wasn't about to let her pay.

Lauren smiled. "Now I have a mission—*I'll* need to dig deeper."

"Lauren."

"Next time we'll talk more." Her smile was sly.

"Not much time for talking. I'm all about my job here."

"I am, too," she said.

Lauren might well be a shark, swimming in dangerous waters for Gabe.

If only his need to protect himself could also protect him from his thoughts of Sophie.

"So, WHAT DO YOU THINK?" Max leaned back in his chair, rocking on its rear legs. He'd sounded nervous and Sophie hesitated to answer.

He'd left his clinic tonight shortly after 5:00 p.m., the earliest since he'd first opened it years ago. As he and Sophie ate dinner, he'd even refrained from talking shop.

"Please don't do that," she said, eyeing the dining room chair. "If Mom was here, she'd tell you why. I shouldn't have to. You're not five years old."

Max kept rocking. "I'm not going to break the chair, which isn't worth much anyway." Most of the furniture in the house was sadly out of date. "Just answer my question."

He wanted to invite Averill over to the house, but Sophie recalled Rachel's comment at the library about the book Max's receptionist had slipped into her bag without checking it out. Had that really happened? Finally, she said, "If you'd like to ask Averill for a meal here, this is your home, too."

"Gabe told me to ask first, but I can tell you're not enthused."

"I, um, really, I'm fine with that."

"If you don't want to cook, we can order in."

"Why would I not be willing to fix dinner?"

"Gabe says I take advantage of you."

Sophie smoothed a hand over her skirt. She remembered lurking in the kitchen that night, fussing over her berry pie, rattling dishes to remind the two men she was still there and could overhear them in the dining room. At the same time her insides had turned into a gooey puddle because Gabe had thought to defend her.

Still, she had an obligation to protect Max. Maybe in a more casual setting she'd be able to gauge Averill's character for herself.

"You do take advantage," she said, but she smiled. "And I let you. You're my favorite brother."

"Aw, Sophie. Tell you what. He's right. I'll order from the café, or we can have a barbecue here. I'll man the grill."

She stared at him. "What am I hearing? The new and improved Maxwell Crane, DVM?"

"Probably not, but since I brought up Gabe, let's talk about him instead. You've had a thing for him for over a year. To be honest, I think it's time you stopped dwelling on some other guy who didn't deserve you, not to mention your traitorous friend. I saw how Gabe looked at you the other night, too. Still. I like him a lot, but I'm not sure I should trust him. With you."

Her heart skipped a beat. So Max, too, had sensed that air of mystery. But attraction on Gabe's part to Sophie? "You know something about Gabe that I should know?"

"Nothing specific," he said, "but what if you and he did start seeing each other—"

"Like you and Averill? Because I'm sure that's what prompted this dinner idea."

"I'm not 'seeing her.'" Max's mouth set. "Don't make too much of the invitation. She's just my receptionist."

"And a little caution might be wise there."

Yet whether Averill was merely an employee or a woman in whom he seemed to be personally interested, how could she tell Max about the possibly stolen book? And why would Averill have taken it when she could have checked it out? The books were free to borrow. What had Rachel actually seen? Maybe Averill had come to the desk, gotten that book earlier when one of the pages was on duty and Rachel was otherwise occupied, then decided later to check out more books. Sophie needed to do a search on the library computer.

To her knowledge Max hadn't dated since Sophie had moved back home. Her brother might blindly follow his heart, but at least *she* knew to be cautious. "I mean, what do you know about Averill? She hasn't been in Barren long enough for my friends to vet her—to make a bad pun. The few times I've met her, she seemed nice and she's very attractive..."

"Yes, she is. I like her. Maybe that's enough." He sighed. "I doubt there's anything to worry about with Averill, but nobody, including me, seems to know more about Gabe than that he's from Texas."

"You don't think that's true?"

"From his laid-back manner, his drawl, his skills on the job, I do. Yet there's an underlying blank. Even though he's my friend, and you'd think we'd delve into each other's lives, with Gabe there is no rest of his story." Max finally righted the chair, its legs thumping down on the dining room carpet, which Sophie had a long-standing itch to change, like the furniture, for something new. He shrugged. "Or rather, I can't put my finger on it."

"As I can't with Averill."

He ignored that. "All I know for sure is, I won't give anyone, including Gabe, the chance to break your heart."

"I'm flattered you care," she said, "but my crush is apparently one-sided."

"Why do you say that? It's not what I saw."

"Gabe may be seeing Lauren Anderson." Perhaps they were having dinner even as she said the words. "And I believe in the adage, 'Once burned, twice shy.' Twice burned," she added, "that's on me."

The night Gabe had come to dinner, Max had seen something that simply wasn't there. Her brief closeness with Gabe in the kitchen had been her imagination, too.

The nearest Sophie would get to Gabe was in a meeting of their finance committee.

AT THE LIBRARY the next morning, Sophie searched their computer system. She recognized those books she'd checked out for Averill but found no record of any other borrowed volumes.

"Solve our mystery?" Rachel asked.

"I wish I had. I hate to think my brother has hired a kleptomaniac." Last night Max had tried to pass off Averill as merely his receptionist at the clinic. He liked her, that was all. No potential romantic interest. Sophie hoped it was that simple. At least until she was able to learn more about her. "Perhaps Averill bought a book at the emporium across the street and then came here."

But Rachel claimed to have seen Averill slip a volume into her bag at the library, shoving it deeper as she added the ones she'd checked out from Sophie.

"I don't want to confront Averill without proof," Sophie said. "I'll keep looking but other than that I guess we'll have to wait and watch—see if it happens again." If it really had before.

Rachel tucked a strand of dark hair behind one ear. "Ooh, this is like a juicy detective story."

Sophie frowned. "Not. I don't need more drama in my life." Last year had been enough for her. She also didn't need to be swayed by her assistant. Rachel seemed to have made up her mind about Averill.

The notion crossed Sophie's mind before she could stop it. Rachel had lost her husband a few years ago and taken this job at the library to "get out of my apartment." She needed to see people, to find a purpose. What if she'd invented the missing book to make herself seem important?

Sophie rejected the idea. She had no reason not to trust Rachel. If anything, she was just overly helpful. Sophie's own insecurity must be showing after Will and Bess's elopement, which had shattered her belief in people, her confidence, her trust.

Instead of prolonging any speculation about Averill, she went into her office—and found a brief email waiting from Finn Donovan. Budget still too large. Please cut somewhere.

Sophie groaned. "Do I look like a miracle worker?" she asked aloud.

She was scouring the budget figures when she heard a voice she recognized at the front desk. Sophie went out to greet the woman.

Willow Bodine Jones turned, all blond hair, cornflower blue eyes, and glowing complexion. "Hey, Sophie, just the woman I came to see."

They hugged, and Sophie said, "Right back at you." They'd been friends for some time. Willow was Zach and Noah Bodine's sister. Like them, she now worked a share of the vast WB land along with her husband Cody. "I've been meaning to call you, thinking you'd be a wonderful addition to my sesquicentennial women's book sale committee."

"Oh, gee, Sophie. I'd like to, but Cody and I are working twelve-hour days. I don't know when I'd find time to attend any meetings. I haven't gone to our Girls' Night Out group for the last three get-togethers. This spring our new business is bursting at the seams. The stalls are full, but we still have people calling us to board and train. We may have to send a few horses to Olivia McCord's barn."

"An enviable situation." Sophie eyed Willow's still-flat stomach. "I hear you're adding to your family as well."

Willow grinned. "Cody is over the moon." He and Willow had had some tough times years ago, including a breakup and reunion before they finally married. "He's sure the baby's a boy." She added, "I'd like a girl, but it's always nice to have a big brother first."

"That's what Max tells me. He thinks I need him in order to function."

Willow rolled her eyes. "Brothers."

"Well, congratulations, little mama." She gave Willow another hug. "If you change your mind about the committee, let me know."

They chatted for a few minutes before Willow seemed to remember why she'd come into the library. "By the way. Cody and I would like to make a pledge for the sesquicentennial."

Sophie straightened. "I have the form right here. Somewhere." She dug through a drawer in the front desk. "Do you need a pen?"

Willow had already drawn one from her bag. She filled in the information, then jotted down a figure that, even reading upside down, made Sophie blink. "Am I seeing right? That's a good chunk of change, Willow."

"We're doing great. Why not share the wealth with Barren? This is going to be a marvelous summer with all the upcoming events…"

"Thank you. I really appreciate not having to twist at least one arm."

"The donations aren't coming in as you'd hoped?"

"We're just getting started. The committee knows that people have other financial commitments, but we'll need a lot more funding to pull this off as we'd like to."

"I can make some calls if you want. I'll fit them in. From home. I'll get my brothers involved."

Sophie thanked Willow again, then walked her to the door. For an instant she felt tempted to ask her what she knew about Averill. Considering their horse training business, she and Cody might have dealt with her via Max and the clinic. Then she thought better of it.

She'd had one success this morning without trying. After her conversation with Rachel about the presumably stolen book and then her struggle with the library budget, her day had been made by Willow's generosity. The Joneses' donation would help.

As Sophie returned to those stubborn budget figures, it was almost enough to make her forget how many other arms she needed to twist. She didn't look forward to that.

CHAPTER SEVEN

"*GQ* PHOTO SHOOT—RIGHT?"

Gabe was examining Critter's injured leg that morning when Noah walked up to the stall door and peered inside. His voice, laced with amusement, had caught Gabe unaware. His footsteps hadn't made a sound, and Gabe had been lost in his thoughts. Startled, Critter could have kicked Gabe's head in. Good thing the horse had a placid nature.

"Must have been for the cover of the next issue," Noah went on.

"Huh?"

"Last night. Saw you walking to your truck from the bunkhouse all gussied up. Designer jeans, a shirt so white it could blind someone, and who bothers to shine his boots unless there's something big going on?"

Gabe could have groaned. "I do."

Noah folded his arms on the stall door, its upper portion open. His dark blond hair caught the overhead light and his hazel eyes danced with mischief. For a man who'd turned his back years ago on Kansas, and his family, to build a cybersecurity firm back East, he looked the part of a rancher himself now. Which he was, in addition to commuting between Barren and New York for his thriving business.

"My mom did teach me and Zach before we were ready for kindergarten how to dress like gentlemen. Never seemed to get it that we spent our time in dirty barns or on the range looking for strays. We didn't care if our jeans had holes from being scraped along a barbed wire fence by some horse or our T-shirts were muddy—until we hit our teens and what the girls thought of us finally sank in." Noah grinned, enjoying himself. "But you, yessir, quite the fashionist-o yesterday."

Gabe ran a hand along the gelding's neck. "I'm no fashion model. Didn't know having dinner in town was a violation. It was after hours, and all the chores were done."

"Settle down. I'm joking."

But Gabe never quite relaxed around Noah or anyone else. And he was still smarting from the interview the night before, which his dinner with Lauren had turned out to be. Even being careful, had he said too much? Gabe had to wonder why she seemed so determined to dig into his life.

"Hey, no offense," Noah said. "Who was the lucky lady?"

"I'm guessing you already know."

"Who, me? I just flew in from New York again yesterday."

Gabe gave Critter a last pat, then went for the door. While waiting for Max to look at the horse, he'd prepare a poultice for the gelding's leg. "Lauren Anderson. I have to wonder why someone so ambitious is here in Barren writing for the *Journal.*"

Gabe pushed by Noah and headed for the feed room where the medications were also kept.

"Hold up," Noah said. "I didn't mean to pry about Lauren. Sorry if I messed with your head. I couldn't resist."

"No offense taken."

"Zach tells me you're looking for donations for some auction. Says he gave you a calf. Being as we're brothers, I'd better try to top him. How'd you like a sweet little mare? Not flashy, but one of the hands quit at the WB and we're looking for a new home for her." He ticked off her good points. "Nice gaits, has no vices, just shy of fifteen hands…"

"Sure. Thanks. It's shaping up to be a good auction."

Noah leaned against the doorframe to the feed room while Gabe busied himself making the poultice. "I'd save her for Teddie, but he's got his pony still and the new colt here. What I'm saying is, she's safe for a beginner."

"I—we—appreciate the donation."

"You've really gotten roped in, haven't you? But then, Sophie's hard to resist. When I see her coming these days, I run the other way. Except for making donations, and the rodeo, I can't do any more. The office in New York is a madhouse, we're opening a branch in Paris, and then there's the wedding."

"You and Zach should have a double wedding."

Noah laughed. "Maybe we will. If Kate joined my mother and Cass in the planning at the WB, might be a good thing from where I'm standing. Get both weddings over with in one day. In one place."

Gabe shot him a look. "You two would do anything for those women."

"Got that right." Which didn't bother Noah at all. "So," he said, "Lauren."

"Her only interest in me is trying to get

a story of some kind—good luck with that. There's nothing to tell."

She wasn't going to learn another thing about him.

Carrying the poultice he'd made, Gabe eased past Noah into the barn aisle.

Noah followed him. "Speaking of that dinner, Kate keeps wondering why you don't come up for supper anymore. Is that because of me?" He paused. "No reason for you to feel excluded. Our engagement doesn't change things at Sweetheart. You're a good foreman, Gabe. I'm glad you're here, especially whenever I can't be. We'll expect you for lunch tomorrow."

Gabe had worried needlessly. He wasn't being pushed aside as he'd feared. Maybe he wasn't seen by everyone as an outsider, and he felt a warm rush inside of what could be called acceptance. He was wanted here at Sweetheart, and for now he belonged. But then, he and Sophie, who feared she didn't belong, were different. She'd left town and come back. For different reasons, he liked being here but couldn't stay forever.

He envied Kate and Noah.

He took the poultice into Critter's stall. Again, Noah was right outside. Obviously, he hadn't finished. "You do make me wonder.

Like other people in this town. Kate, for sure. But I don't care where a man comes from or what he's done. My brother-in-law Cody spent time in prison. I only care if you do your job."

So it was not only Kate who seemed to have doubts about him. Or Lauren Anderson. Noah was somewhat suspicious, too, if in a more minor way.

Which gave him an idea. He'd offered to help Sophie with her campaign for the award, though after his conversation with Lauren, he'd rather avoid the spotlight. But unlike him, Sophie wasn't hiding anything. To better her chances, she could use some serious PR. And with Sophie centerstage, he could stay safely in the background.

TOWARD THE END OF the day Sophie had just shut down her computer when Gabe walked into the library, seeming to fill the high-ceilinged space with his broad shoulders and tall, lean frame. In dusty jeans and a black-and-white checked shirt with pearl buttons, he looked every inch the cowboy he was.

For Sophie, that made a nice change from her ex-boyfriend Will's big-city look.

It made her want to trust Gabe. *Watch out.* That wasn't a good idea.

She took out the pencil she'd stuck into her messy bun, then told herself to *keep it light. Don't let him see how you feel.* "Need a good book on animal husbandry?"

"Not unless Teddie's interest of the week is cows." He didn't quite smile. "I need to talk to you. You still mad at me?"

"I was never mad." Sophie took refuge behind the front desk. At almost five o'clock, there were few patrons left, and Rachel was on the opposite side of the main room, tidying up the tables. They wouldn't be easily overheard.

"Aren't you going to ask, then, how my dinner with Lauren went?"

"No," she said, quelling the urge to do just that.

"She's gunning for you."

"No surprise."

"She wants that award, Sophie."

"So do I, but that depends on the voters— the citizens of Barren."

He used an old political saying. "I plan to vote early and often."

"Ha ha," she said, feeling a little thrill race down her spine. Did he mean vote for her?

"I've been thinking. If you want to win, you need to start getting out there, let people see you, meet and greet. Shake hands and kiss babies. Lauren does and she's good at it. She's winning people over."

She tensed. She'd been expecting this issue to arise. "I see plenty of people right here. Every day."

"Not everyone in Barren reads books."

"True, but between this job and my work for the sesquicentennial, when would I find time?" She was still wrestling with the library budget, and had another headache. She smoothed a slight wrinkle in her blouse, which had a lacy jabot tumbling down its front, and in KC had been one of her favorites. Gabe tracked the motion, then studied her suit before his eyes met hers again.

"You claim people see you as an outsider. I may be looking at one reason why."

Sophie squirmed under his regard. "Oh, now you're a fashion expert?"

"According to Noah Bodine, yeah."

"What does that mean?"

"Private joke. Sophie, that's a knockout suit, but how many women do you encounter here or on the street dressed like you are?"

Sophie hesitated. Claudia Monroe, maybe. "You mean I don't seem…approachable?"

Gabe didn't answer her question except to

say, "What if you wore jeans or a skirt now and then?"

"Why should I change my appearance to win an award? That seems shallow." Still, Claudia had also pointed out the difference between her and Miss Bramley. "My predecessor wore stout shoes, ankle-length skirts and her hair in a bun."

"So do you—the hair at least."

"Are you saying that even in suits, I'm a stereotype of the spinster librarian?"

"I do like your bun. It's…classy."

He might have said sloppy. Every morning Sophie's practical hairstyle started out neat and tidy, then gradually disassembled itself during the day. "You have a point. What prompted this, Gabe?"

"Last night," he admitted, "I dressed up a bit for dinner. A habit of mine from boyhood—my father had his standards—and Noah teased me about it today. Made me think. Wait a minute, what if Sophie's sending the wrong message?"

She glanced down at her skirt. "Maybe I should look around, notice what our patrons are wearing, my friends… In KC I wore suits and heels all the time, but you're saying I'm kind of stuck there?"

Not only in her choice of clothes, but in still

feeling that sense of Will and Bess's betrayal. Had all her suits, which she'd chosen herself and loved, become like armor meant to protect her emotionally? Gabe didn't say that, though.

"You're right. I need to go shopping," she said at last.

"Never a sacrifice, is it?"

"No," she admitted with a smile.

He added, "Now and then, you could let down your hair, too—literally, I mean."

"My clothes are a start, even getting out there with people, but what else can I do to regain acceptance here in Barren?" Sophie thought for a moment. Then, "Hey, I have another idea. Most people here are ranch-related in some way. Even people like Earl at the hardware store or Max who spends most of his time with cattle or horses." She could feel her gaze brighten. "What if I roughed up my image a little? In a different way? Mixed with some cowhands, cowgirls? Learned some of their everyday tasks? Did some chores? I could ask Nell Ransom—"

"Sophie, that's *not* a good idea."

She jabbed a finger at his chest. "Put your money where your mouth is, mister. Even better, Kate's a good friend of mine." Working with her, of course, would mean being near

Gabe. She hadn't considered that before she spoke. She'd already voiced the suggestion, though, and couldn't, or wouldn't, take it back. "What's wrong with Sweetheart Ranch?"

His gaze had shuttered. "Doing what there?"

Sophie shrugged. "What I said. I don't know. Cleaning stalls—"

"Mucking." His mouth looked tight.

"Okay, obviously I need to learn the proper terms. I could polish saddles, bridles—"

"What do you know about any of that? I'm not putting you down. It's just impractical. You grew up in town. You have no experience. And Kate and I, maybe a few hands would be the only ones who saw you. We already have one new kid who needs to learn the ropes. How would that improve *your* image?"

"Word gets around. Everyone in town would hear about a different side of me, the local side. Because you're right, even Lizzie Maguire's mother Claudia sees me as big-city." And since he'd be at Sweetheart, too, Sophie would have an up-close view of Gabe. She didn't need to act on her secret attraction to him, but why not indulge her hopeless fantasy while she worked, preferably with Kate? That sounded safe enough. It wasn't as if she'd ever need to trust him with her heart.

"This is just weird," Gabe said.

"I think it's perfect."

"Sophie. Ranches can be dangerous places." Or did he mean, for his own reasons? Was he afraid she might throw herself at him?

"It's not as if I'll be toting a gun, shooting at varmints—"

"Varmints?" Gabe couldn't keep from grinning. "Where did you get that?"

"I'm a librarian. I know these things."

"Not about Sweetheart Ranch." Sophie just looked at Gabe until, finally, he shook his head. "Your funeral."

"I'll give Kate a call."

IN HIS FREE time Gabe had been working on the silent auction, their first fundraiser for the weeklong sesquicentennial in July. He'd been making good progress until he'd stopped at the library and Sophie suggested spending time at Sweetheart Ranch. Near him. Wasn't his being on her finance committee enough proximity? If only Kate had objected to Sophie's plan, but she'd thought it was a great idea.

Kate had laughed. "Sophie on a ranch?"

"I know," Gabe had said.

"This I've got to see."

Now, a day later, in the barn he'd haggled

on the phone with his father for the past hour. Gabe had dreaded making the call, but that morning he'd seen a stock report on TV, which had finally prompted him. By the time the call ended, he'd felt as if he'd been the victim of an interrogation by the Spanish Inquisition.

"Why are you still in Kansas when you should be here, Gabriel."

"Dad, I told you—years ago—about that rig. The same one that's still spreading oil all over the Gulf right now. There were serious maintenance issues on the rig even then. The safety protocols weren't being followed. When my friend Aaron came to me, I could tell from the look in his eyes that he was scared. He told me so I could tell you."

"Which you did. Or was he simply using you as he did to get that job in the first place?"

Gabe had met Aaron when they were both kids, their fathers working for Brynne Energy. Each December the company threw a big Christmas party for the employees and their families, and Gabe and Aaron had hit it off that first night. With Gabe's father as CEO and Aaron's a member of the drilling crew, they didn't run in the same circles. But over the years they'd met up again at those holiday events, and it was true that Gabe had been instrumental years later, after Aaron's dad had died, in helping him get his first job on the oil rig. As adults they occasionally kept in touch. Though he couldn't say they would ever be close friends, it wasn't fair for his father to question Aaron's motives now.

"And what did you do with that information, Dad?"

"After he spoke to you, I talked to my chief of operations," his father said, sounding defensive.

"You trusted someone else to take action. Which apparently they did not."

"Gabe, if things were lax on the rig, how do you know that didn't change after you spoke with this friend of yours? I am the CEO of one of the largest energy outfits in this country. I built Brynne literally from the ground up, starting with one well, and you've sure benefitted from that. Your guy was blowing smoke—"

Gabe rubbed his neck. "I'm trying to protect you. If Aaron decides to talk, chances are I'll be interviewed, even deposed. Or have to testify in court if it comes to that. I'd have no choice then but to tell what I know—what he told me, which doesn't make you look good—or perjure myself." At the silence from the other end, he added, "He's your real ticking time bomb but you refuse to see that."

"And you're supposed to be part of this corporation. Its next CEO. I have worked my entire life to make that happen, but instead you'd rather hide out on some run-down ranch—"

"That's right," Gabe muttered, "and under a different name, for your own good."

His father had hung up on him.

But until all the investigations ended and an agreement with Brynne was worked out, Gabe would stay where he was. If he had to step forward, didn't his father realize it would look as if he'd mismanaged his company? Ignored the warnings about what might happen that finally did with the spill? Neglected his employees and gotten people hurt, a few killed? He blew out a frustrated breath just as Kate wandered down the barn aisle. Had she overheard the conversation? Gabe had thought he was alone.

"Sorry to barge in. Troubles at home? You said, 'for your own good.'"

So she hadn't heard the rest. "You could say that. My dad goes off like a firecracker, but he'll settle down." Gabe hoped.

He was half waiting for the phone to ring. It would be Jilly again this time.

Kate said, "You know the most important

thing to me is home, family." She touched his tensed forearm. "I lost my mom when I wasn't much older than Teddie is now, and I wouldn't wish that abandonment on anyone. You should fix things if you can. Noah's home. He and I will manage without you."

Gabe felt torn between staying in Kansas, which he should, and trying to talk sense to his dad.

He'd avoided making that call for the same reason he kept away from Midland. Roman candles didn't begin to describe the reception he would likely get from his father once he reached Texas, but it seemed Jilly had assessed the situation well. In two words, not good.

Maybe Kate was right. He could feel himself weakening.

"I'd only be gone a few days. I can be back late Sunday."

"This is already Friday," she said. "Take as long as you need."

Or should he stay, call Aaron instead, try to determine if he meant to come forward? If Aaron kept silent, Gabe wouldn't have as much reason to keep hiding at Sweetheart or to use his mother's maiden name. But should he take that chance either?

The stress didn't make his decision any easier. And yet, above all... Chester Dean Wyatt was his father. Gabe couldn't abandon him, as Kate's mother had her. He was needed at home. He'd just have to be careful, slip into Texas then out.

"My dad's always been short-tempered. I'll straighten him out. I appreciate this, Kate."

"Don't mention it. Come back when you're ready."

Gabe went off to pack his bag.

With luck, he wouldn't be there long enough to get noticed by anyone except his father and Jilly.

CHAPTER EIGHT

"COWBOY BOOTS."

Which to Gabe's father should seem like no big deal. Many men in Midland, if not most, and in Dallas, wore boots, but on that same Friday night Gabe had heard the sour tone in his father's voice. He set his bag down in the front hall, a cavernous space that soared above a white marble floor to the elaborate vaulted ceiling. The oval entryway of the Midland mansion showcased a spiraling flight of broad stairs to the second-floor landing where, as a kid, Gabe had sailed paper airplanes from the railing and been scolded for making noise that might disturb his ailing mother.

"Hey, Dad."

Chester Dean—"Chet," to his friends— Wyatt came down those steps. Still without an ounce of extra fat on his wiry frame, and as tall as Gabe, he stood for a moment, assessing Gabe's attire. "Boots, jeans, denim shirt… you look the part."

Gabe had considered wearing a suit—a lone remnant of his former life when he'd spent several years at Brynne as a junior manager—but hadn't wanted to send the wrong message. He hadn't lasted long and he wasn't home to stay. It had been years since he'd quit that job, long before the oil spill. To his father's displeasure, after that he'd worked at various ranches until he ended up in Kansas. Yet even his clothes made him a target for Chet's anger and deep disappointment. Why wouldn't he see that Gabe was trying to safeguard him?

"Didn't we just talk on the phone?" Chet's Texas drawl got deeper. "Thought I was seeing things when you opened this door. How long has it been?"

"I don't keep track."

"Eighteen months," his dad said for him. "Your mother must be rolling in her grave. When are you going to come to your senses? Realize where you belong—in good times and bad? Take your rightful place in this company?"

Well, at least he'd come straight to the point again.

"Dad, come on. My coming here for more than this weekend could hurt you."

Chet's brown eyes darkened. He ran a hand

through his still-thick hair, the same shade as Gabe's. He had what must be a three-hundred-dollar haircut while Gabe had been cutting his own. His father's eyes flashed. "Why didn't you tell me you were coming? I have a board meeting tonight, then dinner." Plans of his own. Nothing new. "That is, if the board doesn't demand my resignation."

"Don't worry about me. I'll make myself a sandwich."

"Jilly won't stand for that."

"After you and I talked, if I can call it that—"

"You decided to come poke me in the eye again. I guess I should feel grateful that you're gainfully employed, not living in my basement playing video games. Spending the trust fund from your mother." Chet pointed a finger. "You know what? I'm sorry I sent you to the best schools, threw away hard-earned cash on riding lessons. You must be the only guy in the state of Kansas who owns a fancy English saddle."

"That's not true."

"Some cowboy."

Gabe gritted his teeth. "In Barren, we ride Western. I've done both."

The saddle his father meant, made of the finest, buttery leather, must still be in the now-unused tack room in the stables on this estate. So was the silver-encrusted parade saddle he'd gotten for his twelfth birthday to use in competitions.

At the bottom of the stairs Chet turned. He started back up. "I don't want to talk. I'll be late for my meeting."

Gabe's mouth hardened. "Then I'll see you when I see you."

The story of their entire relationship. What had he thought he might accomplish?

For a long moment he stood there, watching his father's stiff back, wishing he hadn't left Sweetheart Ranch. What good could come of this brief visit? His dad considered him to be a traitor. His skull was thicker than Gabe had imagined, and he couldn't fix anything as Kate had advised, least of all their roles as father and son. He wouldn't see his dad again while he was here, or they'd come to blows.

"Are you two quarreling?" At the top of the stairs, Jilly had appeared, and Gabe's heart turned over. As his father brushed past her, she touched his shoulder but sent Gabe a look.

He met her on the landing, folded her into a fierce hug and held on. She was the glue that kept their splintered family, such as it was, together.

"Why a board meeting tonight?" Gabe asked her. Surely they wouldn't want his father to step down.

"More damage control." She sighed. "The company stock has taken a serious hit."

"I saw that on the news. What's going on with this Senate investigation on Brynne, Jilly? Why can't *he* see that I can only hurt him? I'm the connection to him that could send this whole thing spiraling out of control." Not to mention Aaron, too, who'd given Gabe the early warning about the rig.

"He does love you," she murmured, "but he was shocked to see you so unexpectedly. He likes to prepare. Why didn't you say you were coming?"

"I knew he was already mad. Giving him warning would have made things worse."

"He's happy to have you home. He just refuses to show it." She drew back, patted his cheek as she used to do when he was little. Her soft blue eyes showed the same compassion. "Still hurts, doesn't it?"

"I'm okay."

"No, you're not. But for now, we'll leave him alone. Tomorrow he'll have had time to think. Let's hope tonight's board meeting goes well.

You can talk again then. He is your father, after all—you have to keep trying."

"NOT THAT WAY." Kate pointed at the grooming brush in Sophie's hand. "You want to go with the grain, not against, of this horse's hide. You were roughing him up, giving him a cowlick. It's no different from combing your own hair. I like the ponytail, by the way."

The gelding's skin quivered, as if the horse was swatting flies.

"Part of my new look." Sophie glanced down at her jeans and the basic brown boots she'd bought at the emporium. Unfortunately, the new clothes didn't feel right and her shirt, which she'd worn in KC, was made of ivory silk. If she planned to work on her image, she needed to do more shopping.

"Sorry, Critter," Sophie said in a soothing voice, keeping a careful distance from the horse.

"Poor guy, he's in generally rough shape. Stepped in a hole and came up lame. Gabe and your brother have been treating him." Kate looked at Sophie. "And how is Max?"

"Busy. Always." She paused. "He has this new receptionist. Averill McCafferty."

Sophie tentatively swiped the brush along

Critter's barrel. She'd never worked around horses before but, thank goodness, Gabe wasn't here today. As she always did on Saturday, she had closed the library at noon. On such a gorgeous late spring afternoon, people were out mowing their lawns, planting flowers, enjoying the sun. For now, she too was trying to relax. Or she had been before she drove out to Sweetheart Ranch and realized Gabe had been right about her inexperience.

"We're having Averill over tomorrow," she said. That would give Sophie a chance to check her out. Maybe she'd discover that Averill was just as nice as she had first thought, nothing more than an avid reader, and the missing book wasn't missing after all. Sophie reminded herself to take a closer look at the library computer records. She focused on Critter's almost-gleaming coat, stepping a bit closer as she groomed him. At her feet a black-and-white border collie gazed up at her with liquid brown eyes. "Hey, boy."

"He wants a cuddle," Kate said with a sad look, as she swept the aisle. "He's such a love-bug. Nobody remembers how old he is, but he's been a ranch dog here for a long time. Sad to say, the other dogs have begun to bully him—as if to drive him out, which sometimes happens with aging or sick animals." Kate set aside the broom to give the dog a scratch behind his ears. "Our house dog Bandit does his best to look out for Rembrandt, but lately his arthritis seems worse, and we've started talking about having to put him down."

"No," Sophie said without thinking. The idea horrified her.

Rembrandt tilted his head as if to tell her he agreed.

"I've talked with Noah who's neutral, but I'll need Gabe's opinion."

"You'd put him to sleep—Rembrandt—because he's old?"

"Sometimes that's a kindness, Sophie. Another lesson for you to learn. Ranchers, farmers, all country people see the cycle of life—birth to death—every day. With Noah's help, even Teddie came to understand that. I wouldn't dare mention this to him yet, though. He's protective of all the animals on Sweetheart and we haven't decided what to do."

Sophie gazed down at the elderly dog. As a kid, she and Max had shared a miniature schnauzer. When their pet had died of old age, they'd been inconsolable for days. She switched position to groom Critter's offside, as uncertain of her movements as she had been when she first entered the barn.

"By the way. Where is Gabe today?"

"Texas, I'm told."

"You doubt that's true?"

"I don't—yet he's not the usual cowpoke, so who knows? He showed up one day holding the want ads from the *Barren Journal*. 'You need a foreman,' he said. 'I'm your guy.' I admired his confidence, and I like his easy manner with the stock. He's a good manager of the other hands. He certainly does his job, but I call Gabe my man of mystery."

"Max thinks so, too, and they're close friends."

"Noah agrees. I've tried to pry more information from Gabe, but there's, like, a sturdy paddock fence around him. As soon as I get near, he shuts down. All I know is, he has some family trouble. He's taken the weekend off to deal with it."

Sophie knew nothing about his family, but she'd also seen that emotional fence go up and had glimpsed his vulnerability.

"What's your interest?" Kate asked, a twinkle in her eye.

"We're working together on the celebration."

"And?"

"Nothing," Sophie said, keeping her gaze on Critter's withers. She brushed a bit too hard, and the horse stamped his foot. "Kate, I'm not very good at this."

"You will be."

Sophie gestured with the brush at Critter. "Do you think he's pretty enough now?"

"He's all but rolling his eyes in gratitude. Gabe won't recognize him. A half hour in the barn's 'salon' makes a horse feel better—just like us at the Cut and Curl."

As they walked toward Critter's stall, Kate leading the gelding because Sophie didn't feel ready to handle him on her own, Kate studied her outfit. "I'd lose the silk shirt, though."

Sophie had realized the same point. She needed to work on her barn wardrobe as much as she did on her nonexistent ranch skills. Still, at the door to Critter's stall, she looked down at Rembrandt. The dog had followed them and brushed against Sophie's leg.

"I'll be back again soon, Kate. If you don't mind."

"Of course not."

"But please. Before I come, don't do anything rash with this poor dog."

"I'LL NEVER BE able to call myself a cowgirl," Sophie admitted. "But I'm giving it a try." On Sunday she and Max had hosted a simple barbecue in the backyard for Averill, then adjourned to the house to escape the growing heat. May was turning into summer too soon.

"I'm afraid of horses," Averill said.

In the living room after dessert, with the ceiling fan on high, Sophie hoped to learn something about Averill's background that might ease her mind.

"I give horses a wide berth myself. Still, it felt...different to get away from the library for an hour or two. And I saw the most adorable dog at Sweetheart."

"Like on most ranches, there's a pack of dogs," Max pointed out. "Which one?"

"Rembrandt."

"That old border collie? I'm surprised he's still there. Kate's been talking about—"

"I know, but I think he has a lot more life left in him."

Max made a face. "Sophie, I'm the vet here. I take care of Sweetheart's animals, large and small. I examined him last month and told Kate to start thinking—"

"Anyway." Sophie shifted the topic. She'd have to ease into the background conversation with Averill another way. "Trying to soften my image in town with some time at the ranch is one thing, but my main focus has to be the sesquicentennial." And the library job that paid her bills.

Max thought for a moment. Averill was sitting on the sofa next to him.

"Put me down for five hundred," he said. "Credit the clinic in the program."

Averill added, "I'm a bit short right now, but please keep me in mind. I just need to settle in first, save more of my pay before I can contribute to the celebration."

Ah, this could be Sophie's chance.

"Averill, what brought you to Barren?" she asked, trying to sound casual.

"I grew up in Farrier where everyone knows your business."

"It's the same here," Sophie pointed out.

"And while that can seem charming—people do care—I finally decided to relocate. Barren's smaller, and I feel…happier here."

"The clinic allows you to meet a lot of new people, I imagine."

"I already have a few great stories." Averill's gaze turned blurry. "Kids are my favorite. They say the cutest things, and they're so sweet with their animals. I'm fond of little

Daisy Hunter, Blossom's daughter, and most of the area ranchers are nice. Their wives, too." Then she corrected herself. "Not that the women ranchers aren't. I really like Nell Ransom. And Willow Jones."

But Averill's eyes looked sorrowful, as if she had some deep, emotional hole inside.

"You must miss your family."

"I do, but there was only me and my mother. Dad died years ago, and she's finally started seeing someone new. I expect they'll get married. She didn't need me hanging around the house any longer like some failure to launch."

Max grinned. "Lucky for me. Averill's the best receptionist I've ever had."

"And there's been some turnover," Sophie murmured. The job didn't provide a great deal of upward mobility and most people left after a year or so. He'd never asked any of the others to the house, though, and now he edged closer to Averill.

"If I had to double her pay, I would in order to keep her."

Averill caught his gaze. "Wow, that's almost too hard to resist. I should ask for a raise this minute, but you didn't have to say that, Max."

To Sophie's surprise, he touched Averill's hand. "You're a treasure."

Sophie stared at him. "Did you work at a vet practice in Farrier, Averill?"

She glanced away. "No, this is a first for me."

"You're good at it." Max held Averill's gaze. Sophie had never seen him this focused on anyone else. Another sign not to be missed, like Max's suggestion of today's barbecue?

She cleared her throat. "You're interested, obviously, in veterinary medicine. Recently you checked out a book on the subject."

Averill's expression remained neutral. "One of the first things I did here was to get a library card. I love to read."

"You're almost as frequent a patron as Teddie Lancaster."

Max said, "I have a bookcase full of vet stuff in my office at the clinic. Feel free to borrow the books anytime. Save you a trip to the library."

Averill glowed. "Should I leave a note when I do—so you'll know books are missing?"

"Nah, I trust you," Max said.

Sophie straightened. Averill had sounded perfectly honest. Maybe she hadn't stolen the missing book and Rachel really had been seeing things.

For now, Sophie retreated. "If you're interested in our sesquicentennial and would like to get involved in your new community here, I have a few slots left on my women's library group. We're planning a book sale." Her newspaper ad had been worth the money. Both the sale and finance committees were full. She'd even convinced Claudia Monroe to work on the Fun Run event.

"Thank you for asking, Sophie." Although Averill didn't volunteer, the lost look in her eyes had disappeared. Perhaps she was embarrassed about her lack of money yet eager to belong and would sign up later.

"Our first fundraiser is coming up, too," Sophie said. "We're accepting donations of goods for a silent auction. Are you a crafter—or have something you no longer need that's in good condition?"

Averill laughed. "I bought a pair of outrageously expensive shoes before I moved. I can't even walk in them, and they've only been worn for a short time on my carpet. Brand-new," she said, "if those will help."

"Of course. Let Gabe Morgan know what you're donating."

"I don't think I know him."

"I'll introduce you," Max offered. "I need

to get to Sweetheart Ranch, do a follow-up on Gabe's horse. Come with me."

"Gabe may not be there," Sophie said. "Kate told me he's gone to Texas."

"We'll go anyway to check on Critter, which will give Averill a chance to see the large animal part of the practice firsthand." He looked at Sophie. "If Rembrandt's around, I'll give him another exam, although I wonder why he's so important to you."

"I just like dogs."

Sophie tried to relax. She'd heard nothing about Averill to worry her.

Yet...had that brief look of loss been an evasion instead?

And if so, why?

CHAPTER NINE

SOPHIE WAS THE first to arrive for the Monday night meeting of her finance committee. There was good news to report on the upcoming auction, but they were far from their goal with general pledges. She was poring over a new spreadsheet when Gabe walked in carrying a saddle. "My," she said, her pulse tripping, "look at you."

Between the saddle and his usual jeans and boots, Gabe had a definite cowboy appeal. An appeal, period.

He dropped the gear on the floor and sat across from her at the table. "I've been using the storage closet here in the community center to pile up smaller items for the auction. Sorry I couldn't collar anyone to help you this past weekend."

"You were in Texas."

He looked sheepish. "Kate says you were at the ranch to work with Critter. I should have let you know before I left." He gestured at his feet. "This is my contribution."

"You're donating the saddle?"

"Anonymously, okay?" He didn't meet Sophie's eyes. The silver-trimmed saddle was obviously expensive, which made her wary of the gift. How could Gabe afford such an ornate rig? The ones she'd seen at Kate's ranch were practical and plain. "I got it for a song at a flea market in Odessa," he said.

"Did you have a nice weekend?"

"I wouldn't call it good. My father and I never get along. The rest of the time there went about as well as our conversation when I first got to the house—an argument, really. After that I didn't see much of him."

"He's a widower, right?"

"My mom died when I was eleven." He told her with fondness in his voice about Jilly who'd stepped in then to mother him, who still did whenever he let her. "I spent most of my time this weekend with Jilly. I was going to stay over till tomorrow, but because of Dad there didn't seem to be any point."

"I'm sorry there's friction between you."

Sophie had wondered about his family, how they lived and what had caused the problem, but Gabe didn't seem to be in the mood to tell her more. "It can't be easy for you, going home, then. Max and I were lucky to have both our parents until I was a junior in high school."

"Not my home anymore. But Jilly was glad to see me."

"You like her."

"I do." He threw off the topic with a shrug. "How was your weekend?"

"Nothing exciting." While they waited for the other committee members to arrive, Sophie fought the urge to ask if he'd enjoyed his dinner with Lauren before he left town. "I worked Saturday morning, as usual, then on Sunday Max had invited his new receptionist over for a barbecue."

Gabe eyed her. "There's a subtext here—he didn't ask you first?"

"He did this time," she assured him.

But her tone must have given her away. Sophie studied the tabletop, her gaze unfocused on the spreadsheet. "I'm not sure I believe some of the things Averill said—or, rather, didn't say. Maybe she's a very private person who doesn't like to share, but that doesn't seem right, either." Sophie wasn't sure she should confide in Gabe but needed to talk to someone about this. "I want to like her, and I have so far, yet there's something…incomplete about Averill. I also think there's more between them than her being his employee." She mentioned their plan to follow up with Gabe's horse at Sweetheart Ranch together. "Field trip," she said.

"I didn't see them at the ranch, but I only got back an hour ago. I barely saw Kate," he told her.

"Averill sat beside him yesterday on the sofa. He touched her hand."

"You mean Maxwell Crane finds love? Tell me why you're suspicious."

"Not suspicious," she said, "just…yes, I guess I am." She met his eyes. "Gabe, this probably isn't my place."

"He's your brother. You're concerned."

Sophie took another breath. "I think… I'm not sure… I'm likely wrong but…she may have stolen a book from the library."

"Stolen?"

She told him what Rachel had said. "That would be our word against Averill's, of course. I don't even know exactly which book may be missing. All I do know are the ones she did check out. But what if she's guilty? And Max is getting close to a woman who's a thief?"

"Not exactly the bank heist of the century," Gabe said, "but I see your point. If true, that's not a good sign for any romance." He hesitated. "I imagine you're making a connection here with your ex. Still, I'm obviously no judge of relationships."

Neither was Sophie. By the time she'd been blindsided by Will and Bess's deception, they were married. Her heart was broken. Perhaps Gabe had been hurt by someone, too.

"I'm sorry things didn't go well with your father." Outside, she heard a car door slam. Voices. People were arriving for the committee meeting. She looked expectantly at Gabe. "What do you think I should do about Averill?"

"Spell it right out. Best approach. See what she says."

"Really? Max would kill me."

"Then ask him before you say anything. Soph—"

He didn't finish. The door swung open, and Cooper Ransom strode in, talking to his wife, Nell. "Later," Gabe said, then stood, picked up the saddle and started for the storage closet.

Sophie had avoided asking him about Lauren, and embarrassing herself, but she also hadn't wanted to dig any further into Gabe's difficult relationship with his father. She had enough questions about her brother's apparent interest in Averill.

She doubted Max would take kindly to any inquiry.

AFTER LAST NIGHT'S committee meeting, and Gabe's advice about Max, Sophie's day didn't go any better than the one before. The library was super busy, a difficult patron registered a complaint about service that gave Sophie a headache, and yet another computer search for the missing book had come up empty.

Then, when she pulled up at the barn after work, she expected to see Kate again. Instead, Gabe was filling water buckets at a tap in the wash stall.

"Can I help?" she asked.

He glanced at her over his shoulder. "Grooming Critter wasn't enough for you?"

"That horse is a darling."

Gabe snorted. "I promise I won't tell him. Might set back his recovery from that lameness to know he's regarded as less than a macho guy."

She peered into the bucket. "How hard can this be?"

"Soph, give it up. I suggested you lighten your image in town, but not this way."

"You don't want me around."

"I didn't say that. I just..." He ran out of words.

"Well, I'm here. You might as well enlighten me. Do you water the horses every afternoon?"

"We keep their buckets full all the time." Gabe swiped a hand across his forehead. He was saved from explaining further or letting Sophie help when Rembrandt loped around the corner from the yard, then made a dash for her, as if he'd been waiting for Sophie.

"Hi, beautiful boy," she crooned, bending to pet him. Rembrandt's tail wagged like a banner.

Gabe groaned. "First you charm my horse. Now that geriatric dog."

Sophie put both hands over the dog's ears. "Don't listen to him, Remi. You're not only gorgeous but as spry as a puppy. I'm your biggest fan."

"Max was already here," Gabe said. "He agrees with Kate about—" he broke off, as if the dog understood him "—you know. Which, of course, didn't mesh with Teddie's view."

"What's yours?"

"Not my dog," he muttered, "but I'm all for letting nature take its course. As long as he's not in any discomfort—Max says he has some arthritis—I say leave him be."

"My hero." The words slipped out before Sophie thought better of them.

Gabe grinned. "Yeah?"

She blushed. "At this moment, definitely. Will you put in a good word for him? I was half-afraid when I drove in that he'd be gone." She added, "Not my dog, either."

"You'd like him to be."

Yes. Sophie, who hadn't made any decision until now, considered this to be a rescue mission before someone took Rembrandt's life. "Well, I do live with a veterinarian."

"Who disagrees with you, I bet."

"I can be persuasive." But what would Max say if she walked in the door with a dog? It seemed odd to her that, as a vet, her brother didn't have a pet. Maybe he'd never recovered after losing their childhood dog. And would Remi be happy with her? She hadn't thought that far. His adjustment from being a ranch dog to a pet in town would be huge.

Before she could reconsider, Gabe nodded toward the barn doors. "Pull out all the stops, then. Here comes Teddie."

Kate's four-year-old son had spotted Sophie and ran up to her. She straightened from

Rembrandt just in time to avoid getting bowled over. Blond-haired Teddie flung both arms around her waist. "Hi, Miss Crane! Did you find the books I want? Mom's going to stop by the libary while she's in town." He frowned behind the black-framed glasses that made his blue eyes look larger. "But you're here."

"My assistant can give her the books." Sophie bit back a smile at Teddie's mispronunciation of the word *library*, which was common with children. "I think I found some real winners for you."

"About atoms?"

The subject was Teddie's newest interest. She ruffled his hair. "Would I let down my best customer? I think we should have a Reader of the Year award."

"I'd win," he said, grinning up at her. "I won the summer reading club last year. I read the most books of anybody."

Gabe was smiling. "Teddie, Miss Crane's interested in Rembrandt here. What do you think? Could she take him home with her?"

"To keep? He belongs to Sweetheart Ranch." Teddie's brow furrowed. "But the other dogs are mean to him. Bandit can't always help him—and once Rembrandt got hurt."

Gabe nodded. "He might be safer somewhere else, then."

"I'd take very good care of him, Teddie," Sophie said. "I promise."

"Like I do Spencer and Lancelot?" He was devoted to his pony and the foal Noah had given him.

"Exactly like that."

"Do you have other dogs at home?"

"None," she said, uncertain whether that was a plus or minus in Teddie's razor-sharp mind.

"I wouldn't want Rembrandt to feel lonesome." He hesitated. "And you prob'ly don't know anything about dogs." Then he brightened. "You can read some books!"

"Yes, I can. So…" She waited for his decision. Gabe was clearly trying not to laugh. Like most people, he had a tender way with Kate's little boy.

"It's your call," Gabe told him.

Releasing his grip on Sophie's waist, Teddie puffed out his chest. "You can have him." He leaned down to hug Rembrandt, whispering in the old dog's ear. "You belong to Miss Crane now. I'll tell her what you like to eat."

"And get his leash for me, if you will."

"He doesn't have a leash. Rembrandt runs with all the dogs. He's not very good at chasing cows 'cause he's older than they are, but he tries."

Again, Sophie faltered. Could Remi transition from living outside or in the barn with lots of freedom to staying inside all day in a crate while she was at the library? But considering the dog's problem with the other ranch dogs, she was willing to let him try.

"Then I think he's ready for retirement, don't you?—and my brother will be right there if Remi gets sick. We have a backyard, too."

Seeming satisfied, Teddie held out his small hand. "It's a deal."

"Come visit him," Sophie said, "whenever you want."

"I will!" Teddie made his goodbyes to Rembrandt, assuring him that the other dogs would never bother him again, then charged off toward a stall where, Sophie presumed, one of his two horses lived.

She turned to Gabe. "Will Kate be okay with this?"

"She'll be happy. She didn't want to make that other decision. I hope you're sure about this because you just got yourself a dog."

"He needs me."

"Ah, Soph." Gabe hooked one hand behind

her neck and drew her close. He kissed the top of her head.

And said, "You do know he's not house-broken?"

CHAPTER TEN

THE NEXT EVENING Gabe rang the front bell at Sophie's house on Cattle Track Lane.

No one answered at first, then suddenly she flung open the door, carrying a bucket and mop in her other hand. "Sophie," Max yelled from inside, "come get this dog! He just did it again."

"I'm coming," she said. "I was about to put the mop away. Is the mess wet or—" She broke off. "Come in, Gabe. You were spot-on. He's not house-trained."

He followed her down the hall to the living room, where Rembrandt stood with his tail between his legs, a shamed expression on his face. Gabe felt sorry for him. As for Sophie...

"Where has the town's head librarian gone? Yesterday you were watering horses, measuring out feed, and tonight you're a vet tech."

"Mother of necessity." She set down the bucket. "I guess Teddie was right. I'll need to read some books—which won't help now."

"If you want to return the dog, I'm sure Kate won't mind."

"But I would. I made my decision. He's Rembrandt Crane now and here to stay."

"That's what you think." Max was on his knees, dabbing at a puddle that was soaking into the carpet. He looked at them over his shoulder.

Sophie set the mop aside. She moved to take the sponge from him, and Max rose, shaking his head at Gabe.

"We've spent two whole evenings this way. Was this your idea?"

"Nope. Are you really going to let her do the dirty work? She did enough at the ranch—"

"And came home with a problem neither of us needs."

Gabe shook his head. "Man, why did you become a vet if you don't like animals?"

"I love animals. But not in my house ruining this rug."

"Think of it as good experience for dealing with other pet parents," Sophie said. "This will develop your compassion."

"Huh."

Gabe grabbed the sponge from her. "Let me finish here. Why don't you take Rembrandt outside? Encourage him to inspect a few bushes instead?"

My hero, she'd told him yesterday. Gabe wanted to live up to that. At the same time, he'd learned at the barn how dangerous that could be. Touched by her gesture about the dog, he'd almost kissed her but settled for a quick peck on top of her head. He shouldn't get any closer to Sophie. In fact, because of Brynne Energy, and because he wasn't staying, he should keep far away.

"Well," he said once Sophie had returned to the house with the dog. "Any luck?"

"It's a work in progress."

By then, Max had disappeared into their home office and shut the door. Gabe heard him on the phone.

"He's talking to Averill," Sophie said, dropping onto a chair. "Every night now."

"From your tone, you haven't changed your mind about her." When she didn't pick up on that subject, Gabe remembered his reason for coming by. "I brought you something. I'll be right back." He trotted out to his truck, returning with a large dog bed.

Sophie groaned. "He prefers Max's easy chair—not mine—which doesn't endear Remi to him, but thank you for the gift."

Gabe sat on the sofa across from her. "It'll get better," he said.

"I do hope so." She sighed. "Max is mad at me."

"No, he's not. He's aggravated."

"Who could tell the difference? I should have asked him first."

"Yeah, but he'll get over it."

"What if he doesn't?"

"You still have every right to adopt that dog. Not that it's easy, I can tell."

"I'm a beginner here, too. Like Remi. I bought him a collar, leash, bowls, doggy treats and a crate, which he didn't seem to take to. Still, I can't let him loose while I'm at the library."

"Keep trying the crate. Rembrandt's probably stressed out. He's never lived in a house before," Gabe pointed out.

"He seems to like staying indoors, though. I'm thankful for that. In fact, he's becoming a real couch potato."

"But he's never been crated until now. If he gets used to it, the crate should give him a sense of security. You did a nice thing, Soph. That dog—" which was now in the crate in the kitchen, as if to think over his social faux pas "—will have a better life here. He really wasn't doing well on the ranch. Made me sad."

Sophie sent him a grateful smile. "Me, too. But let's bypass my new dog problems. My house isn't the only place filling up." She sat straighter in the chair. "The community center closet is now crammed with horse paraphernalia, quilts, hand-knitted hats, mittens and scarves that will come in handy next winter when the first snow flies, canned goods and homemade chocolates for the auction."

"On the day of the event, Sam Hunter's John Deere will be moved from his barn to the renovated fairgrounds, joined by Barney Caldwell's vintage Mustang. Forgot to tell you, someone else just donated a vacation at their timeshare near Padre Island."

"Wow, that's great," Sophie said, then yawned.

Gabe stood. The event was scheduled for mid-June, three weeks away. "I should go. You did too much yesterday and with Remi tonight. Get some sleep."

She walked him to the door. "I'm pretty good at filling water buckets, right?"

He nodded. "Feeding horses, too—at least you're working on all that, and in town I heard someone mention you and Sweetheart Ranch."

"Who was it?"

"Well, you know, I meant Kate—we all went to dinner at the café—but the word is out."

SOPHIE WAS STANDING in line at the café the next morning, waiting to order her daily coffee before work when Clara McMann, whose friendly face always cheered her, stepped up behind Sophie. The older woman had a heart of gold.

Sophie turned. "Clara. You're out early."

She patted her graying hair. "Not as early as you. You're ahead of me in line."

"Next." The barista called Sophie.

"My regular, thanks. No, wait. Give me the Super-Duper today."

"Big night?" Clara asked at her shoulder.

Sophie stifled a yawn. "You might say that. I was up and down with my dog."

"I heard you'd taken in an old ranch collie."

"He's having a bit of an adjustment." And despite Gabe's advice, Max now refused to help, leaving Sophie to clean up all the messes. "So is my brother, I'm afraid. He didn't want a dog." She added, "We had one once when we were kids. He doesn't want the responsibility."

Clara's brown gaze held hers. "Max does tend to focus on his own work. A good thing for me and Hadley who swear by him as our vet." Clara's former foster kid, now an impressively large man who looked as if he could handle anything, ran the McMann ranch with her. He was on Sophie's finance committee. Hadley Smith was pretty much Clara's adopted son now. Along with his wife, their baby, and his twins from a previous marriage, Clara who'd been a widow for years had a family again. "Poor animal, but do you really think the dog can become a house pet?"

"I'm trying. Him? Not as much." Remi didn't seem to get the idea about using the yard to do his business, and they were playing a game of in-out, in-out most of the time.

Sophie had gotten her coffee and was about to look for a table and wait for Clara when someone else tapped her on the shoulder. Sophie turned. "Jasmine, I haven't seen you since I came back to Barren." She didn't get the chance to ask how her former high school classmate was doing. The woman's weak smile vanished as she eyed Sophie up and down.

"Fancy suit," she said, then gestured at her own faded jeans and shirt. "But then, most of us didn't leave town to become a big-city hotshot."

The snide comment wasn't a compliment

and made Sophie's already shaken confidence take a fresh nosedive. She and Jasmine had been cheerleaders together, but she didn't get to answer before Jasmine spoke again. "I can't imagine you staying this time, either. By Christmas, I bet you'll be moving on to greener pastures." Then she grabbed her coffee from the counter and fled.

Clearly, the message was *You don't belong here. You're not one of us*.

Her cup rattling in her hands, Sophie took the chair across from Clara, who'd managed to get them a table.

Clara asked, "What was that about?"

"Us being rivals, I suppose, when we were in high school."

"Hmm." Clara gazed after Jasmine, who'd reached the door then left the café. "Not the way you expected to start your day?"

"No," Sophie agreed.

"Everyone in town is acting strange, especially with the celebration approaching. Including me. I shouldn't have volunteered again—we're so busy at the ranch—but I'm also hosting bingo night soon at the community center. You wouldn't want to come?"

"I don't play, Clara." The regular event was attended mostly by older members of the community who loved those game nights. Plus, Sophie had Rembrandt. She'd never imagined how close a pet could be to having a child, as if she knew about either one. "I'm swamped with work plus the sesquicentennial—"

"Goodness, and I know you're up for Citizen of the Year. Congratulations, dear."

"In order to win, I was advised to change my image." Sophie told her about the chores she was learning to do at Sweetheart Ranch. Then another idea popped into her mind. "If I didn't dislike public speaking, I'd come talk to your gathering."

"You'd undoubtedly rack up some votes."

Tempted, yet still reluctant, Sophie wished she hadn't spoken. She stirred her coffee. Really, she'd been daydreaming out loud. Yes, she was trying to change her image, but to actually give a talk… "I know this will sound silly, but when I was in school, we had to do book reports, get up in class in front of everybody. I was always on the verge of being sick from nerves. I'd lie awake the night before, heart pounding, wishing I would die before morning. My mom had to shove me on the school bus. Every time."

Clara laid a hand on hers. "But these are your fellow townspeople"

"Many of whom no longer feel I belong here. Jasmine, for instance."

Clara sipped her latte. "I like your idea. This would be good exposure, Sophie. Really, how bad could it be?"

She pushed her coffee aside. "If I didn't remember the day all my classmates started to snicker? Not bad, maybe. But I sat down that one time, my face on fire—and felt the cold wooden seat of my desk on the back of my legs. I'd gone to the bathroom before my talk, and the hem of my skirt had gotten caught in the waistband."

"Oh, dear." Clara laughed. "Embarrassing, I'm sure, but not fatal. I'd be willing to bet most kids have had an equally daunting experience." She added, "My life from the age of ten to eighteen—in the dark ages—was torture. One social blunder after another. I was an awkward child, so I understand how you felt then."

"But this is now, right?" And Sophie was no longer a shy girl. Was that what Clara had meant?

Clara's silence spoke for her.

"My chance to toot my own horn," Sophie went on. "To tell people how qualified I am for the award. Talk about the important job I have."

"The library is the backbone of this community."

"And about all the committees I'm on, the church—" She broke off. "Still, I'd hardly be introducing myself. People see me at work all the time. And eye me with suspicion, as if to say, like Jasmine, when am I going to take off again for some big city? I'm not exactly accepted here now, and I can't blame them…" She trailed off again.

Where had her confidence as an adult gone?

Sophie knew, and Will and Bess's betrayal was hard to forget. But if she wanted to become Citizen of the Year, to feel a true part of Barren again, she had to take Gabe's advice and play a more public role. This could be another way to prove herself. Show people like Claudia and Jasmine that she intended to win. A few new clothes wouldn't be enough. Neither was learning how to pick a horse's hooves. "I'll do it," she said. "You talked me into it."

Clara looked sly. "You did that yourself, dear."

Sophie laughed. She'd been gently maneuvered by a pro, and she could imagine Clara guiding a much younger Hadley Smith in the same fashion. "Clara, if I wanted a campaign manager, I'd definitely hire you."

AVERILL WAS TIDYING up at the clinic the next morning, watching the door and waiting for Max to arrive while she ruminated over last Sunday's barbecue.

I wish Sophie liked me. Averill had long ago developed a sixth sense about how people viewed her. During the meal, and later in the living room, she'd fidgeted under Sophie's steady regard, hoping she didn't say the wrong thing.

Was it in her best interest—or Max's—to keep dreaming she could be more than his receptionist? He didn't need Averill messing up his life, and in contrast to his sister, who was in the running to become Barren's best citizen—wouldn't you know?—Averill didn't measure up.

She didn't want to make another mistake, that word not beginning to cover it.

Max breezed through the door, and a wave of warmth ran through her despite the warning she'd given herself. Although he might be clueless at times, he was a fine-looking man, and she loved the sound of his voice. She was obviously smitten.

"'Morning," he said. "Looks to be a hot one. What's on our schedule?"

Our. Averill studied the computer screen. "You need to recheck that cow at the NLS. Then you're due at the Circle H to see how their horse Blue is doing after the surgery on his leg. And Kate Lancaster is worried about her mare's cough. She wants you to look at Lady."

"That will bring us to lunchtime," he said. "We could meet at the café or Jack's, if you'd rather."

Averill stared at him. *We.* "What about your other appointments? And if I'm not here at lunch, who would man this desk?"

"Candy," he said, referring to his vet tech. Max came around behind the counter, looked over her shoulder. "We should be back for my two o'clock." He grinned, his face reflected in the computer screen. "Just in time to talk with Mrs. Hingle."

Averill had barely heard a word he said after *we could meet at the café.* Often, Max grabbed a fast-food burger somewhere or, worse, rummaged around in his truck for a wrinkled apple or bag of chips. "You really want to have lunch with me?"

"Why not?"

"Max, maybe that isn't the best idea."

"Why not?" he said again.

Averill hesitated. "I'd love to join you for lunch but—" *you're an upstanding member of the community while I'm—*

"What?"

"Nothing," she said, losing her nerve. There was no way she could tell him more about herself than she already had. Growing up in Farrier. Losing her father, although she hadn't said why. Wanting more for herself, which all sounded good. "I...don't want to spoil our, um, working relationship."

Max turned her around. "Averill, is this about Sophie? Last Sunday?"

"No, but other people might talk."

"I'm not ashamed to be seen with you. Why would I be?"

She couldn't meet his eyes. Why had he said *ashamed*?

"If that's what you meant," he added, his puzzled gaze fixed on hers. A car pulled up out front, and an elderly woman got out. "Arrgh," Max said. "Look who's here. Mrs. Hingle."

"Her appointment's not until two."

"I'll see Hingle now," he told Averill, half

smiling. "I can put off stopping at the NLS till tomorrow." The door opened and the woman rushed inside, lugging a large cat carrier and puffing with the effort.

"My Beauty's gaining weight again," said Mrs. Hingle.

"Take her into Room 3. I'll be right there." His eyes dancing, Max looked at Averill. "See you at the café. Tell Candy to answer the phones."

She could hear him chatting with Mrs. Hingle as he entered the exam room, doing his best to calm her. As he did at least twice a week, he would try to convince her that her cat wasn't eating too much but expecting kittens. A fact of life that Mrs. Hingle refused to accept. "Such a good girl," she crooned to her pet.

Shaking her head, Averill turned back to the computer to readjust Max's schedule.

Then, still hearing the low murmur of their voices through the closed door, she sat back in her chair and reached for a book she'd left face down on the shelf.

She wanted this job. But Max…

Averill knew she was getting in too deep when she was the wrong person for him. If she needed proof, it was right there on the spine of that book.

Survivor Guilt: Coping After Senseless Tragedy.

CHAPTER ELEVEN

"TURN ON YOUR TV."

Gabe had answered Jilly's call this morning with one hand while he fed Critter a carrot through the stall bars with the other. "What's up?"

"You'll see."

"Jilly, I'm in the barn. Working." He glanced at his watch. It read just after eight o'clock, and the sun outside was already ablaze as it climbed into the hazy blue sky. "I don't have a television set out here."

"The Senate investigation is done."

"Finished?"

"That's certainly the appropriate word. Brynne—your father—may be indicted."

Gabe's stomach sank. "No surprise, but still…"

"What can he *possibly* do to salvage this?"

He looked around to make sure no one else was in the barn to overhear. The only sounds were those of other horses shifting, stamping a foot, munching grain. He fed the rest of the carrot to Critter, as if Gabe could ease his mind with such a mundane task. "Have you all talked to his lawyers?"

"As we speak," she said. "He's been in meetings since the news broke at six a.m., but of course I'm not there. I'm at home, pacing this solarium and imagining a man's life falling apart." Her voice trembled. "A man I happen to care about."

As if Gabe didn't.

Shoot. If only his dad had listened to him. "He should have followed up better after he talked to one of his underlings. How could he trust someone else, including his COO, to handle things?"

"Meaning Gerald Bixby," she said. "He wasn't the best employee." Gabe wondered if she might be crying.

"Jilly."

"*You* need to be here for him."

He gave Critter a last pat through the bars. "It's not that simple. There must be reporters crawling all over that house, hanging out in front of headquarters, pushing microphones in anyone's face who walks past." Gabe could envision the trucks, the cameras, the chaos. Aaron might well be watching the coverage, too, pondering whether he should come forward.

"I'm a prisoner at the moment," Jilly admitted. "You'd abandon your own father to those wolves? I'm disappointed in you." *Again*, although she didn't say that. This unnatural disaster had affected his relationship with Jilly, too.

"The one way I can help or support him is to keep doing what I'm doing."

"Where is your loyalty, *Gabriel*?"

When she used his full name, and spoke in italics, Gabe knew he was in trouble. "Jilly, it's *because* I care about him that I'm staying here. If, God forbid, my friend Aaron who first blew the whistle—to me—decides to talk, that would be the coup de grâce. Dad's name wouldn't be the only one involved then, so would mine, and I'd have no choice legally but to talk as well. What I know can't possibly help him. Maybe after the formal agreement is reached—"

"Never mind," she said, her tone flat. "Why think talking to you now would turn out better than your last visit home? I shouldn't have called."

"Jilly."

But as he walked away from Critter's stall, Gabe was talking to empty air.

Jilly had been right about one thing. He couldn't hide forever.

Soon, he expected things to really hit the fan. Someone—even Lauren—would discover Gabe's relation to his father and to Brynne Energy. There'd be reporters then on Sweetheart Ranch who would make Lauren's queries at dinner that night seem like a game.

It was only a matter of time, which was running out.

FOR THE REST of the morning, Sophie focused on this month's book order, slimmer than in April. She might as well get used to what would have to be a reduced collection as far as new books were concerned. She was lost in reading *Library Review* when she heard Gabe's voice.

"Sophie here?"

"In her office," Rachel said, probably pointing in that direction.

"Hey." Gabe appeared in her open doorway, leaning a shoulder against the frame. He'd left his Stetson somewhere and his head was bare, the sun through Sophie's windows streaming over his mink-dark hair.

"Hey, yourself."

"I was over at the café earlier for coffee. Clara said you've agreed to give a speech."

"I'm not sure it will be a good speech, but yes."

He eyed her casual wear. "You planning to come out to the ranch later?"

"Probably not today. I need to finish a book order and then talk to Finn about the budget."

He studied his boots, his mouth drawn into a line. "Could that wait? Can you take a few hours off?"

She glanced at her computer. "Gabe, has something happened?"

"I just…need someone to talk to." Sophie wasn't certain she was the right choice, but how could she say no to the man of her dreams? Even when, despite Max's opinion, she felt sure Gabe didn't see her in the same way? When, because of Will, she shouldn't want him to?

"Of course."

"You don't need to take your car. I'll bring you back later."

On the way to Sweetheart, he stayed lost in his own thoughts until Sophie couldn't stand the silence any longer. She'd never seen him in anything except a laid-back mood. "What's wrong, Gabe?"

But he didn't answer. "Tell you what," he said instead. "I need to clear my head and you should keep up with your ranch-y things. Have you ever ridden?" He must know that answer.

"Never." Sophie tried not to shudder. This was getting strange. Clearly, Gabe was troubled and yet when she tried to probe a bit, he clammed up. "Kate can vouch for that. I groom horses from as far away as I can manage. When I helped you feed, they were safely behind bars."

"Tenderfoot." He didn't smile as they reached the barn. "You want to change that, right? When you passed his place today, Earl at the hardware store said he liked that denim skirt you're wearing. Another score on the softer image card."

"I can't wear this skirt to ride."

"Kate has jeans. You can borrow a pair."

Having run out of excuses, and wanting to find out what was bothering Gabe, Sophie relented. "Okay, fine. But wait until this gets around town. Because there's no way I can stay on a horse for more than two minutes. You'll probably have to pick me up off the ground."

When Gabe finished saddling their horses,

her heart was beating a little too fast. He would ride Critter for the first time since his roan gelding had gone lame, "to see how he does. Max cleared him for light exercise," Gabe said as he led the pair out into the sun. "You need a leg up?"

Sophie had grown up with friends who rode, even had their own horses, but she was not only a tenderfoot, as Gabe had said. She was a town girl. She'd paid little attention to the terms people used.

"I don't even know what that means."

"Here. I'll show you. You can mount on your own next time."

"I doubt there'll be a next time," Sophie murmured, distracted by Gabe's touch. He cupped his hand around her lower leg, then boosted her into the saddle. He'd chosen for her a gentle chestnut mare named Precious, claiming she was "bombproof."

"All set?" Gabe stepped back after adjusting her stirrups. "Keep the ball of this foot right where I put it. The other one, too. You'll be fine. Precious will take care of you."

"Gabe. How do I steer?"

He laughed. "You're as precious as that horse's name." He reached up to properly place her left hand on the reins against the horse's neck. "This way to go right, this way to go left. Pull back to stop—but easy does it. She has a soft mouth."

He told her how to nudge Precious to start forward. Amazingly, that worked, but Sophie was glad to ride in a straight line beside Gabe. If they needed to turn, he could tell her, then lead the way. "Just pretend you're on cruise control," he said.

They left the yard at a loose walk, which also suited her fine.

The mare wasn't a large horse, but it still seemed a long way down to Sophie.

"The things I do for friendship," she muttered.

Gabe laughed again. "We'll turn you into a cowgirl yet."

They entered the nearest pasture, Gabe leaning over to unlock then close the gate without losing his balance. He sat deep in his saddle. "How come I'm perched on this mare's back while you look like a centaur?" Sophie wanted to know.

"You'll have a good seat. Just be patient."

But Gabe looked as if he'd been born in the saddle. "How long have you been riding?"

"Right now? About four minutes."

Sophie rolled her eyes. "I meant in your life?"

"All of it, pretty much." He told her about working as a kid on a Texas spread, developing his skills, "realizing my heart's really in cattle and horses..." He didn't go on.

"Cowboy," she said.

For a while they rode across the flat plain of Sweetheart Ranch, birds singing in the trees, the nearby creek burbling in its bed, the sky overhead that brilliant Kansas blue.

"Big sky," Sophie said. It felt good to be out of her office.

"Not only in Montana."

"What about Texas?" Maybe she'd get a better clue to his background and whatever was troubling him.

"There, too," he told her, his hands light on the reins, but said no more.

"Do you miss home?"

"Sure, sometimes. I like it here, though." His mouth tightened. "I take things one day at a time."

"I'm guessing today wasn't especially good—before you saddled Critter."

"Until I kidnapped you from the library," he said, flashing her a thin smile.

"Gabe, you didn't come in just to take me riding."

He drew a breath. "I had bad news today. Something to do with my dad again."

"Is he ill?"

"Sick at heart, you could say. No, he's fine otherwise."

"Then what—"

"I can't tell you anything more about that."

"You said you needed to talk. All right, then. Basic facts. What about home itself—Texas?"

He didn't seem to have a problem with that subject although Sophie had the feeling he picked and chose what to tell her. "I was born in Dallas. My mother wasn't very well, and she had a rough delivery. They never had more children. For half of my childhood, she got increasingly worse, then became bedridden. After she died," Gabe said, studying the far horizon, "Jilly—the woman I told you about— raised me. Now she probably regrets that."

"I'm sure not, Gabe." She reached out, brushing his arm.

"Anyway, I grew up, went to college. Knocked around for a while, managed to get myself engaged. Which didn't work out. I'm sorry for how that ended."

"Is that when you left Texas?"

"Soon after. I decided I'd be happier anywhere else at the time." That seemed to Sophie like only one part of the story. At least she'd gotten something out of him. "Ended up here at Sweetheart."

"You weren't into your father's business?" Sophie tried. "The gas station?"

Gabe stared at the herd of Angus in the distance. "Where'd you get that idea?"

"I don't know. You said something about your dad and the oil industry, and for some reason I assumed he had a gas station." She felt as if she were pulling teeth. "Or did I hear that somewhere else?"

He shrugged. "Texas is oil. But it's cows and horses and agriculture, too." Gabe glanced at her. "You ready to try a lope?"

"What's that?"

"Like a canter." Neither of which meant anything to Sophie. "It may be a little bouncy."

"Wait," Sophie began, but he'd already taken off, poking Critter with his heels then riding slightly ahead of her and ending the conversation. Of course, being a herd animal, Precious took the gelding's lead. Sophie's whole body jumped up and down rhythmically in the saddle, and she couldn't catch her breath. *How do I stop this thing?* Would the mare obey her or keep following Gabe? "Help! I don't know what I'm doing!"

Sophie knew what he'd done, though. After asking for her listening ear, he'd given her the bare bones of his personal history. Just like Averill. What wouldn't he tell her? About his dad?

Gabe drew up immediately. "You're doing fine. Sorry I took you by surprise."

Yes, he had. Because she'd become convinced that underneath his easygoing manner, he really was hiding something.

"And here I thought I was going to help you with a problem."

"I'm okay. Irritated, that's all. I didn't mean to lead you on." Yet he'd certainly done that. "I always feel better after a ride." He turned his horse back toward Sweetheart's barn. The horses pricked up their ears. "They've had enough for today. You, too," he said, "but first time out, I can already see you have light hands."

Was that good? Sophie bit back a sigh. She'd learned very little about Gabe. It was as if he'd invited her, intending to talk, then changed his mind or couldn't bring himself to say more. She'd have done better staying at the library to complete her book order. Now all she had to show for their outing would be a sore behind tonight.

CHAPTER TWELVE

"HOW DID I talk myself into this?" Sophie asked Gabe.

"You'll be great."

At the community center they sat in the back of the room. Sophie shifted in her chair, praying for a sudden hurricane or flash flood that would send people scurrying for their cars. A week after her first horseback ride, at least her tender bottom had healed. But despite her talk with Clara at the café, she should have said no about tonight. Instead, the room had filled up, and at the table in front Clara was reading off bingo numbers.

"B15."

Sophie heard a flurry of low conversation as the excited gamers checked their boards.

"G54."

Sam Hunter's hand shot up. "Ha, got it!"

A moment later Cooper's mother, Merry, sitting close to Ned Sutherland, her second husband and owner of the NLS Ranch, fairly danced in her chair. "I need one more, Clara."

Sophie's hands were damp. When this game ended, she would have to walk forward and begin to speak. She hoped everyone in the room took that moment to avail themselves of the coffee and pastries from the table against the side wall or chose the lull between games to visit the restroom.

"N31."

Gabe, who'd insisted on coming with her tonight, as if to make up for his mood last week, looked down at Sophie's jiggling foot. "Stop making yourself nervous."

"I couldn't be more anxious." She glanced around as if to find the nearest exit. "If I had any chance to win that award, it ends here."

"Soph. Cut it out."

Her fan club of one wouldn't give up, but Max, its other member, had begged off tonight, claiming a veterinary emergency on the other side of Farrier. He'd try to make it later, he'd said, but not to count on him. For once, Sophie was glad he'd unintentionally neglected her. If only the rest of the people here were strangers...yet the whole point was to show the attendees that she was still a valuable part of their community. Worthy of the award.

Gabe reached for her hand, then seemed to think better of it. "If you stumble, you have the printout to glance at. Just be yourself."

"O70."

"Bingo!" someone shouted.

"Bernice Caldwell," Gabe said under his breath. She was seated beside Claudia Monroe, her closest friend. They would probably tell those who weren't here if Sophie's campaign speech flopped.

The first game had ended, and a few people scraped back their chairs, then headed toward the coffee. At the podium Clara was preparing for the next game—then looked up, straight at Sophie. "Before we begin again, this is a good time to welcome Sophie Crane, one of this year's nominees for Citizen of the Year. Sophie, please come up to say a few words."

Her stomach clenched. She had worn her light gray suit, pants with a jacket that nipped in at the waist and had a scalloped peplum, over a white scoop-necked top. Businesslike yet feminine. "I can't," she said to Gabe.

"Go on. If you need a quick boost, look at me. I'll give you a thumbs-up." With a warm hand on her back, he practically pushed her out of her chair, and before she could take another breath Sophie was weaving her way through the room—and there was Rachel in the front row, saying, "Go, Sophie!"

The experience from her school days, which she'd told Clara about, replayed in her brain. Sophie hesitated.

She would have preferred not to see any familiar faces tonight. Her friends would already vote for her. People like Claudia and Bernice might be a tougher sell. Her hands were shaking so hard she had to clamp them against her sides. At the podium, she gazed out at the thirty or so people there and cleared her throat, twice. "Ahem. Thank you, Clara." She waited until Clara had taken her seat, prompting others to do the same. When the shuffling of chairs finally ended, Sophie started over. "Good evening, friends. It's great to see so many of you here tonight. I appreciate this opportunity to tell you more about…myself."

Sophie had memorized her speech, but the next words vanished from her brain. The short silence seemed to last a year. She looked down at the print copy.

"As you all, um, know, I'm a Barren native. Like many of you, I've lived here all my life, right there in my parents' house on Cattle Track Lane. Wow, thirty years."

She half expected someone to point out that

she'd left town for several of those years, but no one, not even Claudia, did.

"Not as long as us, dearie," Sam Hunter called out.

Everyone laughed. Which, unexpectedly, helped to calm Sophie's nerves.

The next twenty minutes passed in a blur of mostly friendly faces, scattered applause, and a few shouted words of encouragement or agreement with what she was saying. Sophie told a few humorous anecdotes as she reviewed her various roles in the community, the pleasure she took in serving, the enjoyment and sense of belonging she felt in her job at the library. She spoke with her fingers mentally crossed and hoping not to be challenged.

"In closing, because this town is so very dear to me, as it is to all of you, I'm honored to have been nominated as Barren's Citizen of the Year. If you feel I've done some good for our town, I would very much appreciate your vote for this award."

A bigger round of applause had just begun when the rear door opened, and Lauren Anderson strode in, dressed to the nines in a snug sheath with an American flag design. And all attention shifted from Sophie.

She swore she heard Gabe groan.

"Evening, ladies and gentlemen." Lauren stalked to the podium. She wore red heels in contrast to Sophie's serviceable black pumps. "Forgive my intrusion on your bingo night—and Ms. Crane's speech. I couldn't resist the chance to stop by. As a nominee myself to be your Citizen of the Year, I'd like to tell you where I've come from and where I intend to go." She gently pushed Sophie aside. "Which is precisely nowhere. From the moment I first saw this town, I fell in love with Barren."

Gabe shifted in his chair and Sophie wondered if that was true. Lauren had ambition stamped all over her. If either of them wanted to move away, it had to be her. But maybe that wasn't fair. Sophie knew little about her. Where had Lauren come from? What made her tick? Sophie walked to the back of the room, feeling many eyes on her.

"Want to go?" Gabe's amber gaze had filled with concern.

"Yes, but I'd better hear what she has to say."

Sophie had tried to speak from her heart, but Lauren's presentation was PR at its finest. By the time she stopped spouting her achievements and told—not asked—people to vote for her, Sophie felt drained. She should have let Gabe steer her out of the community center beforehand to her car and pour what was left of her into her driver's seat.

"You really did well," he kept saying as they crossed the parking lot now.

Sophie rummaged in her bag for her keys. "Until Lauren showed up."

"No one will take her seriously."

"Gabe, she's, like, perfect."

His mouth quirked. "You didn't find her outfit to be over-the-top?"

"A bit, perhaps." Her confidence level, which couldn't be beaten, was another matter.

"You looked more serious." His gaze swept her from head to toe. "Focused."

"But her speech—"

"Sounded as if she were running for president. I watched the audience. By the time they leave this parking lot, they'll have forgotten every word she said." In the dark she could barely see him shake his head. "You were more genuine. You're one of them. She's not."

"Now you're being too kind." Sure, but that didn't mean Gabe had to play protective big brother in Max's place. "Really, you should have stayed home."

"Hang in there, Soph. Next time you face a different crowd, you won't be as nervous."

She hesitated. Maybe he was right. She did

need to make more public appearances, rebuild her confidence, or Lauren might win the award. "You know, I've been thinking. What if I do some flyers, distribute them around town? I can only give so many speeches, but a flyer could reach more people."

"Great idea."

Gabe opened her driver's door. For a long moment, as cars rolled by them, creating a soft whoosh of sound, and someone's horn tooted, he stood there. So did Sophie, drinking in the sheen of his hair under the arc lights, seeing the warm glint in his eyes. When his gaze slipped to her mouth, so briefly she wondered if she'd imagined it, Sophie's heart sang.

But only for a moment.

It was a good thing that, because of Will and Bess, her trust was gone.

And that Gabe was Max's friend. Which was why he cared about her. As a friend too.

She needed to remember that.

Because for a single second she'd thought Gabe was about to kiss her.

CARRYING ANOTHER BATCH of the new flyers Sophie had had printed up in the week following her bingo speech, Gabe stepped inside the hardware store. They had divided the chore in half, which he was fitting in with his other tasks in town for the ranch.

"Hey, Earl."

"Gabe. Haven't seen you in a while," the shop's owner said.

Earl, who was getting on in years, could be absentminded. "I was here three days ago when I stopped by for that horse liniment you sell. Great stuff, by the way."

"I make it myself."

"Brought you these flyers you agreed to take then."

"I'll hand 'em out to everybody who comes in." Earl added, "I like Sophie. She's a good one. Don't make many like her."

"No, they don't."

"She's sure a pretty picture, too."

"Yes, she is."

Earl's mouth turned down. "That reporter over at the newspaper give me a bunch of sheets twice this size yesterday—hot pink— to hand out. Dumped 'em in the trash."

Gabe fought not to smile. That could be called cheating, but he agreed with Earl about Lauren who'd waylaid Gabe in the parking lot after bingo night. Sophie had just driven off and Gabe had been staring after her car, half wishing he'd kissed her, when Lauren approached him out of the dark like some ninja warrior.

"Gabe, I'm glad I caught you."

"Why?" he couldn't help saying.

She sent him that megawatt smile. "I'm not asking you to have dinner." If she had, Gabe would have said no this time. Lauren gestured toward one of the few remaining cars in the lot. "I can't seem to get my rental started. Could you take a look?"

"I'm not much of a mechanic—but sure." He couldn't very well leave her alone at night in the empty lot. He followed Lauren to the compact sedan nearby.

"I write a mean column but I'm out of my depth. I could use a tip from Heloise or Google with this car." She tapped her knuckles against the trunk lid.

"Hit the remote." Gabe opened the driver's door and slipped inside, having to adjust the seat for his greater height. When he tried the ignition, the engine fired right up. "You forgot to have it in Park first. That's all."

"I feel so stupid."

"Not at all," although Gabe wondered how she'd started the car before. Had she been putting him on? Inventing an excuse to talk to him again? No other explanation made sense.

"Rentals can be confusing." Gabe had traded his Lexus SUV for a pickup before he moved to Kansas, and it had taken time to get used to it.

She gave him another charming smile.

"While I have you," she said idly, "I've run out of locals for my column, 'Who's Who in Barren?' You'd be a refreshing change from the mayor, his administrative aide, some council members and our new sheriff." Her latest piece had been about Murphy, the lawyer, another nominee for Citizen of the Year. And she'd done a veritable hit job on the guy.

"Lauren, I'd rather not." He shrugged. "I guess you find me intriguing, but there's not much more here than my job as Kate Lancaster's foreman. Pretty average stuff."

"I disagree."

Gabe shifted his weight from one foot to the other and stared down at his boots in the dark. If he refused, which he wanted to do, Lauren would become more suspicious about him than she already seemed to be. He could almost see her reporter's nose twitching at the thought of what she must smell as a major story. Gabe detected an air of desperation about her, and Lauren only confirmed that.

She added, "I promise to be gentle."

"To be honest, I value my privacy." Which was part of the truth.

"Yes—and you make me wonder why."

As a matter of self-protection, Gabe started to say no, then suddenly changed his mind. He didn't like how Lauren had tried to steal Sophie's thunder on bingo night. He smiled. "I'm sure you know Sophie Crane and I are friends. What if something comes out of my mouth to give her a plug for Citizen of the Year?"

"I can always edit," Lauren murmured. "Will you do it?"

Gabe had finally scheduled the interview, but the date had been nagging at him ever since. Maybe he should prepare beforehand. That way he could control which details of his life he was willing to share. Control the interview. At the most Lauren would have one boring column to write.

He hoped that would get her off his tail. He might also find out more about Lauren.

Gabe stacked Sophie's flyers on the counter now. Earl had gone into the back room to organize some stock that had come in that morning. But as Gabe had driven down Main Street, parking every so often to drop another bunch of flyers at various shops, he'd wished he hadn't passed himself off as something he was not to safeguard his father. Then he could be straight with Lauren, and even more important, with Sophie. As they worked together on the sesquicentennial and now at Sweetheart, it was becoming harder to suppress the truth. What would Sophie think—what would everyone else in town think?—if they knew Gabe was next in line to run Brynne Energy? That he'd lied to everyone.

Gabe's blackout on television news had ended with Jilly's last call about the investigation. Every night he sat glued to the screen and the network anchor, but either the story had gotten eclipsed for now by some political scandal of the moment, or more likely the government was still gathering evidence to build their case before a release to the public in a typical media red alert: BREAKING NEWS! BRYNNE CEO INDICTED OVER OIL SPILL.

When that broke, he wouldn't be able to hide any longer behind the lie he'd been living. When he did come clean, that would probably mean losing his friend Max…and Sophie.

With her firm belief in honesty, and after the betrayal she'd suffered from her ex, she would never trust Gabe.

CHAPTER THIRTEEN

THE WINNERS OF the silent auction—the sesquicentennial's initial event—were to be announced today, and two weeks after her speech at bingo night, Sophie's part would be minor. But what if the committee didn't take in enough money? At the start the bids for items had been brisk, even generous, but they had tapered off over the last few days.

Standing at a table near the bandstand, wearing tan pants and a toast-brown tee, one of the few business casual outfits from her closet, Sophie greeted people who'd stopped to make last-minute bids before the booth closed at noon.

"Ten minutes," she told Clara after checking her watch. The older woman, Sophie's assistant today, loved such events and had also become heavily involved in planning this year's rodeo in addition to the final night of that week's banquet.

"I wonder whose bid will win the tractor?" Clara asked. "That's our biggest prize."

"Except for Barney Caldwell's Mustang." The other items, like a week's vacation at a time share near Padre Island, were less valuable, although they'd gotten the most attention.

"I think Hadley bid on several things."

"Where did he find the time?" Sophie asked. "He and Jenna have to deal with his twins, the ranch, and their own baby."

"A miracle, that one," Clara said. "When I think how long Jenna yearned to have a child of her own…thought she never could, and it warms my heart to see how happy she is now. Hadley too," she added. "He overcame his bad beginnings. My foster son has become a fine man. He's a wonderful father, and Jenna couldn't ask for a better husband." She paused. "Of course, she dotes on his twins as if they too were hers."

"A blended family—" Sophie broke off as someone approached the table. "Ah, Nell."

"Jean Bodine topped our bids." But Nell grinned. "Cooper really wants that tractor." She studied the sheets lined up on the table. "I'd rather win these jars of home-canned food. Wanda Hancock's pickles are the best. In fact, Jack's put them on the menu at Bon

Appetit." She hastily scribbled her name on the item sheets along with her and Cooper's newest bids.

Not many other people were wandering toward their table now. "Good luck," Sophie said, just as Ned Sutherland, arm in arm with Cooper's mother, approached, both still acting like newlyweds. There was a lot of that in Barren and, with two weddings to come, there would soon be more.

"I'll put in another bid," Ned announced after checking the list, "on the Mustang."

Sophie glanced toward the bandstand where Gabe, as head of the fundraiser, caught her eye. He tapped the microphone. "All right, folks." A sharp feedback squeal emitted from the speakers. "Gather around. Thanks for coming out today. First, I'm pleased to announce that we've had terrific interest in this event, a great kickoff for all the sesquicentennial week celebrations. The bidding is now closed. Let's get this party started."

Sophie carried the bid sheets to the podium. The high school band, seated nearby, struck up the "Star-Spangled Banner," and every man and woman stood with hands over their hearts. The American flag waved proudly, as more and more voices joined in to sing the national anthem, which ended in an explosion of cheers and whistles. Barren was a patriotic town.

Gabe raised his voice to be heard above the crowd. "Before I begin to announce the winners, I want to take a moment to thank Sophie Crane—stick up a hand, Sophie, to show us where you are—for her devoted efforts of her time and spirit to make this happen."

Applause. Clara nudged her in the side.

Sophie waved and smiled, but Gabe went on. "Many of you were at bingo night where Sophie spoke about her nomination to become Barren's Citizen of the Year. You'll be seeing a lot more of her in the coming days and I hope you'll listen to what she has to say." He scanned the top page of bids. "Our first winner is… Claudia Monroe! Congratulations, you've won a dozen jars of home-canned corn, carrots and beets. Courtesy of Annabelle Donovan. Oh, and some excellent dill pickles from Wanda Hancock."

Nell had been outbid again.

Gabe's shout-outs continued. Derek Moran, who'd wrecked his snazzy speed-yellow truck not long ago, was the new owner of Barney Caldwell's vintage Mustang. Sophie saw Barney, in town from KC for the weekend to visit his mother, roll his eyes as Derek started toward the table where Sophie was handling the money.

After his troubles with the law years ago, Derek appeared to be turning his life around—the ruined truck aside. He plunked down his money and grinned. Sophie handed him the keys to the classic Mustang, and a few moments later, blowing the horn, he drove off in the car.

Gabe's saddle went to a teenage boy who'd been given a horse for his birthday. The calf Zach had donated now belonged to a ten-year-old girl from a nearby farm. Noah's gentle mare went to a family with an autistic son who was taking therapeutic riding lessons.

Shadow Wilson, Derek's sister, won the gorgeous quilt that had been lovingly sewn by a group of ladies from the church. By the time all but one of the winners had collected their prizes, Gabe's voice sounded raw.

Clara leaned over to Sophie. "I'd listen to him if all he could do was whisper in my ear," she said, poking Sophie again. "Don't tell me you haven't noticed him."

"You're shameful." But Sophie didn't disagree.

Another shriek sounded from the speakers

as Gabe read the final item's winner. "And the John Deere goes to—Jean Bodine!"

"Woo-hoo!" Jean, the matriarch of the WB ranch next to Sweetheart, danced a little jig. She was Noah, Zach and Willow's mother. "Are you sure you read that right, Gabe?"

"It's all yours."

Jean hardly needed the tractor. The WB, a successful enterprise, owned lots of pricey, modern equipment. Sophie knew that Zach had recently purchased a shiny new Massey Ferguson.

Jean turned to call out, "Cody, come on up—get the keys to this thing!"

Looking stunned, Cody Jones glanced toward the restored John Deere gleaming in the sun. He was Willow's husband and Jean's son-in-law.

"It's my gift to you and Willow," she said. "Those horses you're training deserve better than that old, run-down rig you've been using. My husband—may he rest in peace—loved it, but it's seen better days."

Cody shouted at his wife. "How sweet is this? Just when our new barn and the outdoor arena have finally been finished? Great timing." He rushed over to hug his mother-in-law.

"My thanks, Jean, and to Sam Hunter for donating this dream of a vehicle."

As Gabe made his last remarks and stepped off the bandstand, Cody and Willow were surrounded by well-wishers. Gabe walked over to the table and slung an arm around Sophie's shoulders, causing Clara to raise her eyebrows. "Pretty big success, huh?"

"Except for you calling me out earlier." And the fact that they'd still need more money.

"Great PR. Don't you know? There is no bad press."

Clara was watching them, her eyes alight. "You two make a good team."

Gabe didn't refute that. "This town will have the best sesquicentennial you ever saw."

The only one, so far.

Sophie said, "By the way, the church women's luncheon next week needed a speaker. I'm going to talk about my nomination."

"Take your A game, Soph."

GABE SHOULD TAKE his own advice. And a couple of days after the auction, he should have insisted on meeting Lauren at the café for coffee to do the interview. Neutral territory. Instead, he walked into the *Barren Journal* offices already on high alert.

He'd been wrong from a personal standpoint about no bad press.

Lauren came out from behind the front counter to take his arm and lead him into the back area where several small offices were located. Lauren's boasted a plain metal desk, an uncomfortable-looking chair and an old steel file cabinet in the corner. Her desk was piled high with papers, some flagged with colorful Post-it stickers. "Not exactly the *New York Times*," she said. "Have a seat."

Gabe had the uneasy feeling he was about to get grilled, so he started the conversation, hoping in part as a distraction to learn more about Lauren. "Is the *Times* on your list of aspirations? The Gray Lady could really make your career." He paused. "Seems I've heard that you used to work for the *Tribune* in Chicago. Barren's kind of a comedown, isn't it? A small-town newspaper?"

"I ran into a spot of trouble there."

"What kind?" Gabe asked, because it didn't appear that she meant to say more.

Lauren played with a pen. "If you must know, I messed up a big story, neglected to check my facts on a very sensitive matter—we had insanely tight deadlines, which is no excuse, is it—and, I'm afraid, I got fired. After that, my résumés seemed to end up in everyone's waste baskets." She raised an eyebrow. "San Francisco, LA, Columbus, Atlanta…after a while I lost count." And heart, Gabe supposed; he felt sorry for her, although the mistake must have been serious.

"No one would give you another chance."

"None—except, of course, the *Barren Journal*. So I packed my overpriced journalism degree and moved here." Lauren's welcoming smile had died, and her sharp blue gaze homed in on him. "But let's not talk about me. That's not why you're here. First, and this is background, I'm curious about your name. Gabe isn't that common, is it?"

He hesitated. "My mother's choice."

"I know about your dad's oil business. What did she do career-wise?"

Gabe's heart stalled. Had Lauren been doing her research, as she'd promised? Morgan, the surname he'd chosen to use, probably wouldn't lead her to his family, but if she'd stumbled across Wyatt, the connection to Brynne, the company itself…

"Mom was a homemaker." True enough. "Her health was never that good, and she died pretty young." The same info he'd given Sophie and others.

"My condolences. You don't like to talk about that, do you?"

"Painful memories," he agreed, examining his boots. The present wasn't great, either. Gabe hadn't spoken to Jilly or his father since her last call over three weeks ago about the Senate investigation. He couldn't decide if that was a good thing, or very bad. Gabe was still waiting for the blow that could reveal his identity.

"So. You left home when?"

"Not right after college. I hung around home for a while." Trying to be a good son, he'd started that climb up the corporate ladder to please his father. If Gabe had never met Aaron as a kid or later been apprised of the maintenance and safety issues on the rig... "But I'd always wanted to be a cowboy." His summer months on a ranch not far from home had been Gabe's escape from the situation with his dad. Working with horses and cows had not only eased his mind. It had made him want to be like the other real hands. He spread his arms. "So here I am. In Barren, Kansas. Doing what I love." That wasn't a lie.

Lauren raised an eyebrow. "You left out a few years. No wife, no children in that past?"

"I'm a confirmed bachelor."

"Gabe, a good-looking man like you?" Lauren glanced down at her jeans and blouse. No flashy outfit today. Her casual clothes suited the environment of the *Journal* offices while Sophie was still mainly wearing suits to work. "You seem to spend a lot of time with Sophie Crane—as friends, you said."

He needed to keep it that way. On bingo night, he'd again been tempted to kiss her but had resisted the urge, yet every time she came to the ranch to learn a few basic skills, ride a horse now and then, that temptation grew stronger. Gabe ought to turn Sophie over to Kate at the barn.

"I'm not looking for more than friendship. I was engaged once," he admitted. "Didn't last."

"A double heartache, then." Her gaze looked sympathetic, though he didn't trust her. "Losing your mother, then your almost-bride…not the worst reason to bury yourself here on a remote ranch."

"I wouldn't call Sweetheart remote." Five miles from town on a straight road.

"But not exactly in the center of things. Which I certainly understand." Lauren fiddled with the pen again. "Of course, to circle back, I do have bigger long-term 'aspirations,' if not at the *Times*. What about you? And pardon me if I don't buy your friendship-only with Sophie."

"Lauren, I'd rather not bring her into this."

"Ah, I knew it. A protective alpha male." Which must make Lauren even more suspicious of their relationship. "You're like a dying breed."

"Not in this area. Lot of ranchers around, guys who can handle a balky steer or a rogue horse…" Or one pesky female reporter.

"You're a tough case. I'm not getting anywhere, am I?"

"It's your show. Ask away." Gabe had prepared that mental list of acceptable questions to answer, ones that couldn't lead Lauren anywhere. But he'd about run out of road. "Told you I was an open book. Maybe you shouldn't trust your instincts. I doubt many people will want to read about my boring life."

"Too boring, maybe."

The words had dropped into the conversation like a hammer striking a nail.

Gabe didn't know how to respond. Anything he might say could only make her more determined to dig even deeper.

"I googled your name," she said. "Do you know how many Gabe Morgans there are in this country?"

"Plenty, I'd guess."

"I need to narrow my search—because I'm not done yet." She stood up behind her desk. "Thanks for coming in. I'll be in touch once I figure out the angle for my story."

LATER THAT DAY, after work, Sophie topped off her gas tank at the local Brynne station then drove out to Sweetheart to take another ride, not just because she was beginning to enjoy that. She hoped to forget for an hour or two about the library budget, Averill, and her own campaign for the award, but in the half hour she and Gabe had been crossing the land on horseback he had said little.

"I can get away for a bit," he'd said when she phoned ahead earlier. "Come on out."

Yet again he hadn't sounded enthused. And his mood hadn't improved.

Was it her new image he didn't like? Sophie had shocked him with her outfit today: a red plaid sleeveless Western-style shirt with pearl buttons, the ubiquitous jeans and a pair of red tasseled boots with decorative studs. The real beginning of her new wardrobe.

Gabe's eyes had widened. "You took me seriously."

"I assumed you were serious."

"I'd have expected Lauren to wear something like that." Then, seeing Sophie's expression fall, he added, "But you're rocking the look, Soph." Gabe pulled his cell from his pocket and snapped her picture. "You can post this on social media, use it on the next batch of flyers." For some reason, after that he'd lapsed into silence again.

What had happened to change his manner from the easygoing cowboy she thought she'd known to a man who kept his own counsel? She made a face at his back.

Not knowing how to reach Gabe, Sophie concentrated on riding. She liked Precious, and the little mare seemed to tolerate her. Sophie didn't fear falling off as much as she had the first time. Still, when she'd expressed confidence, Gabe had cautioned her not to rest on her laurels. With horses, you never knew what might happen.

Sophie tried again to talk to him about the auction's success and the dwindling donations to the sesquicentennial's general fund, but he answered in grunts and monosyllables until she couldn't take it anymore.

"Gabe, you don't seem like yourself today."

Turning in his saddle, he blinked. "Sorry. I haven't heard from my dad and that worries me. I've called but keep getting his voice mail. Oh," he said as if he'd just thought of it, "and today—not the best reminder—would have been my wedding anniversary."

Sophie said, "No wonder you're quiet. Do you still…care about her?"

"We don't speak. Her decision, but I can't blame her. Leaving a woman who's just had the final fitting on her wedding dress didn't make me popular. I should have found a better way to let Iris down."

"As if there could be."

"Yeah, there's that. Or I might have realized earlier that it would never work with our different lifestyle goals."

"Maybe this isn't the time to bring this up—but did you get your invitation to the wedding at the WB? Kate and Noah decided on a double wedding with Zach and Cass." She rode up beside him. "Kate didn't tell you?"

"Actually, in passing I'd mentioned a double wedding to Noah—since all the planning was getting to him. Didn't expect them to take that suggestion." Gabe rode off, saying he needed to check on a cow in the next pasture that was recovering from a hoof problem. Sophie viewed that as an escape. She watched the stiff set of his shoulders, the tension in his normally relaxed posture.

When she caught up to him, his mood had shifted yet again as if he realized he wasn't being a good companion.

"I'm happy for the four of them. Almost sickening, isn't it," he said, "how mushy Zach and Noah get?"

"I envy them. I don't intend to be planning a wedding anytime soon but…"

"Ouch," Gabe said. "After your ex, you mean."

Sophie's hands tightened on her reins, but she shouldn't be as closemouthed as Gabe. Still, what was there to say? "I have nothing else to tell except what you already know. Will and Bess got married. End of story."

Gabe frowned. "And that left you shattered, afraid to trust."

All right, if he wanted to know the truth… "I'd like to trust *you*, but all I'm getting are mixed messages. You say it's okay for me to come riding, then act as if you don't want me here. You start to talk about the issue with your dad, then stop."

He sighed. "I don't mean to take my mood out on you. It's not just Dad or my former fiancée. I had an interview with Lauren earlier today. That's been sticking in my craw, but at least I ended up learning enough about her to understand her ambition—which is partly a need to redeem herself." Gabe told Sophie about the story Lauren had bungled. "Now, to put herself in a better light as a reporter, she seems to be on a mission to discover some secret about me, a scandal or whatever."

"Is there one?"

Gabe's gaze shifted away from her. "No." He pointed. "See that small rise in the distance? There's a creek beyond with shade trees. The horses need a break."

And he was gone again.

Sophie wished she'd gone straight home after work or stayed late to fret over the budget numbers instead. But her thoughts remained on Gabe, and she wondered about his mood. There must be more to that than he'd told her.

CHAPTER FOURTEEN

"OH, MY GOODNESS," Willow Jones said, twirling her index finger for Sophie to turn around. They were in Farrier the morning after her frustrating ride with Gabe, and Sophie was trying on dresses. Her first cowgirl outfits had gone over well, and she'd picked up a few more casual pieces after the silent auction, but his positive reaction had reminded her that she also needed to soften her image at work or whenever she spoke to local groups.

After sending her updated budget numbers to Finn, she'd taken a half day off to meet Willow at this shop that carried more stylish clothes than the emporium in Barren.

"Sophie, that is simply stunning on you. Business smart," Willow said, "and for summer, cool." She gestured at the natural-colored buttons that trimmed the off-white linen sheath. "Add a tan bag, some killer heels—no, make them wedges—and you'll be set."

She added, "I do love your suits, but Gabe was right. Barren's not a suit kind of town."

Sophie had to agree, and this shopping trip provided the perfect opportunity for change. She'd definitely used her city style from KC to keep people at a distance. Time for something different. Feeling excited, Sophie went back into the dressing room, changed into her jeans and T-shirt, then paid for the dress. "I have a bag at home that will work."

"Then shoes next," Willow tucked her hand through Sophie's arm. "After that, let's get lunch. I rarely take time to eat as I should, and with the baby coming I need to. I'm also having too much fun to go home and work."

"Me, too," Sophie said. "I haven't yet adjusted to the reality—that the library, like most these days, is in worse financial condition than last year. That's not Finn's fault, either."

Although Sophie would have preferred to buy a pair of white flats or kitten heels, she and Willow found some lovely jute-wrapped wedges with cork heels at the store next door.

Then they popped across the street in midday traffic to a tiny storefront restaurant that Willow claimed served the best tacos in Kansas.

After their orders came, Sophie dug in. "These are yummy. All in all, a successful morning.

And a nice change of pace. I used to shop every Saturday in KC—as you've seen from my suit collection."

"You should pick up a sundress or two for the sesquicentennial doings. By then, it'll be hot, hot, hot." Willow studied the dessert menu. "I really shouldn't, but I'm having the flan next."

"Then so will I."

Over dessert, the talk turned to Sophie's riding lessons, if she could call them that.

"I'm not sure I'll go again," she said, recalling Gabe's changeable moods. "My job's been pretty busy, and after today with you my new image is on its way, which should help in my campaign for the award. Besides, if I wanted to spend time with a grumpy man, I'd stay home. After work, Max isn't fit to talk to either sometimes."

"Why was Gabe grouchy?"

"Don't ask me. But I'm not fond of his new Jekyll-and-Hyde routine."

"That surprises me. Kate says Gabe's easy to be with. He certainly has that cowboy look most women in town swoon over." She cocked an eyebrow. "If I wasn't with Cody…"

Despite her awkward ride with Gabe, which had gone up and down emotionally like a merry-go-round, Sophie felt a spurt of jealousy. "But you are. Speaking of the WB—I got my wedding invitation."

"You're coming."

"I wouldn't miss it." Not that Sophie, as she'd told Gabe, was fond of weddings. She'd have to clamp down then on any memories of that selfie from Las Vegas. Or her own silly fantasy about Gabe, who probably hadn't thought about kissing her at all after bingo night.

Willow grinned. "You should see my mother—no, scratch that. When I left this morning, her hair was sticking up in all directions, looking as if it were about to burst into flames. She had her T-shirt on backward and there was a hole—not the fashion kind—in her jeans. Imagine that." Jean was normally careful about her appearance. "If she survives planning this double hitch event, I'll be amazed."

"She does try for perfection."

"At the same time, she's so super-happy about my brothers and their brides that she can burst into tears at any moment."

"Weddings are an emotional time." Sophie toyed with the last of her flan. "Or almost-weddings." She mentioned Gabe's non-anniversary yesterday, in part to keep from thinking about her own fate with Will. The loss of her friendship with Bess.

She and Willow were on the street, saying their goodbyes, when something seemed to occur to Willow. In the middle of a hug, she said, "Wait a minute. You're one of us Barren women. No interest in Gabe? Seriously?"

"As a friend," Sophie murmured, distracted by the fact that Willow viewed her as belonging here. But then, Sophie had never been shunned by Willow or any of their other friends, only people like Jasmine, Claudia and Bernice.

The realization surprised Sophie.

"Ha," Willow said. "Even grumpy, you have to admit Gabe's terrific eye candy."

But for Sophie, and her own well-being, he needed to remain off-limits.

GABE POUNDED UP the stone steps to the library, prepared to eat crow. He'd given Sophie a few days to cool off, but he'd been out of line at Sweetheart. She'd clearly been irritated with him, and he owed her an apology. It wasn't her fault the walls seemed to be closing in on Gabe. That there were things he couldn't tell her.

As he opened the main doors, he removed his Stetson and took a deep breath.

Sophie wasn't at either of her usual posts behind the front desk or in her office.

"You just missed her," Rachel Whittaker told him. "She's giving a talk at the sheriff's department."

Gabe was impressed. Bingo night, the church luncheon, now law enforcement. After Sophie's initial reluctance to campaign, she'd taken the bit between her teeth. He liked her new look, too. Those red boots were killer.

"Thanks. I'll try to catch her there."

Rachel's mouth tightened. "If you ask me— which no one did—she should do something about Averill McCafferty instead."

"What about her?" Gabe didn't know her or Rachel, and he was surprised she would bring that up. All he knew was that Max appeared to have an interest in Averill. And that, as Sophie had said, there seemed to be a missing book.

"Perhaps you could urge Sophie to take a stand."

"Not my business," he muttered, but Gabe made a mental note. He'd mention this to Sophie because why was her assistant using him as a go-between?

Gabe put on his hat, tipped it in Rachel's direction and left the library. He jogged down the steps to his truck parked out front.

And missed Sophie at the sheriff's department, too.

Gabe had no choice but to finish his chores in town.

He'd see her later.

Since the silent auction Gabe had refocused his attention on getting more donations to the general fund for the sesquicentennial, and he'd been approaching as many people as he could. So had Sophie. He'd done okay, if not as well as she had, but the latest numbers Sophie had showed him meant he needed to do more.

Gabe liked the fact that Sophie had seemed to enjoy their last ride together, if not his mood. He couldn't call that an official riding lesson, and when they were back at the barn she'd hopped down without needing his assistance, given the mare a last pat on the neck, then tossed her reins at Gabe. He'd watched her stomp off to her car, not that he could blame her. He'd been lousy company, and she had every right to be annoyed with him. He shouldn't have taken his sour mood out on Sophie.

He also wished he hadn't told her about Lauren hunting for a secret.

Is there one? Sophie had asked.

Gabe didn't like hiding things from her, but

he had no choice. Yet how could he spend even more time with her and not risk blurting out a confession? Gabe knew what would happen then. For now, his apology would have to be enough.

AVERILL AND SOPHIE collected their used coffee cups and plates then carried them into the kitchen while Max stayed in the living room to finish his apple pie. He'd invited Averill for an impromptu dinner tonight before the movie they planned to see—and Averill's stomach was in knots. She'd barely picked at her meal.

"Thanks, Averill. You didn't have to help."

"I was happy to." Even the polite words sounded weak. She never knew what to say to Sophie. When she set a cup and saucer on the tiled counter, they rattled. Her hands were shaking.

"This is your first actual date with Max?"

"Except a quick lunch once. He had to cancel twice before. You know." She shrugged. "His patients come first, as they should."

"That's my brother. I can't fault him for his dedication. After all, the clinic is his livelihood as well as his passion, but if you ask me he needs to get a life."

Did that mean Sophie approved of their relationship? They both cared about Max. Maybe she and Sophie were forming a bond.

"Part of my job is trying to see that he gets some free time now and then." Of course, Averill had a selfish interest there. Tonight's movie, for example. Was she more anxious about their date or his sister's probing questions? Sophie had every right to be curious about Averill, to protect her brother. But what if she realized Averill had walked off with a book she hadn't bothered to check out? Sophie hadn't confronted her, but that didn't mean anything. Or the bigger question: What if she somehow learned about Averill's past? Farrier wasn't that far from Barren. Maybe she should have moved to Denver or Chicago instead.

"Are you okay?" Sophie was staring at her, the last dessert plate in hand.

"Fine. Just a little twitchy about the movie and all."

"Max doesn't bite."

"I hope not." Averill held out her arm. "Remi, though…" He'd nipped at her earlier.

Sophie winced. "That tug-of-war with his rope toy amped him up. I apologize on his behalf. He gets carried away." She inspected the small wound on Averill's forearm. "You should clean this before you and Max leave."

Averill heard him stirring in the living room, telling the dog in a firm voice to lie down. Instead, before she could answer Sophie, Remi trotted into the kitchen, tongue lolling, to lean against Sophie's leg.

"You're his mom," Max said from the doorway. "Control him. He already bit Averill."

She hurried to defend the dog. "It's my fault. I stirred him up."

"Is it your fault he left another puddle on the carpet?"

"Again?" Sophie said, groaning. "I'll clean up. You and Averill don't want to be late for your movie. Let me get my first aid kit, though." She hurried off, leaving Averill with Max.

"This dog. I think he's decided to test my love of animals." But Max leaned down to stroke Remi's head. The dog had collapsed on the floor, his brown eyes clearly reflecting his guilt. "What are we going to do with you, huh?"

Averill felt a surge of adrenaline, alarm flooding through her. She thought he'd meant her, but Remi's tail swished against the tiles and Max gazed down at him almost fondly. "I hate to admit this, but I'm getting used to having him around."

Sophie returned with a small box containing a bottle of antiseptic and bandages.

Rising to his feet, Max took over to clean Averill's wound.

"Really, don't fuss. He barely nipped me. I'm fine," she kept telling him.

"You don't want to risk infection. Animal bites can be dangerous."

"It's nothing," she insisted as he applied a bandage with a whimsical Sponge Bob design.

Max rolled his eyes. "Sophie's pick."

"There's no reason even a bandage can't be fun," his sister said.

He glanced at his watch. "We'd better go. The movie starts in half an hour." Max kissed Sophie's cheek. "Thanks for dinner," which Averill quickly echoed.

"Wouldn't hurt to get Remi out of the house now and then," Max added. "The backyard's okay, but he's used to open spaces. Plenty of appealing bushes—"

"I'll take him to Sweetheart with me tomorrow."

"Still playing cowgirl?" Max couldn't hide his grin as he took Averill's hand. They walked toward the front door. She could feel Sophie's gaze on their backs. She had been nothing but kind to Averill, despite the unwanted questions, but did she approve of this first date?

"I'm a natural," Sophie called after them.

Which made even Averill laugh.

For tonight, with Max, she would try to forget about the book—and her own guilt.

CHAPTER FIFTEEN

THE NEXT AFTERNOON Sophie came to the barn when Gabe had just finished feeding horses. The other hands were out on the range, checking calves and counting the herd. Gabe still had serious doubts about Johnny, the new kid, but he was riding with more experienced cowboys. Maybe he'd learn something.

After he'd missed finding Sophie at the sheriff's office yesterday, then finished his errands, Gabe had driven by her house, but she hadn't been home yet. So he'd temporarily given up and come back to the ranch. Alone with her now, he had to make his apology. How to start?

"I wondered if you'd come again."

Not answering, she stood in the aisle, arms crossed. Gabe stood several feet away, his pose similar, as if they were two gunfighters at the OK Corral.

"I'm really sorry, Soph. I was a beast the other day."

"True."

"I went to the library—did Rachel tell you?— but you weren't there."

"She told me. I wasn't going to come ride again—even if I have to admit it's rather fun." She didn't crack a smile. "But Gabe, I know you were concerned about your father..."

"No excuse. And there are other things on my mind right now, too."

"Things you can't tell me."

He picked at the dirt floor with the toe of his boot. "I wish I could."

"Any relationship—including friendship— can't survive without honesty."

"Trust, too," he agreed, knowing how important that was to her, feeling worse with every word. "So here's me being honest, okay?" He could tell her this much. "I really like you, Sophie." The tense atmosphere between them didn't seem to warrant using his preferred nickname for her. "If things were different... Maybe someday—"

"Maybe never."

"I'm not lying to you," exactly, Gabe thought. He just wasn't telling the whole truth. He supposed that wouldn't win him any points.

"A sin of omission, then?"

Boy, she could be tough. Which he deserved. A year ago, Sophie had come home like a whipped dog with its tail between its legs, her confidence destroyed along with her trust in Will and Bess. He didn't dare risk making that worse.

Gabe was about to speak—what would he say?—when he heard a sharp bark followed by a series of yips and howls from various ranch dogs.

Sophie turned. "I left Remi in the car. I was going to ask if it's all right if he takes a run while I'm here."

"Sure." Gabe gestured toward the barnyard where half a dozen dogs, all shapes and sizes, were milling around Sophie's sedan. "Better hurry or you'll have scratches on your door."

Released from confinement, Remi bounded out to meet his old friends and Sophie gaped at the happy reunion.

"I thought the other dogs didn't like him," she said.

"They're fickle. He's no bother since he doesn't live here now and compete for food and attention. We'll keep an eye out, but he should be okay." Gabe paused. "Let him run. You ready to take a quick ride?"

"That's why I'm here." The brief interruption by the dogs had softened the tone of Sophie's voice. Clearly, she was a woman who didn't hold a grudge, even if she hadn't quite forgiven him, either.

"Then it's high time you learned to saddle your own horse."

Gabe decided to make it fast before she changed her mind. Or he did. He went to get Critter and Precious from their stalls, snapping them into the crossties in the barn aisle. He gathered his saddle from the tack room and the one Sophie had borrowed before. "Pull those bridles off the end two hooks, will you?"

Sophie seemed excited, yet anxious, to learn. After he'd saddled Critter, Gabe walked up behind her. She was grooming Precious. Gabe's chest brushed against her back, and a warm glow settled inside him. He'd never stood this close to Sophie while not facing her.

This wasn't the best idea. Yet he couldn't seem to move back.

"Think you can lift the weight of this saddle?"

"How much weight?"

"Forty pounds or so. Take hold like this, then swing the rig up and onto her back. Gently."

Sophie hesitated. "What if I drop it?"

"I won't let you." Gabe took some of the weight, allowing Sophie to complete the motion until the saddle landed lightly. The horse's hide quivered. "Too high on her withers." He covered her hands with his. "Let it slide back, find its natural position. There," he said. "Now you've got it. Perfect."

Gabe's heart was beating like a steel drum. His mouth nestled close to Sophie's ear, and he could smell the faint scent of the soap she'd used, or some light perfume.

"What next?"

Distracted by his nearness to her, he'd lost focus. "Uh—the cinch." *How about I forget this before I get myself in trouble? Step away.* Instead, Gabe reached under the mare for the webbed strap. When he straightened, his shoulder brushed Sophie. He showed her how to put the cinch through the various fittings, then helped her tighten it.

"Can she breathe? I don't want to hurt her."

"You won't. She blows up. Takes a deep one then holds her breath. Lots of horses do."

"That's pretty crafty."

"You bet. Once we get her bridle on, you can walk her in the yard. Then we'll tighten it again after she's let out the air she's been holding."

Their fingers tangled as they worked, and Gabe helped Sophie do the bridle. He praised her effort but didn't hesitate to correct her. "See these little wrinkles at the corners of her lips? Precious has a tender mouth. You don't want to leave the bit there or she'll end up being a puller, tugging on the reins to make herself comfortable." His hand on hers, Sophie's soft skin against his more callused palm, he helped her adjust the bit. Almost finished. Before he really lost his head and did something he'd regret. Gabe was still lying to her, the worst as far as Sophie was concerned. Once she knew...

She turned to face him, and they were standing even closer than before. He clamped his mouth shut to not say the wrong thing, let alone kiss her as he wanted to do. Badly.

Oblivious to his inner struggle, she beamed with pride. "I told Max I'm a natural."

He glanced at her red shirt and boots. "Now you've got the skills to match that outfit."

He shouldn't encourage her. This was madness, spending time together, riding, wanting...but they weren't at odds now, so all he said was, "Go, cowgirl."

GIRLS' NIGHT OUT, a regular social event with her circle of friends, would give Sophie an opportunity to campaign, if she could, as well as enjoy herself for one evening. Sophie had run home to change after her ride with Gabe, who would probably be around Sweetheart tonight since Kate was hosting. She hoped she didn't run into him so soon, before she had time to digest that interlude in the barn when he'd shown her how to saddle Precious.

"I missed so many meetings when I was away from Barren," Sophie told Kate, setting a batch of flyers on the coffee table. "I've skipped a few since I got back." And always, she wondered. Was she accepted by the group again? "Would you mind me giving a short talk tonight? I feel awkward, as if I'd be using my friends to get votes."

"Doesn't any politician?"

"I'm not running for office." Sophie took a seat on Kate's comfy sofa. She'd been the first to arrive, but in no time the house filled with women chattering, laughing, teasing each other and the sounds of covered dishes clattering onto the kitchen counter where Kate had put out napkins, plates and silverware. Shadow Wilson was opening a bottle of wine. Olivia McCord was giving Annabelle advice about her horse Prancer. Nell discussed pregnancy with Willow. These were lifelong friends, and Sophie shouldn't feel uncomfortable asking for their help, fearing they might reject her.

"Talk all you want," Kate said.

Jenna Smith asked, "Where's Noah tonight?" The men usually disappeared during these gatherings.

"Catching up on paperwork in the office. Door closed. Teddie's asleep, although don't be surprised if he makes a sudden appearance." Kate rushed back into the kitchen to take something that smelled heavenly from the oven.

"That boy never tires," Lizzie Maguire told the others with a laugh. "My four kids can't compete with such energy. And that's saying a lot."

"I bet Teddie's reading under the covers." Shadow poured wine into waiting glasses. "That's what my Ava does when she's not FaceTiming with her friends until midnight."

"Teenagers," several women murmured at once.

Sophie followed everyone from the living room into the kitchen to cluster around the center island. "I'm sticking with my dog." Perhaps forever. Maybe she'd never marry, have children. By the time she considered doing so, Gabe might be long gone, and she'd cautioned herself to stay clear. Then there was the inconvenient truth that after his own failed engagement, he probably wasn't thinking about marriage, either. With her.

Kate turned, a potholder in hand. "You're keeping Rembrandt? I'm glad you've given him another lease on life, but he's not exactly a house pet."

"Tell me." She regaled the group with tales of Remi's house training and Max's frustration. "We've finally made some progress and I love Remi to pieces." Sophie glanced at Kate's Australian shepherd. Bandit was asleep on the floor, his tail thumping in some dream. A lot of dog lovers in Barren.

Shadow clinked glasses with Sophie. "Just saying, but if I were you, I'd prefer loving someone human."

A chorus of voices rang out. "Any suggestions?"

Their teasing didn't bother Sophie. It did make her feel a part of things, not an outsider but one of this circle of old friends again. She'd missed them. If they'd been with her in KC, maybe with their help she would have seen the signs of betrayal with Will and Bess before Vegas.

Sophie tried to shift the topic. "I'd rather talk about Kate and Noah's wedding."

"I wouldn't." Kate took a baking pan from the oven. "The tension is getting fierce."

Sophie turned to Cass who'd eloped with Noah's brother and was already a Bodine. This second time her mother-in-law would see them repeat their vows. "I meant, yours, too. A double wedding's pretty exciting." And the event was fast approaching.

"Zach doesn't think so. I swear, he lives in the WB's barn these days."

Kate agreed. "Noah's planning another business trip to New York so I can finish the plans with Cass and Jean. I'm to let him know when they're done. Quote, unquote."

Willow grinned as she refused a glass of wine. "Sophie's just in her resting phase. Who can blame her after that selfie from Vegas?"

Everyone groaned. Kate put an arm around Sophie's shoulders.

Apparently, they all knew about the betrayal she'd suffered, the humiliation and loss of two people she'd called friends—more than that, in Will's case. A year ago, Willow's comments would have brought shame but, Sophie realized, now she felt mostly irritation.

"Oh, please." Her nose wrinkled. "Let's not go there."

Kate said, "Maybe you're wrong, Willow—

about Sophie resting. She's been spending time here at Sweetheart with a certain hunky foreman of mine."

"Gabe's teaching me horsemanship."

"You're riding?" Olivia looked surprised.

"And learning my way around a barn. With Kate's help, too," she added quickly. "Trying at the same time to improve my image in Barren."

"What's wrong with it?" Annabelle asked.

"If I want to win the award—to be Citizen of the Year—I need to seem more, well, approachable. To look like people here rather than in downtown Kansas City."

"Sounds good," Shadow murmured, "but I'm not buying it. Anyone else?" she asked, looking around. "Lauren Anderson may need to convince Barren that she's one of us—but not you, Sophie."

"Others disagree."

"Don't tell me you're listening to Bernice Caldwell? Or her sidekick?" Meaning Lizzie's mother.

"Well…"

"And what's with Lauren anyway?" Shadow asked. "She sure tries hard, but I get the feeling she's not exactly who she says she is. I mean, why—if she's such a hotshot reporter—is she working in Barren? The *Journal's* not exactly the national newspaper of record."

"I don't know," Sophie said, "but despite her 'edge,' I want to like her. There's something kind of vulnerable about Lauren."

"Don't be that nice. She's your chief competition for the award. Why does she even want to be Citizen of the Year? I can't see her staying long."

Annabelle frowned. "Oh, Shadow, give Lauren a chance."

But Shadow had an edge of her own. "Sophie, I'm not fooled, either, by your riding lessons or this new country girl pose of yours." She gestured at Sophie's casual tee and denim skirt with her red boots. "It's definitely cute, but I'm with Kate. The attraction here is Gabe Morgan."

A few of her friends hooted.

Sophie's face heated. Earlier in the barn she'd stood physically closer to Gabe than ever before, and the memory of his strong form pressed against her would likely keep her awake all night. The feel of his hands on hers as they adjusted the saddle. The clean scent of him filling her nostrils. His shoulder bumping her, then his mouth just short of touching hers.

"We're friends—" Sophie's standard answer—"which is Gabe's only interest in me."

"And if you believe that…" someone said.

But Sophie had to. She hadn't liked Gabe's moods or his defensiveness, the way he shut down about his past or about his problems with his father. She had the impression, too, that he was—or had been—far more at one time than a ranch foreman. For one thing, there was the expensive-looking saddle he'd donated for auction. Anonymously. His evasiveness, claiming he'd bought it cheap at a flea market. Sophie was no expert, but did he think she hadn't noticed, when he'd come to dinner early on that his dress jeans weren't the typical cowboy Wranglers but a designer brand? It was as if working for Kate was his cover.

"Come on," Blossom Hunter piped up. "We all know Sophie's had him in her sights since she came back to Barren. And why not?"

As their teasing went on, and Sophie's color deepened, Kate stepped in. "Give her a break, ladies. Let's eat before Sophie gives us her campaign speech."

Relieved not to be the center of attention, Sophie was even happier when, just as she began her after-dinner talk, Teddie appeared at the bottom of the stairs, blinking sleep from his eyes behind his thick black glasses frames. "Hey. What're you guys doing?"

Suddenly, the attention shifted from her to Kate's adorable little boy.

Then Bandit woke up to cover Teddie's face with kisses, and every woman in the room melted into a puddle of emotion. Sophie joined them.

Her nerves were gone, if not her memory of the barn and Gabe's nearness, which, she told herself, couldn't mean a thing. She wouldn't let it.

The last thing she needed was a man who, like Will, hid his true intentions. In the end, Gabe would probably send her a text, too, on his way out of town. One shocking betrayal was one too many and, along with the loss of her parents, which had felt in part like a sudden abandonment, more than enough. Even if part of her wanted to trust Gabe, the rest knew better.

He wasn't talking. She wouldn't risk getting hurt again.

CHAPTER SIXTEEN

GABE ACTIVATED HIS FaceTime icon, then waited for Jilly to accept the call.

How much time did he have left? Since the Senate investigation had ended nearly a month ago, there'd still been no news, no word of any indictments, no names put forth that would blow what Gabe had come to think of as his disguise. He'd thus far avoided Lauren, who kept calling about the unfinished feature article on him. He did his work at Sweetheart and continued to canvass the townspeople for donations to the sesquicentennial fund.

He felt as if he were living with swords above his head. And then, there was that episode in the barn yesterday with Sophie when he'd nearly lost his head again and kissed her.

"Gabe." At last Jilly's face appeared onscreen.

"Hey, what's happening?"

She made a face. "Nothing. I'd almost rather

have the authorities at our door. The tension is unbearable."

"I guess the feds are still getting their ducks in order."

"Well, and as you know, the board meeting when you were here didn't go well. They didn't demand your father's resignation then, but there are those who still would. And here? This house feels like a tomb."

"Dad's working all the time?"

"That wouldn't be unusual," she said, "but, no. He's been home a lot more than he ever has been. Holed up in his office, working the phones, conferring with his legal team. Worrying himself to death."

"And likely unhappy with me. Reporters hanging around outside the house like they were?"

"Not as many—until the next news breaks." She sighed. "I don't know how much longer I can lie awake at night, listening to him pace the hall by the bedroom. He has terrible dark circles under his eyes. He doesn't eat well."

"You look tired, too." He'd never noticed the hollows in her cheeks before, and the distressed look in her eyes tore at his heart. Each time he heard the increasingly defeated tone of her voice, frustration and guilt ate at him inside. "I already asked once, but why don't you come spend some time with me on the ranch?"

She smiled wanly. "A ranch was always your means of escape."

Was that true of Sweetheart, too? And Gabe was indeed hiding out not just in this bunkhouse but within himself? The way he hid his awareness of Sophie—or tried to?

"I shouldn't blame you," Jilly began.

"Yet you do." And there was something else going on here. At the beginning of their conversation, Jilly had said *I'd almost rather have the authorities at our door.*

"This company is your birthright, Gabriel. Still a family-controlled corporation. Who better would Chet leave it to? You may like that ranch, feel safe there, even think you're protecting him, but is that all?"

"I don't know what you mean."

"Maybe, unconsciously, you're punishing him for what you still see as his indifference when you were growing up. And after your mother died—"

"It's not that simple. So far Aaron has stayed quiet, but there's no telling if that will last. Every day now I scour the headlines, afraid I'll find my worst nightmare on the TV screen or in some newspaper. He works for Brynne. He was passionate about the issues he saw on that rig. I wouldn't blame him for deciding to point fingers." Jilly might, though; she already felt Gabe was being disloyal.

"If that man comes forward, I will stand by Chet. Nothing can shake my faith in him."

He gazed at her image on the screen, seeing the changes the years had made, a few lines, the slight gray in her hair, but she was still an attractive woman with a great heart who'd all but given her life to Chester Dean Wyatt.

"What aren't you saying, Jilly?"

Gabe recalled the shift she'd made from the bedroom she'd occupied near his as a child—where he'd slept the weekend of his trip home—into larger rooms. His father's. He remembered the hand Jilly had put on his dad's shoulder when Gabe climbed the stairs from the entry hall.

"You're not still living there," he said, "just because it's become home, or because you've become the virtual lady of the house."

"No," she admitted, looking away from the camera. Gabe glimpsed tears in her eyes.

"You *really* care about him." Why hadn't he seen that before?

Jilly didn't hesitate. "I love your father. Yes."

"He couldn't ask for anyone better," Gabe said.

"Then I have your blessing?"

"Did you ever doubt you would?"

"No," she murmured, sounding relieved. She blinked back the tears. "I don't think I did."

That didn't change things between Gabe and his father, but for the first time in a while, he didn't feel that sword hovering quite so near his neck.

Once the spill was fully contained, the damage somehow dealt with, maybe his dad and Jilly could find happiness together.

Then Gabe could stay in Barren without that ever-present sense of dread. He'd take the chance then to let Sophie know how he felt. He would tell her the truth.

HAND IN HAND with Max, Averill walked from Bon Appetit, where'd they had dinner, to his truck in the parking lot behind the restaurant. Twice tonight he'd glanced at the readout on his phone then ignored the incoming call. His gaze had focused on her face, and Averill, who didn't have experience, thought she saw the beginning of…could it be love? "I think I make you happy," she said.

"You think?" he asked, a playful note in his voice that had become familiar.

This wasn't the neglectful, take-people-for-granted Max that others knew.

With Averill he was different, seemingly less preoccupied with patients, treatment plans, medications, emergencies. He didn't overlook her as some said he did Sophie.

Max unlocked his truck's door and helped her up onto the passenger seat. Averill had worn a dress tonight with two-inch heels, wishing she'd kept the gorgeous pair of spikes she'd donated to the auction. This was the fourth consecutive date she'd had with Max in as many days, beginning the night he'd taken her to the movies and paid little attention to the story on-screen.

For a long moment he studied her in the arc lights, glanced at her mouth. He didn't kiss her, but Averill sensed he wanted to. Again. Then, to her disappointment, he straightened and twisted the ignition key.

They were headed for her apartment when Max abruptly pulled into the parking area near the creek. At ten o'clock the town had already gone to sleep, and Averill had seen the lights go off at Bon Appetit, which had apparently closed for the night. One arm draped over the steering wheel now, Max turned to her.

Swiftly he leaned over, closing the distance between them, and lightly pressed his lips to hers. Averill startled a bit, even though she'd been hoping for another kiss, then willed herself to relax. All she had to do was forget the lies she had told him, forget his sister and everyone in this town, the book she'd taken from Sophie's library in a vain attempt to fix her life. But things were moving too fast. She mustn't lead him on.

Max said, "I should have waited until we got to your place. But I couldn't." He returned for a second kiss, his arms around Averill, eyes closed. He looked as if he were in heaven. So was she.

Torn between sinking into the kiss and pulling away, she tensed.

"What's wrong?" he asked.

"Old baggage, I suppose. My family kind of ruined my ability to go with the flow."

To do the very thing *she* wanted to. Fresh guilt moved through her instead.

Max drew back in his seat. "You don't say much about Farrier. I assumed there are bad memories. Might help to talk about them."

"Maxwell Crane, therapist? Sophie would

be shocked. Besides, you haven't had any success counseling Mrs. Hingle about her cat's pregnancy."

She'd tried to lighten the conversation, but Max remained serious. "I still want to know, Averill." He paused. "I haven't been one for serious relationships before, but if we're going to move forward like I want to—"

She laid a hand over his lips. "Max, I'm not at a point when I can take this—us—any further. It wouldn't be fair to you."

"I can decide for myself whether it's fair." He played with the steering wheel. "I thought I wasn't alone here, that you wanted me to kiss you tonight as much as you did before."

She heard the wounded tone in his voice.

Averill touched his hand. "I did, but maybe I shouldn't have said yes to our first date." It had seemed harmless then. She'd never dreamed he'd want to take her out again. She couldn't afford to keep seeing him now. Yet how could she not when he lifted her from grief every time she did? Still, in the end, her everlasting guilt would ruin what they already had. "There are things you don't know about me. Things I don't want to tell anyone."

"You mean about your father? You mentioned him before."

"He's part of it, yes." Her pulse skipped a beat. She couldn't let Max get closer to the truth she needed to hide. If he knew, he'd never want to see her again. She would lose her job, too, the emotional refuge she'd found here in Barren. "Let's just say ours wasn't the happiest home. I learned to be closed around people. I'm sorry I flinched when you kissed me." Unable to go on, she studied her lap.

Max touched a finger to her chin, gently lifted until he could look into her eyes.

"Averill, you know me. Better than you think," he said. "I would never hurt you. Whatever there is, you should tell me."

"I can't. I can't," she repeated. "I'm sorry, Max. Please, take me home."

SOPHIE HAD NO sooner reached her office on Monday than Rachel slipped out from behind the front desk and poked her head in Sophie's door. "Averill McCafferty's here."

Sophie had also been waiting for Averill to come in again. She and Max were seeing each other every night after work. Last Saturday—two nights ago—they'd gone to dinner at Jack's restaurant. But Sophie didn't share Rachel's level of concern. So far, she'd seen nothing to alarm her. She rose from her desk. "I'll handle this, thank you, Rachel."

Her assistant meant well, but she seemed a bit too eager to solve the issue of the missing book. Maybe Rachel was only trying to prove her worth in this job. Still, the situation was a tricky one, and she hoped Rachel was wrong.

As she might expect, Averill wandered into the fiction stacks to peruse the New Books shelf. She didn't seem to find anything she liked before coming back into the aisle. *Please don't take anything.*

Despite Rachel's opinion, Sophie did like Averill, especially the way she treated Max, and she hated to get put in the bad position of having to call out his new girlfriend. Her first caution to Max about Averill hadn't been well received. If Sophie was responsible for breaking his heart just when he was becoming a happier person...

Sophie knew how that felt. She wanted to learn the truth but didn't want to upset Max.

Averill was now in the nonfiction section where she picked up one book, studied the jacket copy, then put it back in place. She was reaching for another when Sophie said just behind her, "The new Grisham is in. I was about to call you."

Averill jumped. "Oh. Sophie, hi. I forgot you were saving that for me."

"I'll leave it on the counter until you're ready to check out." Sophie had slightly emphasized the last words. "Take your time."

Sophie crossed the room again to the desk. "I can't believe you just let her know she's being watched," Rachel said.

Sophie felt a twinge of guilt. "If she's doing nothing she shouldn't, that won't matter."

"You don't believe me about that book?"

"I don't *want* to believe she's stealing from us," Sophie admitted. "She and Max—he's taking time for himself and leading a more balanced life. How could I destroy that?"

But Rachel's look told Sophie she'd blown their quasi-investigation.

And why did Averill focus on that shelf? Like libraries across the country, Barren used the Dewey decimal system of categorizing books, which consisted of ten major classes, each with ten divisions, again with ten sections in numerical order that made shelving easier. The 360-section related to social problems and services. Self-help and rehabilitation. Maybe Averill knew someone, a family member perhaps, with an addiction issue. She had hinted at her less-than-happy home life in Farrier. What if she had taken a book on such a sensitive subject from that very shelf? Other people had done the same sort of thing, hoping to avoid embarrassment at the checkout desk. Eventually, the books usually got returned in the night drop. In that case, Sophie could empathize. Perhaps Averill didn't want Max, or anyone, to know she had a painful secret meant to protect someone else.

She lost track of Averill when Finn Donovan walked into the library. Sophie could tell from the way his keen gaze took in the room that he wasn't here to borrow a book in the nearby 350s about public administration. He was looking for her. "Mr. Mayor," she said, coming out of the biography section, 920, across the way.

"Sophie. Can we talk?"

Uh-oh. This could only concern the library budget. After she'd sent him her numbers, Finn must have found another category to slash. "Of course." She led the way to her office, her heels soundless on the tile floor. With today's soften-her-image skirt and blouse, she wore the cork-soled wedges she'd bought with Willow in Farrier. Sophie had discovered she liked dressing down a bit and felt more a part of things. Was it possible her suits had been a pose, not only a shield, and this was instead her true style? Sophie shut the door behind them, then motioned Finn to a chair.

"You peeved at me?" His keen powers of observation came from experience. He'd been a cop in Chicago before tragedy had taken his wife and son's lives. Finn had moved to Barren where he'd first found a new role as Stewart County's sheriff. He'd also found love again with Annabelle, and her daughter Emmie completed their family. No, that wasn't right. They'd welcome another addition, Annabelle had told her, which hadn't happened yet.

"Not peeved, more resigned. I'll be making a sign soon," Sophie told Finn, "to alert my patrons that there will be no more Saturday hours."

He shifted in his chair. "I know I asked a lot of you. My first attempt to balance the city budget as mayor. I may have been a bit zealous."

"Finn, I had to cut my book-buying budget in half."

"Let me finish." He held up a hand. "I come in peace. I wanted to let you know. I've looked at the numbers again, and I'm going to propose to the council that we give back a little of what we—I—took away."

"Are you serious?"

"In my current position, I'm way busier than I was writing parking tickets on Main Street or arresting teenagers for toilet-papering the trees on Halloween. Yeah, I'm serious. I wouldn't waste time even to get in your good graces again."

"How much money?"

The modest amount Finn mentioned lifted Sophie's spirits. She did a quick mental calculation. "That's better, enough at least so I won't need to close the library on Saturdays."

Finn glanced at the ceiling. "If only that solved the rest of our problems."

Sophie straightened in her desk chair, sensing Finn was about to drop another shoe.

"The general fund for the sesquicentennial," he said. "Let's talk about that, too."

"I know we're still running short, and my report tonight to the committee will reflect that, but there are outstanding pledges. Those will be honored soon, I hope."

"If not, we'll need to cut corners. The fireworks, possibly, and Jack Hancock will have to change his menu for the final dinner. We won't be able to afford steak. Looks like rubber chicken or pork barbecue from where I'm sitting." He added, "Oh, and a few people have canceled their donations. There goes the Fun Run before the carnival."

The 5K race was done with partners. It was one of the most popular events at other town celebrations. Yet how much money would eliminating that save?

"It does sound like a lot to pull off. Maybe, as someone suggested, we went overboard with our initial planning."

"Many of our fine citizens will disagree. I hate to disappoint them."

Sophie did, too. "When the finance committee meets, maybe we can all try to come up with a way to salvage things."

Finn rose from the chair. "I hope so. I want to do right by Barren, be a good mayor for this town, but I might be in over my head."

"I'm sorry I gave you a hard time," Sophie said, walking him out. "I know our next year's budget is one issue—not the only one. Keep trying, Finn." He was still new to the job, getting his bearings. She wouldn't burden him further.

They passed by the desk where Rachel was checking out Averill's books, the John Grisham included.

"Yeah," Finn said, "I will try, but there are days—today—when I'm sorry I took this job."

"You did bring me good news," Sophie reminded the mayor.

And perhaps tonight Gabe might announce a generous new pledge from someone that he'd forgotten to tell her about, but the meeting was no longer on her mind when Sophie returned to the front desk. Averill had gone, and Rachel had a newly determined look on her face.

"There's another book missing," she told Sophie.

CHAPTER SEVENTEEN

FINANCE COMMITTEE MEETINGS would never be Gabe's favorite way to spend an evening, and Finn Donovan, seated next to him tonight, seemed to be in a grim mood. Normally, the new mayor, like Gabe, was even-tempered.

"What," Gabe asked under his breath, "did you get an advance copy of Sophie's report?"

But other members were filing into the room and, without responding, Finn rose to greet them. Then Sophie walked in, a downcast look on her face, too. She eased into a chair across from Gabe who wondered if she regretted their ride last week. "You saddle-sore again?"

Instead of answering, she shoved the new report across the table to him. "Prepare yourself. I'm afraid our efforts have fallen short. I know you tried."

Gabe scanned the sheet, then flipped to the bottom number.

"That's all we have now? Total?"

"Some people changed their minds and can't

contribute. If others don't fulfill the pledges they made—"

"The celebrations will have to be curtailed."

"Finn and I discussed this earlier. Not to repeat myself—" Abruptly, Sophie stood, then called the meeting to order. "I'm afraid I have bad news," she began. "Each of you has a copy here of my latest report. I've been pounding the pavement, some of you have, too, and Gabe has done more than his share. But along with fewer pledges and the dwindling amounts on others, we're not in good enough shape. I'm now throwing the meeting open for suggestions. How can we save this?"

Unfortunately, there were few ideas that made sense this far along in the planning, with most committees filled and the events already scheduled. Sophie said, "I'll twist some more arms, but I've noticed that people tend to avoid me when they see me coming. They're weary of the hype."

"Do they want these celebrations or not?" Cooper Ransom asked. "If another dozen stepped up to pledge even a relatively modest amount, if a few more reconsidered and honored their original pledges, we could get these numbers in line."

Gabe didn't relish that task. Those people

who refused weren't the only ones who would feel tapped out, and the closer the sesquicentennial got, the more tensions would rise. For a second, he considered calling his dad, asking for a donation from Brynne in exchange for prominent placement in the program as a corporate sponsor. The rodeo entrants could wear the company logo on their shirts. But was that a preposterous idea? Not only would he likely be rejected, but if his father did agree, Gabe would be shining a spotlight on his own relationship to the company.

When the meeting finally ended, Sophie looked as unhappy as Finn had, but Gabe didn't know how to cheer her. "Hey, cowgirl. It's always darkest before the dawn."

"Really? You're reduced to banal aphorisms?"

"Big words—I know, I know, you're a librarian. I mean it, though."

"What else can we possibly do, Gabe? We can all try to put a good face on things, but unless magic happens, there will be no Fun Run, no fireworks…and I don't know what else."

"Soph, I hate to see you so worried."

"I hate that we haven't been able to meet our goal for donations."

"Could the town council free up more cash? They gave us a nice start."

"I doubt that. Finn's already done what he can there. Besides—" she couldn't help a brief smile "—he may restore part of my library budget. I don't want to rock any boats."

"Then for now why not get your mind off the problem? You coming to Sweetheart tomorrow? I think you should ride. Always takes my mind off any troublesome issue."

Well, not quite. He hadn't been the best companion before, and he never got away from his fear that Aaron would talk, that time was truly running out and Sophie would soon know he'd lied about who he was. He could tell something else was bothering her, too.

"Maybe you're right," she said with a sigh.

"Let me do more thinking. I might come up with something so we don't have to cut events."

He already had. The notion hadn't occurred to him until now. His father wasn't Gabe's only source of a sizable donation.

There was one other person he could tap.

AVERILL COULD IMAGINE living permanently in Barren. She liked Max's house on Cattle Track Lane, liked her own little apartment across town where they were snuggled up on her sofa, his arm around her as they both tried to watch a movie on TV. Max had taken her home the other night, as Averill had asked him to do, and she'd known that was the best decision she could make. It wasn't wise to see him so much after work. Kissing was not good at all.

But then, unable to help herself, she'd relented and apologized to Max for her odd behavior on Saturday night.

"What do you think?" He took another potato chip from the bag they were sharing. "I've seen old films like *Cheaper by the Dozen* before—my mom was a big fan—but even this remake doesn't work for me. I mean, twelve kids?" He tilted his head to meet her eyes. "How many children do you want to have?"

As if she and Max could last that long. She leaned her head on his shoulder. She'd known the ending before their movie even started.

"I don't plan to have a family."

"No? Why not? You'd be a fantastic mother. You're so good with my clients, my small patients, and around large animals," he added.

Averill felt the blood rush from her head. "Max, I told you. I have a lot of stuff to work out. The last thing I need is to start thinking about marriage or babies." The words caught in her throat. "With anyone."

His arm dropped from around her shoulders. "I'd never thought seriously about that either before." His gaze turned somber. "Or am I on the wrong track? I thought after your freak-out, we were moving again toward a solid place in our relationship."

Averill stiffened. She always feared letting down her guard, spilling all the details about her past in Farrier. A life she wished she could forget. If it hadn't been for her...

An image of five-year-old Lucie flitted through her mind.

"You and me? Please don't," she said, withdrawing to her side of the sofa. A new life with Max, babies, would remind her every day of the sorrow she had caused. Even with the help of the books she'd "borrowed" from the library, which were another source of guilt, there was no way through that dark tunnel.

For a second, she wished he was the preoccupied-with-his-own-work Maxwell Crane she'd first met. "Max, we haven't known each other that long. And I'd rather talk about that raise you once mentioned."

"Averill, I'm not going to propose tonight, but I'd like to have a real discussion about us. Soon."

He moved closer again. The chip bag

crunched between them, but Max didn't seem to notice. He had that look in his eyes, the one she shouldn't respond to but always did.

She was in his arms before she could try to protect him from herself, and Max's kiss was making her forget again—almost—her own reasons to feel guilty.

She and Max wouldn't last. But for now, tonight… Averill kissed him back.

DELUSIONS OF GRANDEUR. That was what the sesquicentennial plans were, Sophie thought as she drove out to Sweetheart the next day. She was wearing her latest "cowgirl" attire: a white shirt with brown piping, tan jeans that should be cooler in the hot sun than dark denim, and sturdy brown roping boots instead of the flashy red she'd worn before. She had added a hat this time, the straw version of a Stetson for late June.

Last night's meeting kept circling through her brain despite her attempt to change the direction of her thoughts. What solution could there be? Neither she nor Gabe wanted to collar those people who hadn't already donated or pledged. And that wasn't the only thing troubling her. There was still the matter of Averill McCafferty and the second missing book, which changed things.

Gabe was in the barnyard, hitching Critter to a rail, when she arrived. "Glad you decided to come today. Let me get Precious, then we'll head out," he said.

Sophie patted Gabe's gelding on her way past. "I'll get her—and saddle up."

"Think you can manage by yourself?"

"I had an excellent teacher."

Gabe didn't contradict her. He waited in the yard while she wrestled the heavy saddle from the tack room to the barn aisle, then hefted it onto the mare's back. The bridle seemed easier this time, although Sophie was gasping for breath when she led Precious out into the hot sun.

Gabe studied her. "You okay with this heat? Maybe we should have ridden earlier."

"I couldn't. My job came first. I'll be fine."

"You need help mounting?"

"I can swing up. Watch me."

Sophie would ride through Hades before she let him boost her into the saddle again, but she was glad she was here. His mood seemed better this time. As he'd said, she needed the getaway, too, and spending time with Gabe was always good—if not for her own well-being.

Sophie remembered the teasing she'd endured about him at Girls' Night Out. She wouldn't daydream about a romantic relationship. Gabe wouldn't stay forever in Barren, and she didn't want another rejection or betrayal of her trust as she'd had with Will and Bess. She could trust Gabe, though, to take her on a harmless horseback ride.

As they rode cross-country, they discussed last night's committee meeting, Gabe's difficulties with a ranch hand who didn't seem to be working out, and finally Averill. "I don't know what to do, Gabe. I did see her in that section—rehab and social problems—but that didn't mean she took anything. When Averill checked out, she borrowed all fiction. But Rachel claims she stole another book."

"She could have slipped one in her bag while you were talking to Finn."

"That's what Rachel said."

"And I almost forgot to tell you. The day I stopped at the library while you were at the sheriff's department giving your talk, she wanted me to urge you to do something about Averill."

"She did?" Sophie frowned. "Why bring you into this?"

"My thought, exactly."

"That wasn't necessary. Besides, I decided to do some more sleuthing myself this morning." Sophie had delved again into the library's computer system, trying to reconcile the inventory from the nonfiction section in question, then methodically searched the actual shelves in a process of elimination. The 360s didn't contain that many books in a small library, and to her dismay Rachel had been right. Several titles that should have been there were not. They hadn't been borrowed, either, according to the system. They were simply gone, and although Sophie wasn't happy now with Rachel, she'd alerted her.

"I admit I want Max to be happy with Averill. I may be blind to the truth I don't want to see."

At that moment, Gabe's horse shied, and he pointed. "Look." An Angus cow had wandered out from a copse of trees by the creek, a newborn calf trailing after her. Gabe steadied Critter. "Let's dismount, check out this baby."

"The cow gave birth in the woods?"

"Cattle like their privacy at such times. So do horses. I can't tell you how many foals I've missed seeing born in the middle of the night. One right here on Sweetheart. Teddie's colt appeared when we even had a stall monitor in use, but the whole event was over before I got there."

Gabe examined the calf, then rose from a crouch, sounding relieved. "Seems fine."

"I've never seen anything cuter," Sophie said. "Except Remi."

He gave the cow a friendly pat on the rump that sent her ambling off into the grass, the calf behind her. Gabe and Sophie turned back to their horses to remount—and Precious jumped. One hoof landed down hard on Sophie's instep, and she cried out.

"Soph. You okay?"

"Uh. Hurts a little, that's all."

"Maybe not. Here, sit down." Gabe tethered the horses to a tree where they seemed happy to graze on the grass. "Take off your boot while you still can. If that foot swells, as it probably will, removing a boot could be a lot more painful. We might have to cut it off."

Sophie's stomach rolled. "These boots are brand-new." She sat down in the spot he'd indicated under a tree. "I'm sure it's nothing."

"Let's have a look." Sunlight filtered through the branches, dappling Gabe's features but not softening his frown. He knelt and took hold of her boot. "I'll try not to hurt you any worse. Yell if you want to."

She held herself rigid. "Cowboys get hurt all the time, right?"

"Pretty much."

Sophie gritted her teeth as he tugged off the boot. "I guess my skills need more work."

"First rule of any barn. Don't spook the horses." But he smiled as he said it. "This doesn't look too bad after all. We'll get you to the barn, put some ice on it. I'll call ahead to Kate. She can meet us there." He turned away to get the horses.

"Gabe, I don't think I can stand up." Sophie had tried, then sunk down again onto the grass. The pain shooting through her foot had made her see black spots in front of her eyes.

"Hey." Gabe's expression looked worried. "Never mind, I'll carry you. You can ride with me. Precious will follow us home."

"What if I…if I can't…"

Another bolt of agony cut off the rest. The dark curtain descended, the sun went out, and Sophie slumped into Gabe's arms.

A few minutes—or an hour?—later she blinked in vague awareness.

Gabe was bending over her. "Thank God. You're back, honey." He'd never used the endearment with her before. He smoothed a trembling hand over Sophie's hair. "You lost consciousness for a few seconds. No wonder, that foot's swelling like a balloon, turning black and blue." He framed her face. "Scared the devil out of me, Soph." Even his voice shook. "Just rest, then we'll get you home when you're able to ride."

"I'm still a rookie," she tried to joke, but a soft sob caught in her throat.

Gabe must see the tears in her eyes, part pain, part humiliation.

"Ah, but you're my rookie."

Wow, two expressions of affection. Was she delirious? Sophie told herself his calling her honey, or saying she was his, didn't mean anything. She'd frightened Gabe, that was all. Then, as his smile faded, she had to change her opinion. His face came closer, his mouth moved toward her lips, and like an answer to her yearlong prayers, Gabe kissed her.

Her pain temporarily eclipsed, Sophie flung her arms around his neck and held on tight, letting him take the kiss deeper, murmuring, or was that whimpering, in his arms? She felt as if she'd been waiting for this all her life. "Gabe." But he was already pulling back.

"I shouldn't have done that. You're hurt— and I take advantage of you?" He surged to his feet, then held out a hand to help Sophie up.

"I'm a jerk," he said as if to himself just when Sophie had been floating on a cloud.

Right then, even on her bad foot, she could have run a marathon across the plains of Sweetheart Ranch. She could have forgotten every bad moment with Will and Bess, their ugly betrayal. She could have trusted him. Completely. But Gabe regretted the kiss.

They rode home in silence, Sophie resting her head against his warm back, hoping the tears didn't soak through his shirt. And let him know just how much she cared.

THE NEXT MORNING, after he'd completed his chores, sent the hands to check the herd for any calves that had evaded getting their vaccinations—and made sure the newborn he and Sophie had found yesterday was still okay—Gabe drove over to Farrier.

He mentally kicked himself the whole way. Why had he given in to impulse, to his fears for her, and kissed Sophie like that? It was hard to tell himself now that she was simply a friend, his best friend's sister. That kiss had nearly blown his head off. It was as if he'd never warned himself not to get involved. But if he *could* tell her everything now, and by some miracle she didn't reject him, would he and Sophie be able to take their relationship deeper? Yet, as always, he ran up against Brynne Energy, his dad, the as-yet-silent Aaron—and Sophie's need for total honesty. Gabe couldn't give her that. Not yet.

So. At the bank, he got a cashier's check for an amount that had made the clerk blink.

At least he could do this one thing for Sophie. If he was careful.

Which didn't work out.

On his way out of the branch where he kept his accounts, he ran into Lauren Anderson.

Hastily, Gabe tucked the check into his shirt pocket.

"You're far from home," she said, and his heart stalled.

"Been doing your homework?" Did she know about Midland now rather than Odessa?

She looked puzzled. "I meant Sweetheart."

Great. He'd just alerted her to the fact that her suspicions about him might be right. If she'd been tempted to give up before, that sharp blue gaze told him she wouldn't now.

"Actually, I'm glad to see you," she said after a brief pause. "We haven't finished that article."

"Lauren, I keep telling you. I'm just a cowboy. There are tons of them in Stewart County."

"You're the one I'm interested in."

"Look. This is pointless. I'm in town to run errands for Kate. I gotta go."

"Errands—and what else?" She was staring at the bank entrance.

"One of them, uh, was a ranch deposit."

"Maybe not only that. I saw you put that check in your pocket."

"Which is my business—not yours."

"Hmm. That's guaranteed to perk up my reporter's instincts. Tell you what. Meet me at the newspaper office tomorrow." She named a time. "Let's do this."

"There is no story," he said through clenched teeth, turned toward his truck, then stopped. If he refused the interview now, after she'd seen the check, she'd be sure he had something to hide.

Man, she was like a dog with a bone. Rembrandt couldn't have been more persistent. Besides, Gabe welcomed the chance himself to dig even deeper into Lauren's background.

"Okay," he said at last. "One short conversation. Then I'm done."

Gabe didn't look back, but he felt Lauren's eyes on him until he pulled away from his parking spot and hightailed it to Barren.

Why was Lauren so determined to investigate Gabe's life? And pick it apart for the truth?

Whatever her reasons, he could give her the scoop of her career.

But, with any luck, he wasn't going to.

CHAPTER EIGHTEEN

"MAX, I CAN'T believe this."

Sophie stared at the cashier's check in her hand. The amount seemed like someone had broken into Fort Knox. With her foot propped up on the sofa, and throbbing, she'd taken yesterday and this morning off. Her badly bruised instep—nothing broken, her doctor, Sawyer McCord, had told her—from two days before wasn't the only reason. Sophie still needed to make sense of that kiss she'd shared with Gabe—and his immediate withdrawal.

But this…the figure made her look again as if she'd been seeing things. It shocked Sophie even more than her nomination for the award weeks ago. A courier had delivered the envelope, but there was no note inside, no return address.

"Why look a gift horse in the mouth?" Max strolled in from the kitchen, blowing on his coffee. "Doesn't that solve your problems with the sesquicentennial?"

"Yes, but who could have—"

"Sometimes people do nice things without needing credit."

For a second Sophie wondered if her brother had sent the check. Max was famous in Barren for donating his services to area ranchers and farmers, single moms and little kids with ailing 4-H stock or sick family pets they couldn't afford to treat, one reason Sophie loved him madly. Max might forget a birthday or fail to show up for dinner, even date the wrong person—Averill, from what Sophie now knew?—yet he had a tender heart.

But she doubted he could afford to write a check in that amount, and he'd already donated.

"You can still have the Fun Run, whatever. Kind of makes my donation look like chump change."

"The committee appreciates every dollar." Sophie waved the check. "But I have to admit, this will really, really help." If only she could resolve the issue with Averill before Max got hurt, assuming she had taken those books in the first place or had a sketchier background than Sophie had thus far learned about.

When her phone rang, she glanced at the screen. It was Janet Turcott, the head librarian in Farrier. On a hunch Sophie had called her after she'd searched Barren's computer and shelves.

"I need to take this, Max."

"Catch you later," he said, grabbed his keys off the hallway table, and headed out to his truck, not to be late for work.

"Hey, Janet. Thanks for returning my call."

"How can I help you, Sophie?"

"Um, I have a patron here in Barren, a regular who loves John Grisham's work. She's originally from Farrier, a voracious reader." Sophie hesitated. "I'm not certain I should even ask, and violate her privacy, but do you know a woman called Averill?" It was an unusual name.

"Averill McCafferty, sure. She's in Barren now?"

"Has been for a while."

Janet's tone softened. "I've known Averill since she was a little girl. She used to come in all the time, choose an armload of books then return them two weeks later and pick out more."

"Sounds like a local boy I know." And Sophie had requested books for Teddie from Farrier before.

She heard the smile in Janet's voice. "Get

them hooked on reading early, huh? By the time she was ten years old, Averill had read every age-appropriate thing we had."

Sophie hesitated. "Did she ever fail to check out a book? Just take it home and never return it?"

"You mean steal from the library? No," Janet said, "but I lost touch with her. Years later, when Averill's life, her family, sadly fell apart, she stopped coming in. I never saw her again."

Sophie's stomach knotted.

There was a short silence. "Averill was a good kid caught up in a tragic situation." Janet added, "I feel uncomfortable saying more. You can read the local newspaper reports from that time or, better still, ask Averill. Has she done something wrong in Barren?"

"My concern is even more personal." Sophie didn't mention Max.

After a few pleasantries about the challenges of running a library in an age that valued social media and endless entertainment options over reading books, they hung up.

Sophie fell back against the sofa cushions. For Max's sake mainly, she'd wanted to know about Averill. A few absent books weren't the end of the world. Her brother had finally found someone he could care about who'd drawn him out of his usual preoccupation with the clinic, and now a missing book or two seemed minor by comparison. A tragic situation, Janet had said. Averill may have taken those very titles about coping with the situation. But had she been involved in something serious enough to make the papers? Perhaps a felony? Even murder?

Sophie hoped not, but she needed to know what that tragedy was. For Max's sake.

LATE THAT AFTERNOON Gabe headed over to Sophie's house to see how she was doing and to clear things up about their kiss. His interview with Lauren earlier hadn't gone as badly as he'd feared, so maybe this wouldn't, either. At least Lauren hadn't delved deeply enough into his background to find his connection to Brynne. Considering the company name, which could lead her to him, it wouldn't take that much more digging.

When Sophie didn't answer the door, he found it open.

"Come in," she called from the living room. "Gabe, hi. I've been confined to this sofa all day. I thought I'd go into work after lunch, but then I felt worse than I did this morning."

"Nothing wrong with taking time off." He handed her the bunch of flowers he'd bought at the local convenience store. "Sorry, these are already wilting—"

"It's the thought that counts. Thank you."

"You still feel bad?"

"Better after some ibuprofen, which I've been eating like candy. Could you do me a favor and put these in water?"

"Sure." Not knowing how to begin about his lapse of judgment with her, he escaped into the kitchen and rummaged for a vase under the sink. Gabe was no flower arranger, but even he knew to cut off a few inches of the stems, add water and ditch a couple of dead blossoms. Then he kind of fluffed the rest before he carried the arrangement into the other room. Sophie looked pretty lying on the sofa under a light blanket, her hair loose around her shoulders. Despite his vow to step back after that kiss, the sight turned his voice husky. "I've rarely seen you with your hair down. I like it."

"Part of my new image," she said, "and your suggestion, but I can't take credit. I didn't have the energy to put my hair up today. Makes leaning on the pillows more comfortable, too."

This was not the way to atone for his behavior. He'd been out of his mind, all right, when he'd kissed her. He'd had to withdraw.

"Sophie, I…" Then he couldn't go on.

"What's up?" she asked after a short silence. "I've never seen you at a loss for words. Or looking guilty like you do now."

Gabe swallowed, hard. "I am guilty."

"For what? Bringing me flowers?"

"For the other day," he managed. "I should never have kissed you."

"You're a very good kisser," she murmured.

"Soph, that's not the point."

Her expression fell. "You didn't take advantage. I let you. I didn't discourage you."

"You didn't know what you were doing. You'd just regained consciousness after scaring me half to death."

"Then you went all chill on me, pulled away, made it clear you wished you hadn't done that." She tried a shrug. "It was just a kiss." As if she meant to convince herself.

Gabe ran a finger around the collar of his shirt. "I don't want to mess up our friendship. That means a lot to me, and I know what you went through in Kansas City."

"You needn't protect me, if that's what you're doing, because of Will and Bess."

"Plus, there's Max—I'm not going to get on his bad side."

"*Plus*," she repeated, "there's that other thing." She wasn't going to let this go. "The cloudy history, which you refuse to tell me—or anyone else—about. I think that's the real point. Am I wrong?"

"No, but nothing has changed there, Sophie."

"You told me before—you can't talk about it."

"And I haven't lied to you." Much.

"You just haven't told the truth."

"Let's not pick this to pieces, okay? I am sorry about the kiss. Your accident, too," he added, turning toward the door. He'd leave it at that, even if she never spoke to him again.

"Gabe." She had straightened on the sofa. "I can't chase after you."

Her tone nearly brought him to his knees. Shaking his head, surrendering, he came back to sit on the end of the couch. "If I could tell you, I would." All too soon that truth would come out anyway, but Gabe wanted to buy all the time he could before that happened. He'd tried to regret their kiss but couldn't.

Why let her keep thinking he did? He'd wanted to kiss her, perhaps from the moment he'd met her. Even knowing how wrong that would be, how it might spoil their relationship or his with Max. End up exposing his lie before Gabe figured out how to deal with that. But what harm could there be now in letting her know something of how he felt?

Gabe took her face in his hands. "Soph, I do care about you. Really care, and I want to be honest, always, but right now I'm in the middle of this thing with my dad. Can you trust me enough to let it go at that? Temporarily?"

"You care about me? As more than a friend?"

"I thought I was a good kisser. That says something, doesn't it?"

Tempted to prove that again, he forced himself to ease back. "How about this? Let's have dinner somewhere tonight. I'll help you hobble into the restaurant. We'll order the best thing on the menu and share a bottle of wine."

"Not if you're the designated driver," she said but with a smile. In fact, Sophie's whole face had lit up, as if he'd offered her the world, and her eyes sparkled like the Hope diamond. "I care about you, too, Gabe. This will be our first date."

And maybe the last if he turned on the TV later and saw Aaron's face. Being short on time, though, had one advantage: it sharpened all feeling. His sense of urgency, his need to see Sophie happy even when he knew he would end up hurting her, made it impossible not to seize the moment.

"A date. Is that what this is?" He agreed it was. "You sure you feel up to it?"

Sophie gestured at her foot. "Doesn't hurt much at all now."

Gabe had another thought. He was jumping into this off a high diving board, but he didn't care right now if there was any water below. "Hey, and about Saturday? That double wedding at the WB? I know it's short notice, but you want to watch Cass and Zach, Noah and Kate get married?"

"With you as my escort?"

"Making up for lost time." Before there was no more to count on.

"Gabe, I'd love to." Then, as if she needed to temper her emotions with a different topic, Sophie leaned over to the end table and picked up the cashier's check—one more thing he was keeping from her that Gabe hoped wouldn't hurt. "In all this excitement, I forgot. Look what came today. Isn't this the best donation ever? I only wish I knew who sent it."

THE NIGHT BEFORE had been magical for Sophie. She'd let down her guard with Gabe, and their dinner at a new Thai restaurant in Farrier, their good-night kisses later, had her dancing a mental jig. Was it possible they could have the kind of relationship she'd dreamed of? What if Sophie *could* trust again? Trust Gabe. Still. She wondered at the truth he seemed to be hiding. Would she be able to accept it when it finally came out?

She was fixing supper, wondering if Max would come home to eat tonight, when her phone rang. Hoping it was Gabe, feeling the same blissful haze she was in, Sophie picked up, one hand stirring the beef goulash she was making. "Hello." She hadn't glanced at the display.

"Sophie, hi. It's me." The familiar female voice made Sophie drop her wooden spoon.

"Bess," she managed to say. Why was she calling? Sophie thought of hanging up, but her former roommate and friend rushed on, her tone raspy.

"I know this is awkward, but I wanted you to know." She cleared her throat, obviously moved. "Will and I..."

Briefly, Sophie thought Bess was calling to tell her they were getting a divorce.

"We had a baby! This afternoon. His name—"

Sophie stopped listening, or rather, hearing,

unable to make sense of the words. She stood, watching the goulash burn in the pan, tears springing to her eyes.

"Nineteen and a half inches long," Bess was saying. "You should see his hair, exactly the same shade as Will's."

Sophie spoke past the lump in her throat. "Bess. Why would you tell me this?"

A silence followed. Sophie heard her shuffling something in the background, the clink of a glass against a table, possibly a hospital stand. "I hate how things ended. I miss you, Sophie."

She was about to harden her heart and say that was too bad when, to make matters worse, Will came on the line. "Sophie. How's it going?" As if he'd never broken that same heart.

Did he expect her to congratulate them? The man who'd claimed he loved her, wanted to marry her, then suddenly, without a word of warning and behind her back, had wed someone else?

"Gee, Will. I'm still trying to make sense of that selfie you sent me from Vegas."

"Oh, that…probably not the best decision I've ever made. But we—"

Bess chimed in. "I know I shouldn't have called. But Sophie, please. Forgive me."

Shaking, unable to say another word, Sophie hung up.

She scraped the burnt contents of the pan into the trash. Ruined, like her relationships with Will, with Bess, whom she'd trusted most in this world, except for Max. There was no comparison between her brother and them.

How insensitive could two people be?

CHAPTER NINETEEN

"YOU'RE AWFUL QUIET." On Saturday Gabe leaned close to Sophie at their table.

Dressed in his best jeans and shirt, his Stetson and polished boots, he'd picked her up an hour before the wedding. Now she was trying to enjoy herself at the reception, but that birth announcement from Bess had shaken her like the selfie from Vegas—rubbing salt in Sophie's wound. What on earth had made her, much less Will, think it was a good idea to call?

Bad enough, but she'd also learned enough from Janet Turcott, the librarian in Farrier, to still be worried about Averill, although she'd had no time to look up those newspaper articles. Or to ask Averill directly. Sophie toyed with the stem of her champagne glass and spied Lauren Anderson not far away with the newspaper's photographer, capturing today's festive occasion. Sophie should have stayed home.

Gabe saw her looking at Lauren. "She's ambitious, all right—not a bad quality—but for good reason. During that interview the other day I learned something else about Lauren. She was not only discredited and fired from her previous job, but the editor, her boss, was also Lauren's fiancé at the time. So, a broken heart as well as the loss of her career. She can be pushy, but I feel for her, Soph."

So did Sophie, whose gaze shifted away from Lauren to focus on her surroundings. Her attempt to enjoy the reception wasn't working, but the WB's double wedding earlier had been beautiful, like most weddings, and the reception had truly pulled out all the stops.

A huge white tent on the front lawn, fairy lights in the trees, filet mignon for dinner, an endless supply of champagne, a great band and two lovely brides. Cass had chosen a filmy white gown with crystal accents. Kate wore a sleek column of ivory satin, simple but stunning. On the large outdoor floor that had been set up nearby, they were now dancing to the first song with their grooms. All four looked so happy that tears filled Sophie's eyes. Solely for them, for Averill, too, or because of Bess's new baby?

"I'm quiet because I heard from my ex and his wife," she finally said.

"That took nerve on their part." Gabe reached for her hand. "What's the word?"

"They just had a baby boy, whom they named after Will."

"Why would they tell you?"

She could hardly speak. "That was my question. Can you believe? Bess tried to resurrect our friendship. Then Will made it a total disaster. I hung up on them."

He squeezed her fingers. "Good for you."

"I'm also glum because I feel bad for Max." He'd come to the wedding alone instead of bringing Averill.

"She had something else to do," he'd said and was now talking to Jean Bodine. The mother of the two grooms hadn't stopped smiling, often through tears, since the wedding march had begun. "I haven't spoken to him yet, but I've learned Averill has some dreadful tragedy in her past." A secret she'd been keeping, as Sophie feared Gabe was, too. "I can't help thinking she's desperate for Max not to know." She hated to believe her brother had been duped as Sophie had by Will and Bess. "Like with the missing books, I don't how to approach this new info."

"Maybe he already knows."

She took a breath. "If so, he would have been upset enough to tell me. Those books may pale in comparison to Averill's past."

Gabe rested his forehead against hers. "Aw, Soph. I'm sorry. You're in a tough spot. What do you think he'll do once he does know?"

"Since she didn't come to this wedding with him, maybe they've already talked about that—and broken up."

"He hasn't seemed like the Max I know today. I wondered if that was because of me. You," Gabe added. "Together."

"I doubt that."

His cell pinged and he pulled it from his pocket. He glanced at the screen, frowned, then put the phone back and drew Sophie from her chair. "A text from Jilly. I'll read it later. Come on, let's dance."

After the two brides and grooms finished their waltz, the floor had opened to the wedding guests, and the strains of a soft ballad rose on the humid summer air.

At the edge of the temporary floor, Gabe stopped. "You're limping. I should have asked. Do you feel okay to dance?"

"My foot's better, but the bruise Precious

left is purple and green today, heading toward yellow."

"Have you seen Sawyer McCord again?"

"He said there was no need to as long as there's improvement. Doc Baxter, who's still holding office hours now and then, agreed." The older man had been a fixture in Barren since Sophie was a child, but he'd sold his practice to Sawyer and was traveling a lot with his wife.

Gabe held her close. His warm touch against her cooler skin never failed to surprise, and delight, her. "I hope you learned that lesson. Precious weighs over half a ton."

"I promise to keep out of her way."

"You're doing great at Sweetheart, though, Soph."

"Who would have thought?" Gabe hadn't, but now, to her delight, several things had changed between them.

In his arms, Sophie floated as best she could while favoring her foot, trying not to think about Averill, or the possibility that this interlude with Gabe might end, too. That she, like Averill and Max, having touched happiness, would be alone again.

"I'm not a fan of 'Moon River,'" Gabe murmured in her ear as they glided across the wooden floor. "Why do they play this at every wedding?"

"It's a pretty tune."

"You *like* it," he said in a mock accusatory tone.

"I used to love weddings." Not anymore, after Will and Bess's deception. "I don't care what songs they play."

"Well, I have my limit." He danced her to the edge of the floor then off into the grass, whirling Sophie toward the cover of the trees.

"Where are we going?"

"Somewhere private. I need to do something."

"What?"

"Something I've been wanting since before Precious stepped on you." Under a cottonwood tree strung with lights, he embraced her again. "This," he said, then took Sophie's mouth with his. The kiss wasn't soft or light, barely touching as it had been that other day, or like the tender good-night kisses after their dinner date, and it wasn't long before Gabe deepened it further until she lost track of their surroundings. Only his arms around her counted, his kiss. Gabe's fingers played with hers. "I didn't regret our first kiss. I just hadn't admitted to myself then how much you matter to me. I want to think it'll be okay."

"What will?"

He didn't answer and Sophie thought his kiss had held a touch of despair.

After a moment he said, "You look terrific, by the way, better to me than either of the brides—as gorgeous as they are. You outshine everyone here, and I'm proud to be the man who brought you."

"I'm proud to be with you, Gabe."

He kissed her again, a mere brushing of their lips this time. "That dress," he told her, "should be outlawed. There's not a guy here who won't vote for you as Citizen of the Year or anything else simply because of it."

Sophie had bought the dress during a second shopping trip with Willow. Off-white with a soft red, green and pale pink floral pattern on the low-cut bodice and repeated in bands around the midriff. The thin straps of the dress were barely visible, the back bare, and the long skirt with deep pockets flowed almost to the floor, covering her bruised foot. She wouldn't have chosen such a style in Kansas City. Strappy sandals with stiletto heels that had dug into the lawn completed her outfit.

Sophie's hair was in a low chignon with loose tendrils around her face.

"I have other attributes, you know."

"Don't get huffy. That's not me viewing you as some object." He toyed with a strand of her hair. "This is me telling you I want you not only because of how you look tonight but also who you are. Barren's head librarian with her hair in an adorably messy bun, the town's best candidate for the award, Sweetheart Ranch's number one cowgirl—"

"Kate won't like you saying that."

"She's busy with Noah." The two were dancing again, Kate's arms around her new husband's neck.

"And Zach," she noticed, "has disappeared with Cass. I don't see them anywhere."

"Guess why." Gabe covered her mouth in yet another kiss. "I really like this new image of yours. Jeans and a pearl-buttoned shirt one day, this dress…"

Without warning Gabe drew back as he had that other day, and for a too-long moment looked at her until Sophie discovered a slight wrinkle in her dress that needed to be smoothed. She'd been blindsided once before. Did Gabe plan to let her down gently? When their romantic relationship had barely started, and after such a sweet lead-in, what was he about to say? *Dinner and this wedding have been nice but let's not take this any further?* At least he wasn't sending her a breakup selfie. But that wasn't his intention at all.

He lifted a hand to her hair, touching the stray tendrils that framed her face. He let one of them sift through his fingers while Sophie stood frozen. "What?" she finally said.

"I love...your hair like this with your bun low at the nape of your neck—like a ballerina—but no." Gabe shook his head. "I like it even more like this," and he began to slowly pull out the pins. Sophie's eyes met his as her hairstyle fell apart in his hands, slipping through his fingers. "Like silk," he murmured.

Apparently, her crush on him wasn't one-sided after all. And Sophie's heart sang.

"Gabe." Her voice sounded breathless. "I'll wear it down again—with this dress. For you."

Her hair brushing her shoulders, she moved back into his arms, and they danced to another ballad in the shadow of the trees. She might never feel this happy again. She wanted to relish these first days of being a new couple, if that was what they were, and to not worry about the future—or even her brother and Averill.

For the first time since she'd come home to Barren, she could foresee a future. After Will and Bess, she'd certainly become gunshy. Maybe, after that birth announcement, and with Gabe now, it was time to put the past behind her.

But the moment didn't last.

Gabe nuzzled her neck, his voice shaken. "You're the best person I know, Soph. Don't ever forget that."

How many times had she dreamed of this, him looking at her as he did tonight? Holding her now? And yet she fretted all over again.

Despite their dinner and this wedding, the dance they'd shared…he'd sounded as if he would never see her again.

AFTER THE WEDDING, Gabe had spent the next day on the phone back and forth with Jilly, all but forgetting at times even the previous night with Sophie. "I'll be there as soon as I can," he'd told Jilly.

But he couldn't just leave. On Monday he'd followed up on some things at the barn, then assigned the job as stand-in foreman to the most experienced of the other hands. Now, the next day, with the intention of filling Max in before he flew out tomorrow and everything went further south, as it was about to, he tracked him down at the clinic. Max was in the supply room, staring at a row of bottles on a shelf.

"Hey."

Max didn't answer. He looked unhappy, as he had at the wedding. Because of Averill? Gabe hoped he wasn't going to make him feel worse.

He leaned against the doorjamb. "You okay, Max?"

"Sure." He picked up a bottle, then set it down again. "What's up?"

Gabe shifted his weight. Jilly's text had sent him reeling. Then he'd unwisely kissed Sophie again, said things he shouldn't have said. He'd taken a chance, unable to stop himself, telling her part of how he felt.

What would happen when he had to explain to her, as well as Max, that he was leaving? He should have told her first, but he was here now.

"I'm, uh, going to have to go back home for a while."

Max scowled. "Right after you started dating Sophie?"

"Yeah. But I want you to know, I'll work things out with her." Somehow.

"From where? Texas?" Max shook his head.

"Or is that a fiction? I value our friendship, and I've overlooked the little lapses, the slips, the evasions. But I'm done turning a blind eye to things." Did he mean about Averill, too? "Who are you, Gabe?"

Gabe studied his boots. "Texas is real, all right."

"Is this about your dad?"

"Yeah," he said again, "and I've had to keep that from you—from Sophie—but any minute now there won't be a secret."

Max flung up a hand. "You're speaking in riddles. You say you want to move ahead with Sophie, but all I hear is more stonewalling. I promised myself I wouldn't let anyone hurt her again. Now you tell me you're just leaving?"

The plans for that hadn't been simple. Jilly had offered to send the company plane for him, but Gabe had nixed that. He'd had to tie things up at Sweetheart, tell Sophie he'd be gone for a while, and he preferred not taking the risk of being noticed a bit longer. Then he'd had trouble booking a commercial flight.

"On Wednesday," he said, which was the first seat he'd been able to get.

"I saw you two at the wedding, dancing off into the trees. Why, Gabe? When she's finally beginning to be herself again, when you must know how she feels about you, why would you do that to her?"

"I said we'll work it out."

"Really? How? Or are you just like that poor excuse for a human being who ran off with Sophie's best friend to Vegas?"

"Maybe it looks that way right now, and I'm sorry." Gabe spun on his heel. He'd made a hash of this with Max. How would he avoid doing the same with her? "I needed... I wanted... I better speak with Sophie."

Gabe knew there was nothing he could say to Max that would make things better. Probably with Sophie, either. Not now. "I hoped you could trust me a while longer, Max. That's what I'm asking you to do. I promise, I'll tell you everything soon."

Right now there was no more to be said.

He walked from the room, down the hall through the clinic, past the empty front desk. Averill didn't appear to be working today. He went out onto the street where he leaned against his truck, his legs having turned to water.

He couldn't have left town without telling Max.

He couldn't go before talking to Sophie. But what if he was too late? What if she already knew? This latest news might have broken by now.

Gabe reached into his pocket, took out his cell and stared at Jilly's message, which had inspired him to speak his mind to Sophie, dance with her, kiss her in the moonlight before he had to run smack into his own fate.

He'd lied again to Sophie at the wedding. It had taken one glance at Jilly's text. To know.

Your friend—Aaron, right—has blown the whistle. He's going to talk. Now what?

AT WORK THAT morning Sophie had a stubborn sense of impending doom. About Gabe, and the strange thing he'd said at the reception, but ever since she'd talked to Janet Turcott, she'd been on edge, too, wondering. What was the nature of the tragedy in which Averill had been involved? She hadn't had time until now to look for the news articles.

Sophie did a Google search. As she read the first report, then the second, and finally another, her eyes widened. "Oh, goodness. No," she murmured, a hand to her mouth. "How terrible." Janet had, if anything, soft-pedaled the tragedy. Averill wasn't part of the felony herself but had suffered a very personal loss that would break anyone and made Sophie's heart ache for her.

Unable to read further, she closed the window on the last article, then rummaged on her desk for a paper she would need later. She was scheduled to speak to her women's library group today about her candidacy for the award. She tried to focus on refining her usual stump speech, which many of the attendees had probably heard, and added a few new details to freshen it.

This would be a busy week. After the wedding, on Sunday the first of the celebration events—a kickoff parade to jointly honor the town and the next day's Fourth of July holiday—had required her complete attention. There would be something every day or night through next Sunday. Still, her thoughts remained on Averill. Max. And Gabe.

She hadn't seen him since Saturday.

As if she'd given her brother's girlfriend a cue, through her open office door she saw Averill walk into the library, return the Grisham book to Rachel with glowing praise for the writer's latest bestseller then go toward the stacks.

"Same MO," Rachel murmured, poking her head in Sophie's door. She'd come from behind the desk as soon as Averill headed for the new fiction shelf. "Wait and see. She does this every time—a few minutes of shuffling through the books there, then heads for that one section in nonfiction."

As Rachel spoke, Averill glanced around, then disappeared at the opposite end of the fiction stacks. Almost instantly, she reappeared in nonfiction. "See?" Rachel said. "The 360s again."

"I'll be with you in a minute." Sophie ran her pencil through a line in her speech, and taking her cue, Rachel left the room. The missing books were an irritation, a possible sign that Averill couldn't be trusted to do the responsible thing, but a tragedy was far worse. And yet...

When she heard someone suddenly cry out, Sophie ran into the main room where she found Averill tussling with Rachel.

"I saw you!" Rachel said, causing every head in the library to turn. "Sophie, I followed her. She's stealing another book!"

"I am not. I was looking at it, that's all."

"Like you've 'looked at' several others before sticking them in your bag." Averill did have a large tote with her.

"You have no evidence," Averill said.

Rachel held up her cell phone. "No? What about this video?"

Averill's face turned ashen. "You recorded me?"

"Everything is documented these days." She held the phone out to Sophie. "Take a look."

Sophie hesitated. Even as she wanted to know the truth, she knew how this might affect Max. "Rachel, I feel like a voyeur."

"You needed proof. Here it is—this is what she's been up to."

And there was Averill on the screen, browsing in the nonfiction section, pulling out one book then putting it back, perusing another... then pushing it down into her bag. The image was blurry enough that Sophie wasn't sure it was Averill. Her stomach dropped. "If I'm seeing right, this isn't good."

Sophie felt half-sick. On the one hand, she should appreciate Rachel's sleuthing. She might want only to prove herself, which Sophie understood. She also knew that Averill had rights.

"What's wrong, Mommy?" a little boy nearby asked, his eyes wide.

"Everything is fine," Sophie assured him and his mother.

"I was about to check out," Averill claimed, her gaze sliding away from Sophie's.

"I'm telling you, Sophie. You didn't believe me that she's a thief, but now—"

"Please," Averill cried, "I haven't taken anything. I like to read, to learn things, that's all."

Rachel grabbed the tote and pulled out the book in question. "I nabbed her before she could add this to her 'collection.'"

"That book was in my tote because I couldn't carry everything otherwise."

Sophie turned to Averill. "Do you still want this?"

"I've changed my mind. No," Averill muttered.

"Then you're free to go after you check out the rest."

"Thanks, Sophie." The slumping of her shoulders told Sophie that Averill was terribly upset. So was Sophie.

"I'll check you out myself."

After Averill left, not having said another word, then rushed down the outside steps, clearly shaken by the unclear video, Sophie went back into her office—and reread the articles on her computer. Neither Gabe nor Max was on her mind now.

Averill's tragedy seemed much more terrible than a few missing books.

CHAPTER TWENTY

SOPHIE WAS STILL thinking about Averill and the video when, shortly before one o'clock and her speech to the library group, she checked the rear door of the community center again. Gabe hadn't shown, breaking his promise to her after the wedding. *Your fan club will be there in force*, he'd said on her doorstep. *Meaning me*.

With the sesquicentennial celebration this week in all its glory—she hoped—she knew the voting for the award would take place tomorrow. This would be Sophie's chance to convince any doubters that she should become Barren's next Citizen of the Year. Her speech was second nature now, and she no longer let her nerves get the best of her.

Today's event should also have a friendly audience. Sophie sat, half listening to the other candidates for the award, all of whom had been invited to speak. Sophie's slot came last.

Gabe would say that was a position of strength. People would remember what she'd said, but he wasn't here. And Lauren stood at the podium, charming everyone. After learning from Gabe about her background, Sophie had a different view of her. She could almost root for Lauren.

When it was her turn, Sophie spoke with confidence, partly on autopilot because she knew the words so well. Weeks ago, she could never have done that. Even Will and Bess's birth announcement hadn't rattled her as much, it turned out, as some selfie from Vegas. That photo, their betrayal, wasn't the baby's fault, and Sophie had since decided to send a gift. As she walked through the parking lot to her car after her speech, someone called her name.

"Sophie, wait up." Lauren was behind her. "Good speech. May the best woman win."

"And the same to you."

"I won't keep you. I imagine you're on your way back to the library, and I'm headed to the *Journal*. Big story—huge—in the making, and my byline will be on it."

"Congratulations."

"The timing couldn't be better." Lauren's smile turned coy. "Don't you want to know what the story is?"

Not really. Lauren was always hunting for a scoop. Angling for the award. And just when

Sophie had felt kindly toward her, Lauren was in her face.

"Go ahead, ask. I know you want to."

"You know no such thing." Sophie picked up her pace. "I have to go."

"It's about someone you know."

Sophie's step faltered. "I don't listen to gossip. I'll wait to read the paper."

"Suit yourself, but…" Lauren stepped in front of her. "Gabe Morgan."

Sophie's pulse jumped. "What about him?"

"He's not who you think he is." Sophie tried to go around her, but Lauren kept pace, determined to have her say. "I saw you with him at the wedding. Dancing, vanishing into the darkness together—" Lauren laughed. "I'm not jealous. I'm married to my computer. Gabe's pretty to look at, but he's a hard case with a story. Thank goodness for Google."

"I have no idea what you're talking about. Whatever dirt you think you've dug up on Gabe, I don't want to hear it."

Still, a small silent alarm had gone off inside, and Sophie, of course, had her own suspicions. She remembered the look on his face when he'd said *don't ever forget that*, as if he wouldn't be here much longer.

"Gabe Morgan is a common name—which

threw me off track at first—but Gabriel Morgan Wyatt is not."

Sophie hadn't known Gabe was short for Gabriel, which didn't seem to suit a Kansas cowboy. But Wyatt?

"Morgan was his mother's maiden name. Railroads in her case. His father married into money, which helped to launch his corporation."

"Corporation?"

"Big oil," Lauren said with a nod of transparent satisfaction that she'd upset Sophie's equilibrium. She was scooping herself to do so. "Brynne Energy."

"Brynne?" Sophie had filled her tank again at the local station this morning.

"The family business." Lauren added. "Chester Dean Wyatt, CEO—and future emeritus, chairman of the board." She smiled, the same expression she'd given Sophie one day at the *Journal* office. And she'd thought Lauren had a romantic interest in Gabe then. Instead, the next story was all she cared about. For good reason, Sophie had to admit.

She could no more have hidden her reaction than she would trust Lauren after all. Or now, it seemed, Gabe himself. "Oh. That oil spill in the Gulf," Sophie realized.

Stunned, she had never imagined a personal link to Gabe. The story hadn't captured her interest other than to read the occasional mention on her TV's crawl and say a prayer for the victims.

"I've shocked you." Lauren continued, "Tons of trouble—I should say barrels and barrels—and your *cowboy* is next in line to run the company. Imagine the money involved.*"*

The money wasn't an issue. His lie was.

Lauren said, "I'll make sure I have all my facts right—this time—but after I break the story in the *Journal and on our social media,* the wire services will pick it up. The news will be everywhere. Worldwide. And so will my name." She added, "This makes my career, or rather remakes it, and I'll be off to the big leagues. *The Washington Post, the New York Times.*"

What about the award? Sophie wanted to ask but, having gone numb, could not. Apparently, being Barren's Citizen of the Year didn't mean much to Lauren after all. Or, perhaps she'd taken as much delight in trying to beat Sophie for the award as she obviously did in exposing Gabe's secret. Breaking the fragile trust Sophie had almost given him.

Right now, the award didn't matter to her, either.

Her mind spinning with the truth Lauren had insisted on telling her, Sophie had frozen in place. *Shocked* wasn't a strong enough word.

Lauren smiled again. "Anyway. Considering your new *relationship* with him, I thought you should know."

But what if Lauren was lying? To be fair, Sophie would have to confront Gabe. She'd assumed, even hoped, any secret might be minor and not on the order of Will and Bess's betrayal. This was even worse. Maybe he had a different explanation. Either that, or she didn't know Gabe at all.

THAT SAME AFTERNOON SOMEONE pounded at Averill's door. "Open up," he called.

It was Max, and her heart plummeted. She didn't want to see anyone, especially him, but after the debacle earlier with Rachel and Sophie at the library, she'd known this was coming. Averill opened the door.

"Why weren't you at work today?" he asked.

"I didn't feel well." She weakly gestured for him to come in.

"Is that why you bailed out on the wedding last Saturday?"

"No," she said. After their talk about babies and marriage, Averill couldn't bring herself to attend, to witness such joy and love. And yesterday she hadn't worked. On Monday, a holiday, the clinic had been closed.

"You should have called, Averill. This morning, after Gabe left—we had words about my sister—I kept hearing the empty silence in the clinic before my first appointment. I knew something must be wrong with you. I worried about you. I closed the office as soon as I could. Have you seen a doctor?"

"It's not physical."

Max looked relieved. "Okay, then what is it? I tried to call you a dozen times only to get your voice mail."

"I didn't check my messages."

He drilled her with a look. "Great. And this morning Mrs. Hingle made me lose the last of my patience with her latest argument that her cat can't possibly be pregnant. I guess she'll find out when the kittens arrive. You and I would have laughed over that." But neither of them was laughing now. "Instead, I couldn't concentrate, and because I wouldn't risk my safety around large animals, I canceled a visit to that pig farmer near Farrier, a vet check on a horse that Cooper Ransom wants to buy, a couple of wellness visits to a newborn calf and a bay foal. You haven't quit on me, have you? On us?" he added, looking as miserable as she felt.

Averill led him into the living room and sank down on the sofa. Her apartment was really a studio with an adjoining postage-stamp-sized bathroom. Her couch opened into a bed. The small space was devoid of any decor and had only basic furniture. The chair he chose to sit on, a bistro table. No pictures on the walls. Averill had attached a photograph of the two of them at the park where they'd had a picnic lunch one day to the refrigerator with a magnet. Other than that, she'd always known that Barren would be temporary. The apartment and Max.

"I've been lying to you."

"Averill, I knew when I hired you that you didn't have experience. You've learned a lot in these past months. Did something happen at the clinic? You gave the wrong dose of some medication to a patient or forgot to order the drugs we're short on…"

"I'm not the person you believe I am." She'd guessed this would happen. "I lied to Sophie, too. I stole books from the library."

Max looked as if he couldn't believe he'd

heard right. "I mean, sure, that's not a good thing, but tell her. Pay for the books, return them, whatever."

"I will, I promise. But please listen, Max."

To her horror, he tried to make a joke. "Don't tell me. You're a serial killer."

Averill felt the blood drain from her face. "Not that far from the truth."

"I shouldn't have said that," he muttered. "You mean, like you really have an alias or something?"

She should have used one. Built a whole new persona for herself. Moved to a different town. But here in Barren she hadn't expected to fall in love with Max. "No, I'm Averill McCafferty all right. I take it the name has never triggered some memory."

"Of what? We only met when you applied for the clinic job."

"I'm from Farrier," she said, "but the rest was a smokescreen. To protect myself."

He couldn't seem to comprehend what she was saying. "Your mother's not seeing some guy and you felt in the way?"

"She is, and I did, and my father always had a bad heart, but we didn't believe we would lose him so soon until I—" She shook her head. "The story about me was in the papers."

"My folks read the *Farrier Record* plus the *Barren Journal*, but Sophie and I canceled the subscriptions after they died. I don't ever remember seeing your name."

"You probably wouldn't recognize it then, but you have a right to know now." Her voice shook. "When I was a junior in high school, my mom and dad had another child. A surprise midlife baby. They'd had trouble conceiving again after I was born and were thrilled with another daughter. They doted on her. So did I. Lucie was adorable, sweet, loving... how could we not? I took care of her every chance I got. Later, that meant summers home from college, on spring break, and occasional weekends whenever they wanted to have a date night. All they had to do was call." For a moment she couldn't go on, then, "One afternoon Mom had a dental appointment and Dad went with her. As a treat, while they were gone, I took Lucie to the mall. They had a giant sand sculpture there every summer, and that year's theme was about princesses. Her favorite, of course, at five years old."

In halting sentences, she told him the rest, her face downcast. "I, um, had this boyfriend at the time. We were on and off a lot, fighting at that point, and I'm sitting on a bench in the mall, on the phone trying not to yell at him, tears dripping down my face, when suddenly I look around—and Lucie was gone."

Max's face looked pale. He must sense what was coming.

"She'd literally disappeared. I couldn't see her anywhere. I dropped the phone with my boyfriend still shouting in my ear. I started running, searching for her, calling her name, feeling more frantic every minute, but I—I couldn't find her."

"Averill," he said.

"It happened so fast. One second, she was on the bench beside me, the next she wasn't. The police did their best, and the community came together, combing the nearby woods…but we never saw her again. To this day I don't know what happened to her. My parents were dev-astated. I wasn't held responsible—but I was, Max. Because of me—some college romance gone bad—my baby sister isn't here anymore." Her voice broke on the last word.

He cleared his throat. "So, after that you left Farrier."

"Not for years, even though my relationship with my mom wasn't good. She won't ever forgive me. I moved into a place of my own, but that didn't seem to help either of us. I was still nearby, so finally I came to Barren. I don't blame her. I'm thirty years old and I can't forgive myself."

"Have you tried counseling?"

"I did at first, so did my parents, but then my dad got sick, and taking care of him took all our time. Know what I think? Lucie's disappearance, the never knowing, killed him, not his heart condition. Mom still barely speaks to me. Once she met that guy, I had to leave home, and as I told you I've become very good at avoidance. It's been my way with you, with Sophie, and everyone else in this town. None of you really know me."

"That's a tragic story, but it's *not* who you are, Averill. You've never been anything but kind, generous, and you're a good worker. I don't know what else to say. How to help you."

He made a move toward the sofa, as if intending to comfort her, but she rose then stepped away. "Max, I let a silly phone conversation with a guy whose face I can't remember now take precedence over keeping my little sister safe. How can you even look at me now? I know how protective you can be with Sophie—even when it seems you're clueless."

"Gabe would agree with you there," he admitted, "but that's not the same."

"To me, it is."

"I don't blame you for what happened." He looked desperate. "I'm not judging you."

"You should."

"Averill, you're a victim, too. I bet you told Lucie to sit right there."

"I was twenty-one years old. An adult. She was only five." She sniffed, her voice trembling. "I'm giving you my notice, Max. I'm sorry, it's effective immediately. You have a position here in Barren, and I don't want to leave you in the lurch, but the clinic has been your life—"

"Before I met you."

She tried to ignore that. "I can only damage your reputation. Once this story comes out, and people in Barren learn who I really am, they could turn their backs on you too."

"Guilt by association? I doubt that." He hesitated. "You're underestimating the people here. And me. You didn't do anything wrong."

"Then you have more faith in your hometown than I do. I knew this would catch up with me eventually. I'm sorry I drew you into my terrible past."

She'd dismissed him, but he didn't rise to leave. Max sat, staring at her. "You don't need to be miserable. Look at what we've had these past months." He tried a crooked smile. "You're my right-hand girl at the clinic. If I'm not inclined to fire you—or to stop seeing you outside the office—why would you quit?" He swallowed. "Averill, this may be the worst time to tell you, but I'm falling in love with you. I don't want to lose you."

Oh, no, Max. Please don't say that. "I was never yours to lose," she forced herself to say.

"You're not thinking clearly."

"I've had plenty of time to think since Lucie wandered off at the mall and someone snatched her. I should never have taken my eyes off her."

"Okay. You made a mistake, but that's what it was. A mistake." He hesitated. "Is that why you didn't want a family? Kids of your own?"

Her mouth quivered. "I couldn't imagine raising a little girl, seeing in her part of Lucie."

"Averill. You're going to live the rest of your life with that guilt?"

"Probably, yes. I've read all the books—including the ones I took from the Barren library. I didn't want to check them out because the evidence would be right there in the library computer with my name, my card number. I didn't want Sophie or Rachel to know." And then Max would find out.

"Other people take out self-help books."

"I'd hoped the books would help but they don't. Neither did counseling."

Averill walked toward the door, and Max had no choice but to follow. She held it open for him, then laid a shaking hand against his cheek.

His eyes were twin pools of hurt. "Don't do this, Averill. We'll get through it together. I want you to be happy."

Her heart cracked in two, yet she couldn't let him sacrifice himself on the altar of her everlasting guilt. "I don't deserve to be happy," she said, then gently closed the door.

CHAPTER TWENTY-ONE

"YOU LIED TO ME, GABE."

Sophie had walked into the barn where he had Critter tied in the aisle, and Gabe heard the words he'd dreaded for months. He'd wanted to tell Sophie right after he'd left Max's clinic that morning, but showing up at the library, while she was at work with Rachel and a bunch of patrons were there, didn't seem the best opportunity. Neither did talking to her at the community center where she'd given her speech. So he hadn't gone there either. After he finished grooming Critter, he'd thought, he would go to her house. But there was no sense denying the truth now.

He fiddled with Critter's bridle. "I did, yeah. I had to, Soph."

"Why?" Her expression fell. "I'd hoped… I wanted to give you the benefit of the doubt." Her mouth hardened, no longer the soft, warm lips he'd kissed. "Instead, you led Max, everyone on this ranch and in Barren—me—to believe your lies. Except, of course, Lauren Anderson."

He groaned. "She told you."

"At least she waited until after I gave my speech. I shouldn't warn you, but she's going to break the story in the *Journal*."

In their stalls the other horses shifted, one whinnying as if in disapproval of Gabe. His lies. He couldn't look at Sophie.

"Was anything you told me true?"

"Most," he said. "The basics. My mother's illness, her death when I was eleven, Jilly stepping in to help raise me, my dad's withdrawal from family life."

"Oh, you mean the father who's in the 'oil business'?"

He stared at the aisle floor.

She pointed a finger at him. "You lulled this entire town into thinking you were just like us. Instead, your father is *Brynne Energy*, including the convenient local station where I get my gas. He runs a giant corporation—supported by people like me—which, I understand, you're going to take over."

His mouth tightened. "That hasn't been determined."

"Whatever that means. Why are you here pretending to be Kate's foreman when your father is in serious trouble? You should be standing by him in Texas where you belong."

Sophie and Jilly agreed there. "I am Kate's foreman."

"Playing a role." She moved closer to Critter, as if seeking shelter. "Really, you should be on the stage—in movies. What kind of man are you, Gabe? Or should I say Gabriel?"

"Soph."

"Don't call me that. Ever again." When he took a step, she held up a trembling hand.

Buying a little time, he unhooked Critter from the crossties, smoothed his forelock, still evading Sophie's gaze. "I get it that you're disappointed in me."

"That doesn't begin to cover it."

"I realize you're probably comparing us with your ex and his Vegas bride. But hear me out. I've been trying to protect my dad. I couldn't go back. I'd have been a key witness along with someone else in the federal government's case against Brynne. Against him. I still am."

"I don't believe you."

At her tone of voice Critter's ears laid flat and he danced a bit. "Watch it," he said. "You'll get stepped on again."

"Another sore foot is no issue right now. I'm already in pain."

"I know, Sophie, I do." Gabe rubbed the back of his neck. "I am too." She hated him—he'd always known she would—so why hold back now? He told Sophie about Aaron. "He's going to talk. When he does, he'll probably point at me to corroborate what he says. He didn't cause that oil spill in the Gulf, I didn't, my father, either. But I can back up what Aaron said then—what he'll say now. We both know things about Brynne that will not help my dad."

"I see." She didn't sound sympathetic.

"Whether or not you think I was wrong to stay here, I do have to go back now. The story's out or will be—not just from Lauren. It's worse than she knows. Jilly warned me in that text I got at the wedding. I was going to tell you then, but I didn't want to ruin that night. I can't say how sorry I am that I didn't tell you before Lauren did."

"I don't believe you," she said again. "You were right, though. I am comparing this to Will and Bess. The difference is, I'm not heartbroken over them anymore. I don't feel bad when I think about their new baby. I actually hope they'll be happy together, all three of them. But you? Because, even after dinner in Farrier, the WB wedding, the…kisses, which were nothing more than lies, too—"

"Sophie, we aren't a lie."

"How dare you. There is no *we*." She drew a deep breath. "I've wasted another year of my life hoping you'd see me as more than a friend. I worked with you on the sesquicentennial, had your support for the award, when all along I was being played again. Why would you do that to me?"

Gabe couldn't speak. Max had asked the same question.

"I almost trusted you not to hurt me like they did." She lifted her head, tears glittering on her lashes. "Max was right to caution me about you. I knew you were holding something back—but nothing like this."

"Sophie—"

"I should have listened to my brother." She gave Critter a tentative pat on the neck. "Have a safe trip back to *Midland*," she muttered then stalked out of the barn, past Critter, past Gabe, into the blinding sun.

He couldn't see her clearly in the light, but he'd heard her words.

I almost trusted you.

HADN'T SHE PROMISED HERSELF, after Will and Bess, she'd never be lied to again? Her vision blurred by unshed tears, Sophie drove into

Barren well above the speed limit, pushing her car—the one filled with Brynne gas— to take her physically as well as emotionally away from Gabe. It wasn't possible to get far enough. She planned never to see him again. She should be laughing at her own gullibility.

On the way home, where she would likely give in to the tears that clogged her throat, she made one stop. At the library, Rachel was behind the front desk. Sophie's heart wasn't in the job right now, but her assistant's obviously was, perhaps even more since that embarrassing scene with Averill.

"While you were speaking at the community center, I started to rebind some of those children's books we pulled from the shelves. The kids tear them apart. It's hard to keep up, and the pile has been growing."

"I know. That chore is endless." After she'd returned from Kansas City, work had saved Sophie; she wished Barren's library could do so again.

As if to further prove her own value, Rachel hurried over to the night depository. "I emptied the bin first thing this morning, but a while ago I heard more books land inside. Might as well get them now before we close for the day."

Rachel hauled out a volume, then held it up for Sophie to see. "Well, look at this."

Sophie went closer to read the spine. *Survivor Guilt: Coping After Senseless Tragedy.*

"It's one of the books Averill took."

Rachel's expression brightened. "Here's another on the same topic. These are the ones that weren't checked out or on the shelves before, the titles you told me about." Something fell out of the book and Rachel scooped it up. "Oh—there's a note."

The folded message was from Averill.

Sophie read over Rachel's shoulder. *Dear Sophie, I'm returning these books, which I never should have taken. I think you'll soon know why I did. I'm glad to have known you, even a little. And sorry to have hurt Max. It's better this way.*

Rachel asked, "What's better?"

"It sounds as if she's leaving town."

And Sophie hadn't yet told Rachel or Max about the Farrier newspaper article. He'd be doubly crushed.

"Averill, I'm afraid, was involved in a dreadful situation when she was younger." Briefly, Sophie explained. "Her poor sister has never been found." The unsolved disappearance was a horrible burden for Averill to bear.

"That tragedy didn't give her the right to steal from us."

"Of course not, but at the moment, knowing what she has to deal with, I'd rather give her a hug than confront her about these books."

"I sensed from the start she was guilty." Rachel added, "These confirm I was right."

Yes, they did, but Averill had indeed returned them. Irritation skittered across Sophie's nerve ends. "Is it more important to you to be right than it is to be fair?"

Rachel's gaze strayed to the long center table in the main room. "I wasn't imagining things, but at least we have the missing books back."

Sophie gentled her tone. "It's not your job to patrol this library or to bring any violators to justice. I welcome your dedication, but I hired you to work the front desk and assist me. Fixating on the books Averill failed to check out wasn't your job, either. It was enough for you to tell me about that."

Rachel sniffed. "I'm sorry. I only wanted to feel useful. I should have let you handle it."

"Yes, you should, but talk to me now, Rachel." Sophie didn't know much about her assistant's personal life. Their only connection had come through the library as boss and employee, but it was obvious Rachel was troubled, and Sophie should have asked sooner.

Rachel's face fell. "As you know, I'm familiar with tragedy, too. Life hasn't been easy since my husband passed away. Living alone in that apartment, without him, not having his birthday, our anniversary to celebrate, or Christmas…" Her lip quivered. "This job means the world to me."

Sophie slipped an arm around her shoulders. "Don't worry. I'm not going to fire you, but if any other problems arise, I'm still head librarian. If you need help, ask." She paused. "Do you have any other outlets besides the library? A social group? A hobby of some kind? A pet?"

"This will sound pathetic, but no," Rachel admitted. "Nothing, and my family lives in a different state." She raised an eyebrow. "Even our dog died soon after Jason did."

"I'm so sorry." At a loss to say more when Rachel seemed about to cry, Sophie tried to lighten the mood. "You can borrow Rembrandt anytime."

Rachel laughed a little, wiping a tear from her cheek. "He still wetting your floors?"

"Not as much. He seems to have gotten the idea that our backyard is his private bathroom.

My bed has become his, and even Max seems to have accepted him. Finally. But do you see what I'm getting at?"

"I think so."

Rachel had made a mistake but nothing on the same order of magnitude as Gabe's. This was Sophie's chance to help her feel better. "I'll tell you what. Why don't you join me next time for my Girls' Night Out meeting? It's a great bunch of local women. You probably know most of them. We have a grand time, lots of food, some wine, and always good conversation."

"I'm not sure. I'd be an add-on. You're all friends while I…"

Sophie smiled. "I won't take no for an answer."

For a moment, Rachel leaned against her. "Thank you. I… I'd like that."

SOPHIE LEFT RACHEL to close the library, glad they'd come to some agreement. Her overzealous assistant was, in fact, a lonely person, probably like Averill. Now if Sophie could only come to terms with Gabe's perfidy.

To her surprise when she got home, Rembrandt wasn't the only one to greet her. As usual he jumped up on Sophie, drooling all over her summer dress, but Max was home early, too.

"Averill and I broke up," he announced, coming from the kitchen as Sophie shut the front door behind her.

"Oh, Max. You seemed so unhappy at the wedding, and I was afraid of this because of something that happened at the library today. You look as sad as I feel." She stroked Remi's head. "For me, it's Gabe."

He winced. "Sorry. I heard he's leaving. And you know what they say—misery loves company. Averill claims she's not who I thought she was," he said. "That's what she thinks anyway."

"Gabe isn't, either." Sophie flipped through the day's mail without really seeing the various flyers and bills. "Turns out he's no cowboy. He's the son of a very wealthy man."

Max blinked. "Gabe?"

"Probably lived in a mansion rather than a bunkhouse. Silly me." She gave Max the bare details, trying to keep her voice steady. Remi finally got down, then fell into a heap on the floor at her feet. "Why couldn't he tell me the truth?"

"Apparently, he didn't tell me, either. Gabe came in this morning but only confused me, talking in riddles. Now I know why." Max paused. "I thought I was just being a good big brother, cautioning you not to trust him too quick."

"You're not shocked, though."

"Not really. I have good instincts, Sophie. He and I never talked much about the nitty-gritty aspects of our lives. I wish I had pushed him harder."

Sophie shook her head. "I don't want to talk about Gabe. It was nice while it lasted." Vast understatement. "Too bad I took him seriously. Tell me about you and Averill."

That story, which he told in a halting voice, was as sad as Averill's personal tragedy. "I'm so sorry, Max."

"But the thing is, she's wrong. I couldn't convince her that we could work things out. I really think she should seek counseling again, try to make sense of what happened to her little sister."

"She's still missing."

Max nodded. "Which seems even harder in a way than it would have been to deal with her…death. I know that sounds weird, but the not knowing destroyed Averill's parents, their relationship with her too. They were all victims. I want to help, but she refuses to let me."

He swiped one hand over his face. "Averill quit her job today. I have the feeling she's probably leaving town as we speak. I don't know how to stop her."

"Max, she returned those missing books to the library." This was not where Sophie wanted their conversation to go, either, but there was no putting that genie back in the bottle. "I, um, actually did know about her sister before." She mentioned the Farrier article. "I should have told you, Max, I would have…" Sophie drew a folded note from her pocket. "This came with the books Averill returned."

Max scanned the note.

"She's sorry she hurt me? Well, there's that," he said. Her once-neglectful brother, wrapped up in his clinic, had finally fallen in love but now seemed broken himself. She wouldn't have wished that on him any more than Max would wish that selfie from Vegas on Sophie.

"Would she go back to Farrier? She really is from there."

"Exactly as she told me. Poor little kid, her sister. Poor Averill," he added.

"What are *you* going to do?"

"I don't know."

"Maybe she'd go to her mother."

"They don't speak to each other."

"She might, though. Go home. You should try to find the address. Maybe Janet Turcott would know. My librarian friend."

"What are you saying? You think we should talk things out?"

"If for no other reason than to reach some kind of closure once you've both had a chance to decompress."

"I can't believe she just gave up on us. Not a good sign," he said, "for a future with someone."

"It happens," Sophie murmured, thinking of that debacle at the barn with Gabe. "Not to hold a pity party here, but I should have been smarter about Gabe. After all, that selfie of Will and Bess did a number on me. I should have guessed history could repeat itself."

Sophie couldn't say more. The threat of tears had closed her throat.

"He's always had a hard time with his dad. But if he goes back, does what he needs—"

"Max. He's scheduled to become Brynne's next CEO. Why on earth would Gabe come back to Kansas, to Sweetheart Ranch, if he can straighten things out with his father, live the high life again in Texas, then take over as planned?" She paused, remembering him saying *that hadn't been determined yet.* "I don't want him to come back."

Max studied her for a long moment. "You sure?"

"Absolutely." But she thought how much Gabe liked being a cowboy, riding horses. He was good at the job, had a real feel for it. Had that been fake, too? "I can't risk breaking my heart all over again. Twice is enough."

"Then I don't think I should take your advice. Try to talk to Averill again. Maybe I shouldn't have trusted her, either. The stolen books, for starters."

"Averill didn't lie to you. She just didn't want to talk about a painful experience." Sophie sighed. "At least give yourself time to figure out what's best."

"You, too, sis." He turned toward the kitchen to get a beer from the refrigerator. "Care to join me?"

"It's five o'clock somewhere."

CHAPTER TWENTY-TWO

"ALL SET, SOPHIE?" said a cloying female voice behind her the next morning.

She turned to find Claudia Monroe standing in the aisle at the café where Sophie had been waiting for her coffee, which she badly needed. Last night she and Max had overdone their pity party—a rare occasion—and Sophie's temples pounded with a new headache. She'd added a few bear claws and the cinnamon bun that Rachel preferred to her usual order, which was taking longer than she'd planned. "Set?" she echoed.

"For our Fun Run, of course."

Sophie wanted to groan. The week's sesquicentennial celebrations had begun, but her heart was no longer in the events. "You're on the committee?"

Claudia gave her a strange look. "You urged me to volunteer."

"Oh. Yes." She'd almost forgotten she had put Claudia to work, hoping to keep her out of Sophie's hair. She still had plenty to do, but after setting herself up for another betrayal like Will and Bess, trying to forget Gabe was her top priority. "Frankly," she said, "I'll be glad when all this is over."

"You must be exhausted. To be honest, I doubted your ability to pull this off, but you've somehow managed." As if Claudia instead was the driving force behind Barren's celebration.

"That's all anyone can do."

Last evening with Max she'd felt closer to him than she had in a long time. For once, he'd given Sophie the same degree of attention she'd always given him. Maybe it had taken the breakup with Averill to wake him up. He was suffering just as Sophie was, not that she was happy about that new bond.

Claudia eyed her blue sleeveless, scoop-necked summer dress that should keep Sophie cool all day. Unfortunately, this morning she felt overheated. Or was it because of Claudia? She couldn't cope with her today. "Of course, a nice suit like the ones you've always worn would be better. That casual look doesn't say professional to me."

"I like it—in fact, I plan to keep it." A remnant, perhaps, of her quasi-relationship with Gabe. That reminder wasn't good to dwell on, but the new style was truly hers by now, and Sophie was no longer dressing to please anyone but herself. She rubbed her throbbing temple. "Claudia, I appreciate the fashion advice, but maybe you could keep it to yourself from now on."

The woman bristled. "Humph."

"Excuse me," Sophie murmured, then stepped up to the counter to get her order. Claudia wasn't the only person in town who'd criticized her in the past year, made her feel like an outsider. Yet others' attitudes had gradually softened along with Sophie's image, and now her friends weren't the only people who seemed to support her.

Leaving Claudia to stew about her comment, Sophie crossed the street and walked the few blocks to the library. She gave Rachel gave her cinnamon bun then passed by into her office. After their conversation about Averill yesterday, their relationship seemed fragile, but Sophie hoped Rachel's first Girls' Night Out meeting later would change that.

She slumped at her desk, then put her head in her hands. *How* to forget Gabe? It had taken her more than a year to get over Will and, in Bess, the loss of her best friend. Maybe she'd never completely get past that Vegas selfie.

Still, she'd ordered an adorable outfit from the Baby Things shop for their firstborn. With luck, that would be her last contact with them.

She tried instead to think about the lies Gabe had told her. *He isn't who you think he is*.

But like Lauren with her intended scoop, which hadn't come out yet, Claudia had been right about this much. Sophie needed to focus on Saturday's Fun Run three days from now.

She and Gabe had signed up together as a team. Bummer.

Looked like she would be running solo now—in every way.

Straightening in her chair, she took a deep breath.

Never mind Claudia. Or any of the others who'd doubted her. Never mind Gabe.

The anonymous donation to the sesquicentennial's general fund had made the entire celebration possible after all, and Sophie said another silent thanks to their mystery benefactor. She had to wonder. If Gabe was as well off as it seemed, could it have been him? At the same time she did feel grateful for the money, she wished she could afford to throw it in his face.

Still, why dwell on that?

In a day or so, after she'd nailed down some

last-minute details, maybe she'd drive out to Sweetheart Ranch. Gabe wouldn't be there now. She'd saddle Precious and take a long ride. By herself. Solo flight. *You go, cowgirl.*

"WELL, WELL. The cowboy shows up. Finally." Gabe's father had met him that morning in the front hall after Gabe fought his way through the press outside.

Gabe's stomach tightened at his dad's tone. Déjà vu from his previous visit, except that his dad looked terrible. He was hollow-cheeked, with blue-gray shadows under his eyes, and must have lost ten pounds. His pricey suit hung on him. He needed another three-hundred-dollar haircut. "Hey."

"What's the happy occasion?"

"Dad, come on. You know I couldn't come before."

"Do I? That was your choice."

"Yeah, but…" He ran out of words. It was no choice.

"Gabe." Jilly glided down the stairs in a silk dressing gown. She embraced him. "I'm glad you've come."

He kissed her cheek. "Me, too." He was persona non grata with Sophie. When he'd told Kate yesterday, even she hadn't been in his corner. "Well," she'd said. "I suppose you have no other option." Pause. "Just go, Gabe."

He wondered if his job would be waiting for him this time. If he'd be able to go back as he planned to. He hadn't stopped replaying Sophie's words in his head the entire trip to Midland. He should never have lied to her; yet how could he not? The basics, as he'd told her, were true, and protecting his father—who didn't seem grateful now—had come first.

At least Lauren hadn't really gotten her scoop after all. She'd delayed too long, and just before the *Barren Journal* edition was due to come out with her version of the story about him and his father, the national news had broken about Brynne Energy's whistleblower, stealing her thunder. Gabe had seen that on his phone right after he landed. Looked like she wouldn't be heading to the *New York Times* anytime soon. Karma, Gabe thought, though it was too bad Lauren had missed that second chance to redeem her career, if at his expense.

"I suppose you've seen the papers, TV," his father said, running a hand through his already-mussed hair, as Gabe often did. "Your friend Aaron is the big item today."

"What has he said?"

"Nothing so far, but I can't count on that."

"We can't," Gabe corrected him and decided to give Aaron a call. He'd been avoiding that yet he needed to test the waters for his father's sake. He wanted to know what they were up against.

"Oh, now you're willing to do your part?"

"That's not fair, Chet," Jilly protested, laying a hand on his forearm.

Gabe supposed he deserved his father's dig, even when his presence wouldn't have been wise before. "What can I do to help?"

"Give Jilly a break, then. Man the phones for a change instead of her. I can't talk to another reporter either."

"Let me grab a shower, some coffee, then sure. Whatever you need."

His father started for the front door, shoulders set, prepared for the blow awaiting him outside from the media. "The board is meeting again, though I don't see how we can do damage control now. If I thought this was bad before, the real storm is about to start. It'll be ten times worse than any hurricane." He sent Gabe a dubious look. "You can use my office."

Clearly, his father doubted he was up to the task ahead of them.

AFTER WORK, Sophie drove toward Sweetheart Ranch. Tonight, she was joining her friends for their latest Girls' Night Out. A chance, she hoped, to forget her troubles. She'd had such high hopes for her and Gabe.

His lies had changed all that.

Trust—the hope that she wouldn't get hurt again—didn't seem to be in Sophie's future.

When she arrived at Kate's house, most people were already there. Sophie took Kate aside. She hadn't seen her since the wedding.

"I was surprised that we're meeting here tonight. Why are you still home? What happened to your honeymoon?"

Kate rolled her eyes. "We had to delay a bit. Noah and his partner are in Europe, dealing with some sudden issue at their new branch office."

"Sorry about that."

"Don't be. I'll be joining Noah soon."

Kate led Sophie into the living room where she was pleased to see Rachel. "Hey, glad you made it," she said, giving her a hug.

"She was hanging back at first, a bit shy, but we finally pried her out of the corner." Kate grinned. "Seriously, welcome, Rachel."

"Thank you. You're sure it's okay for me to be here?"

"Of course. We're an ever-expanding group. There's always room for more."

Pretty soon Rachel had been drawn into the crowd and was laughing over some joke with Blossom Hunter. The two clinked wineglasses in a toast.

Annabelle put an arm around Sophie's shoulders. "Girl, I can see you're not in the spirit tonight. Anything I can do?"

"Not really. I, uh, have the whole sesquicentennial celebration in my head, remembering this thing I forgot to do, that detail I missed."

"No one will care if something gets overlooked—and by the way, the 5K will be awesome. Finn and I are already laughing about our showing this coming Saturday. Our Emmie will probably come in ahead of us. Which will be nearly dead last."

"Me too. It'll be fun, literally," Sophie said. Once she stopped worrying about the number of water bottles along the route—were there enough?—she might be able to enjoy herself.

The upcoming Fun Run took part of her mind off the now-dead issue of Gabe. "Excitement in Barren is at an all-time high," she told Annabelle, "and even some late pledges have come in to further boost the celebration's budget. With those and our largest donation, we may end up with a profit."

Annabelle offered Sophie a glass of wine from those grouped on an end table. "Several people have told me what a good job you're doing. Even Claudia and her bosom buddy, Bernice. And doesn't the carnival set up tomorrow?"

Sophie nodded. "They were rolling into town when I left the library."

"Imagine how thrilled the kids will be. If there's cotton candy—oh, and doughnuts, her perennial favorite—Emmie will be happy. She's not as thrilled about all the rides." Annabelle's gaze sobered. "So, about you, madam chairperson of almost every committee, what's the matter? You really seem down."

"Just tired." But Annabelle, her gaze sharp, wasn't buying that.

"I didn't see Gabe here when I pulled in." A loaded statement if there ever was one.

"He's gone to Texas again. For good, I imagine."

Annabelle's eyebrows rose. "Kate must be losing her mind without her foreman. And Noah's not here. Plus, wouldn't you know, she told me one of Sweetheart's other hands just quit."

Sophie didn't think before saying, "Maybe I should offer to help."

Annabelle grinned. "And use your new cow-girl skills?"

"Minimal as they are, but I could muck a few stalls for Kate. Groom horses. Take some of the workload off her shoulders."

"With the celebration in full swing? Sure, in your spare time."

"There is none," Sophie agreed, taking a sip of her wine. Kate's living room was filled with people Sophie loved, and she felt their love for her, specifically with Annabelle now, begin to ease her heartache. She would survive.

"So. About Gabe." Annabelle bent to catch Sophie's gaze. "What aren't you telling me?"

Sophie's throat tightened. "He lied to me. Haven't you seen the news on TV?"

"Wow, your relationship actually hit the air-waves?"

Annabelle's teasing tone didn't make Sophie smile. "I can't pretend another minute," she confessed. "I really liked him, Annabelle. But instead of the laid-back cowboy I thought I was falling for, he's a fraud. Worse than that, he's…" For a moment she couldn't go on. "Brynne Energy," she managed at last. "His father…"

Annabelle's mouth dropped open. "You mean Gabe's dad owns that big oil company? The one that, yeah, is on every news station in the country."

"The very same. I can't understand why he'd come to Sweetheart to work for Kate."

"From what you're saying, at the very least he could have bought his own ranch."

"He's a good cowboy." Sophie blinked, hard. "He's just not a very good person."

"Ah, Sophie." Again, Annabelle put an arm around her. "Don't you dare cry. He's not worth it. Maybe I should put Finn on his trail. Once a lawman, always a lawman," she said, "even when he's now mayor."

Sophie dashed a tear from her eye. "How could I have been that stupid to believe him after—"

"Will the Weasel? And Miss Stab-Her-Best-Friend-In-The-Back?"

Sophie had to laugh. It was either that or end up blubbering for the whole room full of her friends to see. Rachel, too. Then Sophie would have every one of them quizzing her, probing about Gabe. Even their support wouldn't keep the tears from coming then. "Thanks. I do love you, Annabelle."

Her once-shy friend had blossomed, in part

because of Finn's love but also the successful career as a travel tour guide she was juggling between home and family.

"Same goes. You'll be okay. Next time, maybe you should try linking up with a local guy."

"There won't be a next time—not for twenty years or more."

"If he didn't treat you well, we'd all run him out of town. Yee-haw."

Sophie hugged her. Across the room Rachel was in the middle of a group of four other women, all talking at the same time. She fit right in. At least Sophie had done one thing right.

"Then," she said, "I half wish Gabe would turn up again."

"Oh, honey, so do I."

GABE'S EARS WERE BURNING. He'd handled phone calls all day, but they'd finally died off around six o'clock and, even though he felt weary, he'd called Aaron.

"Hey, man. Long time," Gabe said when the oil worker answered. He'd wondered if he would or would shut Gabe out now.

"I've been expecting this call. What a mess, huh?"

"And getting worse. Obviously, I saw you mentioned as the Brynne whistleblower. What are you going to tell the feds?"

His tone hardened. "The truth. I warned you about that rig years ago. You said you'd take care of the matter—but nothing changed. Now, just as predicted, people have been injured or killed. And oil is still gushing into the Gulf exactly as I told you it would."

Aaron was right, but Gabe reminded him that he'd told his father back then as promised, and it wasn't his dad who had dropped the ball. "I know he bears the final brunt of responsibility as CEO, but I care what happens to him. Personally. You may hold his future—and that of Brynne—in your hands."

"What, you begging me to keep quiet? I already came forward."

"I'm not trying to influence you, Aaron. You say what you must. But when the feds grill you—my dad's lawyers too and they all try to destroy your credibility—that will mean outing me."

"They can't damage my credibility as a witness. I *knew* what was going on, saw it firsthand. I told *you*. I tried to prevent that spill, and three of my pals from that rig are still in the hospital."

Gabe pinched the bridge of his nose. "I'm sorry to hear that. I tried, too, Aaron."

"For them alone, I can't stay silent."

"I understand. But it looks bad for Brynne."

"Don't expect sympathy. Besides, Daddy has deep pockets, right? What's a billion-dollar fine or more to him?"

"His reputation is on the line." But it was true, there was no real defense. If Chet hadn't been Gabe's father, he'd have sided completely with Aaron. Maybe he shouldn't have called, which might only make things worse. Gabe could sense Aaron shaking his head.

"You'd really stick by him? If I were you, I'd come clean, then wash my hands of that company. Last I heard, you weren't part of things there anyway. I was, in fact, hoping you'd turn your back on Brynne. Separate yourself from the whole enterprise—and him."

"He's still my father." Gabe remembered once telling Sophie, *You're in a tough spot.* Now he was too. Rock and a hard place.

"Yeah, and according to you, he never gave a dog's rump about his own son. Lots of luck, Gabe. It was nice knowing you. Don't call me again."

He hung up, leaving Gabe to wish he'd never met Aaron when they were kids at that long-ago company Christmas party.

CHAPTER TWENTY-THREE

"I WONDER IF Gabe's ever coming back?" As she spoke, Kate came from the feed room into the barn aisle where Sophie was struggling to saddle Precious. "I told him to go, but the guy Gabe 'promoted' for now isn't cutting it."

The horse didn't want to cooperate and kept dancing in the crossties, evading Sophie's touch. She calmed Precious, then reached under the mare's belly for the dangling cinch strap.

"I haven't heard a word from Gabe since he left," Kate went on. "I'm tempted to call his cell and fire him. But considering the news he told me, maybe he's already quit."

She didn't seem to notice that Sophie hadn't responded.

"I was shorthanded before that kid Johnny quit on me, too." She paused. "I called the newspaper earlier to place an ad to hire a new hand, but I got Lauren and told her never mind. I don't want to talk to that woman."

"I'm surprised she's still in Barren."

"She doesn't have much choice since the Brynne story broke—not in the *Journal*. It was too late to pull her own article, but it sure fell flat. Not the scoop she'd hoped for."

"We've had our issues, but I also know what makes Lauren seem difficult to other people." Sophie pulled the cinch tighter. "You may be right. Why would Gabe want to come back? He can't need the money." Which didn't explain his being here in the first place. "Ugh, but he warned me. This horse blows up every time."

"Let me help." Kate, being more experienced, deftly finished saddling Precious. "Good girl. You behave for Sophie. She's feeling bad."

"Did I say that?"

"Your face says it all, as it did the other night, but cheer up. Gabe shouldn't be on either of our minds now."

And yet, two days after he'd left, for Sophie he was.

"About the award instead, I voted—for you, of course," Kate said.

"Thanks. And I voted for myself."

"I can't imagine Lauren winning. There are those who already suspected her of using this town and its citizens to get ahead. Writing those columns to pad her résumé. I think your chances to win are better than good."

"Her reporting took a bad turn before Barren. She wanted to jump-start her career again. We'll soon see."

Kate studied her again. "But this award's not why your face looks downcast, right?"

True, Sophie had finished her campaign, done all she could. The rest was in the voters' hands. Her conflict with Gabe, learning who he really was, had overtaken all other thoughts. She didn't quite answer Kate. "My brother's been moping around the house, too. Coming home early, going into the clinic late, canceling appointments except for emergencies... He's devastated about Averill."

"That's sad. They made a nice couple."

"Yes, but Averill's awfully damaged. From what I learned about her sister's disappearance and the family's breakdown, I doubt she and Max could be happy together." Still. Sophie had urged him to at least follow up with her for closure. "I used to get upset with Max for being clueless about anything except his work, but I hate seeing him this way."

Kate took the bridle from Sophie, who promptly took it back. "I can do this," she said. "My purpose in coming to Sweetheart in the first place was to learn how to tack up this horse—among other ranch-y chores. After my ride, I can stay. You need another hand and for today I'm it or I'll try to be." She urged Precious to open her mouth, then eased the bridle in, checking to make sure there were no wrinkles around her tender lips.

Kate stepped back. "Okay, let me get Lady ready. I'm coming with you. I could use a break—and as we ride, we can check fence. Another cowgirl skill for you to learn."

That seemed like an excuse to Sophie. As much as she liked Kate, she had wanted to take her solo ride. Kate must be as concerned about her mood as Sophie was about Max.

And try as she might, Sophie couldn't quite forget Gabe, the good parts like the teasing way he'd had with her, the soft light on his hair at dinner that one night, dancing with him at Kate's wedding…even his calling her Soph. At least he'd finally confessed to the lies he'd told her. That had taken courage.

"Okay, spill," Kate said as they went through the gate into the near pasture. "I know you're worried about your brother, but you've said very little about Gabe. Before he left for Texas and the news came out, I'd thought you two were taking friendship to a higher level."

"Oh great, did everybody at the WB weddings see us walk toward those trees?"

Kate waggled her eyebrows. "The signs were there. And remember, I'm still a newlywed. Even Teddie rolls his eyes when Noah and I get lovey-dovey." She grinned. "Which is most of the time."

Sophie envied them. She'd had her own visions of Gabe, the two of them together, hand in hand, riding side by side, searching each other's eyes, discovering love. "I never learn my lesson," she said with a sigh. "After Will and Bess—"

"That was different. You got fooled."

"Yes, but by Gabe, too." Sophie told her about their last confrontation.

Kate looked thoughtful. "Are you that certain he's the villain here? I'd say his father is the one who's responsible. Isn't it possible Gabe got caught in the middle?"

"He *lied*, Kate."

"About what, exactly? The town he comes from? Maybe you're not seeing this clearly. I wouldn't defend Gabe if he was some ne'er-do-well drifter who'd turned up with a phony job résumé, possibly like Johnny. Being a cowboy wasn't Gabe's first career—I understand now he was originally being trained to take over Brynne Energy—but it's surely the job of his heart. He's the best foreman this ranch has ever had." Kate reined Lady around a rock nearly hidden by the grass. "It seems to me Gabe has put down roots here. Look how he helped you with the award campaign, jumped in with the sesquicentennial. Does that seem like a man who couldn't wait to leave Barren— to become CEO in a place he fled over a year and a half ago?"

Sophie pondered that as they neared a section of fence that had sagged to the ground. Kate dismounted to inspect the damage. "Looks like some of our ladies have left the building, probably grazing now on WB land. Fickle cows."

"Which is pretty much the same land as Sweetheart."

Kate couldn't disagree. "If Noah had his way, my spread would be part of the WB. But I value my independence. We can cooperate, but this will always be Sweetheart Ranch. Even though he keeps reminding me that I'm a Bodine now, too. I'll send one of the boys out to fix this fence." Kate remounted her horse. "Oh, and bless his heart, Noah has asked to adopt Teddie. He'll be part of Noah's family, too. Our family."

"You're a lucky woman, Kate."

She grinned. "Indeed I am. Noah's problem—the one I mentioned at our Girls' meeting—has been resolved. Teddie and I are flying out tomorrow, meeting him in Paris. Amazing, huh?"

"I thought you didn't like to fly."

"Until—well, Noah. I'm slowly changing my mind," she said. "We've already been to New York several times, and Teddie and I have our passports. While we're gone Zach can help here. He and Cass decided not to take a wedding trip. After all, they had one in the Bahamas when they eloped last winter." Kate added, "I'm so excited. I mean, *Paris*. We'll start there then travel to see the chateaux, the cathedrals…"

"Sounds wonderful."

But Sophie's heart ached. Once, she'd fantasized about being with Gabe forever, marrying him and having children. That had been mostly in her own mind, at least until lately when it had begun to seem possible, yet he'd betrayed her just as Will and Bess had.

To her dismay Kate picked up the topic again. "What about you, Sophie? And Gabe?"

"He hurt me."

"Noah has hurt me, too, at times. I mean, I

blamed him for my first husband's death—unfairly, I came to see. Getting hurt can be part of any relationship, Sophie. It's how we move on from that, which matters. Are you going to nurse your bad feelings about Gabe, the lies he told to protect his father and Brynne—not to hurt you—or do something to make things better?"

"Right now, I need to focus on the celebration. After that…"

Kate said, "At least call him. Talk it out." Her gaze had gentled. "You love him, don't you?"

Without answering, Sophie rode on ahead, biting her lip against a fresh flood of tears. She had never said those words, and he hadn't, either. She'd urged Max to see Averill once more, not to carry with him the same regret Sophie had about Will and Bess. Should she do the same about Gabe?

Odessa, not Midland, was his only real lie, as Kate had pointed out. Even Morgan was part of his true name. His mother's illness, her death, his dad's withdrawal. Jilly's love. Assuming they were all true, he'd had a sad childhood, a lonely one. Who was she to judge his actions now? Perhaps he'd returned to Texas not only because of Brynne Energy but in the hope of some reconciliation with his father.

Sophie's parents had died instantly in that head-on crash. With no goodbyes. Leaving her and Max to care for each other. If she had the same chance as Gabe, could see them again to tell them how much she loved them… But she did not. How could she blame him for seizing such an opportunity while there was still time?

It wasn't only about protecting his dad, then, who had lawyers to safeguard his interests. It was about Gabe's love for, his loyalty to, his surviving parent.

As for Brynne…

That hasn't been determined, he'd said. What if Gabe had gone home to make his peace, to help resolve the oil spill, with every intention of coming back?

Was she holding that one lie against him, like the selfie from Will and Bess? Was she going to dwell on them the rest of her life? Prevent herself from finding happiness? As she'd said to Rachel, was it more important for Sophie to be right—even self-righteous— than to be fair?

She turned back to see Kate waiting for her.

What if, instead of her rejection, Sophie had given Gabe her trust?

WITH A WEARY sigh Gabe sat back in his father's desk chair the next night. He glared at the landline phone as if willing it to ring. He'd had one idea that might save the situation with Brynne, specifically with his father, but the wait was killing him.

Aaron had talked, all right.

Which meant so had Gabe, who'd spent much of the time since his arrival being grilled by federal agents and lawyers. Today being Saturday, he'd missed the Fun Run with Sophie in Barren. Tonight he'd had way too much caffeine, a fresh cup sitting on the desk before him now. He rubbed a hand over his face. "Why doesn't Bixby call? He's the guy Dad told about Aaron's concerns, the negligence on the rig." Brynne's former chief of operations might be able to shed some light on things.

Chet's defense team had tried to reach him without success, so Gabe had decided to give it a try. In his dad's office he'd come across an old email address. But Bixby wasn't answering Gabe's pleas either to produce that much-needed evidence. An old memo, notes from a meeting, whatever might help. "He can tell the authorities now that, yes, Dad knew about the long-standing problems there—and tried to deal with them."

"Bixby?" Jilly said. "How could he possibly help? Which might implicate him?" Years ago, when she had worked for Brynne, her office was in the same executive wing where his father presided over the company. "He was never the best fit for the position, always tended to pass the buck to someone else. Even so, the fact remains that Chet knew what was going on. The massive fines we expect won't be any less." She paused. "Which are richly deserved, I'm sorry to say."

"I know," he said. This wasn't about money, or Brynne's reputation. People's lives had been lost, but it was the only thing Gabe could think of to help his dad. He'd sacrificed his relationship with Sophie to do so. "We don't get along, but I can't watch Dad deteriorate any further. Why the hell doesn't this phone ring?"

"Gabe." She reached across the desk to squeeze his hand, which was clenched into a fist. "You've done your best. If we never hear, he still appreciates your effort."

"And yours? I don't know how he'd have managed without you here."

"We love each other," she said. "With love anything is possible."

Gabe gazed at her for a moment. He wished that was true for him and Sophie. But, as he'd predicted, to Sophie he must seem worse now to her than Will and Bess.

"You're the best thing that ever happened to Dad, Jilly. When Mom got sick, you didn't hesitate to be there for her."

"That was my privilege. She was my best friend. How could I have done anything less than care for her, day and night, until..." She cleared her throat. "Then, afterward, you needed me. You had lost your mother at such a tender age. My heart went out to you, and your father, well, he simply couldn't cope. If Chet wanted to call me your nanny for appearances' sake, I didn't mind."

"You never left," he pointed out with a half smile.

"I always loved him. Not that I let him know until the time was right. Unless he finally manages to kick me out—which he's tried to do during this disaster at Brynne—I'm staying."

They'd probably been sharing his dad's suite for some time.

"Why don't you marry him?"

"He hasn't asked me."

"Then maybe you should ask him—women do these days."

She laughed. "I've thought about it. I don't think his traditional ego could take that."

Relieved to be talking about something other than the oil spill fallout, Gabe offered to ask his father in an old-fashioned way what his intentions were, but Jilly was staring at him hard enough to make Gabe squirm.

"All right," she said, "enough. Your father and I will work that out. I can see—I've always been able to gauge your moods—that part of you is here worrying about us, hoping for that phone call, while the rest is back in Kansas. Who is she?"

Gabe shook his head. "Uh-uh. Remember when I was seventeen, dating that lifeguard at the community pool? You tried to give me advice about her—"

"I'm still giving advice. When you came home last time, I saw that you were happier than I've seen you in a long time except about your father. Now I can tell you've left someone behind. Someone you care about very much."

He didn't even try to equivocate. "Sophie Crane."

"Crane," she repeated. "Is she your friend Max's—"

"Sister. Yep." He explained his deception in Barren, at Sweetheart, with Kate and most importantly with Sophie. "She gave me my walking papers."

Jilly leaned forward. "Really."

"Yep," he said again. "Anyway, everything except Brynne is on my back burner."

"Really," Jilly echoed. "That's not what I see."

"Doesn't matter. I lied to her—and honesty is even more important to Sophie than to most people."

"Does she know how you feel?"

"What is this, seventh grade? Jilly, let it be. I'm trying to. For now."

"Not succeeding very well, from where I'm sitting. Assuming she cares about you, too, don't you think she deserves an update from Midland? Why not open a conversation? You need support, just as your father does."

"I have you for that."

Jilly smiled. "How do you know I have enough energy for both of you?"

"You always have." He tilted his head. "You've been like a second mother to me—almost more than Mom, who was sick so much. But I have to handle Sophie by myself." Not that he knew how.

The phone rang, and with a glance at Jilly, he picked up. This could be the call he'd been waiting for, though for an instant he hoped it might be Sophie. "Hello?"

"Gabriel?"

"Yes." He held his breath. The woman's voice sounded reedy, thin.

"This is Rowena Bixby—Gerald's wife. Widow, I mean."

Gabe groaned inwardly. The guy was dead. "My sympathies," he murmured and meant that even when he also knew that avenue had been their last hope. Where could he and Jilly and his father turn now?

"I would have called sooner, but I've been away visiting my grandchildren. I'm sorry to be the bearer of bad news, but there is no memo, no notes of any kind. I'm sure of that. I remember your father did speak to Gerald in person then. Neither of them wanted any record of possible negligence on that rig at that point. Chet asked him to follow up, but my husband felt certain that this whistleblower who has come forward, I understand, had some agenda of his own."

"Meaning?" Gabe asked.

"I believe you're friends with the man. Gerald told me he had used your influence to first get that job on the rig and that he was angling for a promotion then. Pointing the finger at his boss on the rig was the way he hoped to get it."

"Yes, I've heard that."

"Gerald believed he would use you again if need be—urge you to pressure Chet."

"But he didn't," Gabe said.

"In any case," Rowena went on, "Gerald decided there were no safety issues on the rig. He was wrong, we know now. And as I said, I can't help you with any follow-up memo because there isn't one, but I did have a vague memory. I looked through my personal emails after you contacted me—the email you used was Gerald's, which I've kept as well—as soon as I got home."

Gabe held his breath until Rowena went on.

"I've found a message that may interest you from Gerald to me while he was on a business trip. I'm looking at it now. In that email he lays out his own reasoning for not pursuing the matter after Chet spoke to him." She read it to him, and Gabe lifted his eyebrows in Jilly's direction. Score. Like a Hail Mary pass.

Gabe's pulse drummed in his ears. "Can you forward that to me?"

"I'd be happy to."

His father's conversation with Bixby had obviously died there with no further follow-up. Gabe shouldn't be surprised. He was sorry to hear of Rowena's widowhood, but why had his father trusted Gerald? He'd sometimes complained about him. Gabe, like Jilly, recalled him as a lazy employee, even inept. His reasoning had been wrong—Aaron wasn't trying for that promotion or using Gabe—but Gerald had been happy to drop the ball.

"Thanks so much, Rowena. I'm sorry this email puts Gerald in a bad light."

"I don't think he'd mind. He liked Chet. I'm sending it now. Please give my regards to your father. I hope the email is what you want."

After he hung up, Gabe sat looking at the computer screen until the email showed in his inbox. To make certain it was what he needed, he opened and reread the attached memo. "We're good," he told Jilly.

She read it, too. "At least this is something. Good job, Gabe."

"Wish that wasn't all we can do," he said. He rose to kiss Jilly good-night, watched her to the door and into the hallway.

"Call her," she said over her shoulder. He heard her footsteps on the stairs, the clunk of the heavy door to his father's bedroom suite. No matter what happened next, she would continue to take loving care of him.

He turned off the lights, then sat in the darkness.

In the morning they'd forward Rowena's email

to the corporation's lawyers. That wouldn't exonerate Chet—as Brynne's CEO, his dad was still ultimately responsible for the oil spill—but might help alleviate his guilt and prove he'd tried to do something about the rig. After that, Gabe would try to think of some way to help the victims of the spill.

But how had he messed up so badly with Sophie? He'd known how she felt about lies, about the pain her ex and her best friend had caused. The tragic loss of her own parents. He wondered if she was still going out now to Sweetheart to ride. Remembered the first day she'd tried to saddle Precious. Remembered their kisses, Sophie's eager response.

If only she could have trusted him…

After so many months of running, he'd faced the music with the investigators and done what he could here. Even if that didn't help, at least he'd stopped hiding. But, ah, Soph. He could imagine her beautiful face, pale hair escaping from that messy bun of hers, see her in those flashy red boots. He could envision the flat Kansas plains, that big blue sky and Sweetheart Ranch. He could almost hear the whinny of horses, Critter, Precious and the others. Smell the summer's sweet new-mown hay.

Gabe straightened. In his head, he was half-way there.

Because, as Jilly had implied, what was he waiting for?

He'd deal with the matter of becoming Brynne's next CEO later.

Gabe wasn't a liar. The greatest truth of all was that he loved Sophie.

If he wanted her, and he did with all his heart, he had to go...home. To Barren.

CHAPTER TWENTY-FOUR

LATER THAT NIGHT, Gabe found his father in the wood-paneled room he called the study. Across from his office, it was his favorite place to relax, often with a snifter of brandy before bed. "Hey," Gabe said, standing in the doorway. One lamp was lit, illuminating the planes and angles of his dad's face. Ice cubes clinked in a glass.

"Want a nightcap?"

"No, I'm good. Dad…" Then he couldn't think what to say. He'd never just entered this room, always waited to be summoned. He'd seen Chet numerous times during this visit, and they'd always seemed to be sizing each other up. Finding fault.

"Something on your mind?"

"Jilly," he said at last.

His father tensed. "She's been on my case ever since this crisis began. Hasn't done much good. I'm still sitting here tonight, like every night, thinking of those men on that rig, the fire…those lost lives. Maybe I should pack it in, Gabe. Sell Brynne—if anyone now would want to buy the company."

"Hang on. Nothing's settled yet." Brynne had offices all over the world, rigs in many countries, thousands of workers who depended on that income.

"I appreciate your digging up that email from Bixby."

"Welcome." Gabe moved from the doorway, dropped onto a big easy chair across from his father. He heard the clink of ice cubes as Chet took another sip. He still looked gray, gaunt and beaten down, but his comment had surprised Gabe.

Chet lifted his glass. "You and I usually ignite sparks off each other, don't we?"

"Yessir."

"Your mother always said we were too much alike. I never saw it—until now."

Gabe didn't know what he meant. He'd come to talk about Jilly.

"Let the lawyers take it from here, Dad. You need rest. I'm glad Jilly's here to take care of you and—"

"That woman. She's been meddling since you were knee-high."

"You do know she loves you?"

"I'm kind of fond of her myself." His eyes twinkled, and a faint smile touched his mouth. "What's your point? You want to take me to task for sharing my rooms with her? That's our business."

"I think you should marry her." The words could apply to him, too; Gabe thought of Sophie, the way he'd left her with tears in her eyes. He hoped to change that.

"Whoa," Chet said, coming upright in his chair. "I was married once. I'm too old to learn to live with someone else."

"You already live with Jilly. Mom's been gone a long time. You're not that old."

"Did I ask for advice, Romeo?"

Gabe's mouth tightened. "Or is it okay with you that she shares this house, stands by you, and you pay her a nice retirement stipend? That's it?"

His father leaned forward, the glass in his hand. "Watch it, Gabriel."

"No, I should have said something long ago." Sophie's image flitted through his mind again. He hadn't done right by her, either. "I love Jilly, too. She deserves better from you. She raised me while you were holed up in your office at Brynne—"

"Know why?" His dad had seemed to deflate before his eyes, as if he'd been holding something inside for a long time. "Because I couldn't bear to be in this house when *she* wasn't here, remembering every day and night there was nothing else I could have done to make her well. Your mother was everything to me and after she passed, I withdrew, went to ground as it were, tried my best to forget that loss—the kind of loss some of those people at Brynne are going through now—and then, Gabe, there was *you*…" He drew a sharp breath. "Eleven years old, with no mother. Bless Jilly for taking over then, keeping her arms around you. I'm not proud of myself, but I couldn't…" He didn't go on.

"It's okay, Dad." He'd never imagined the depth of his father's sorrow, so like his own at the time. Even now, he still missed his mother. "Jilly pulled me through," he said. "I think she pulled you, too."

His voice had become hoarse. "That's no reason for me to marry her."

"Unless you love her." *Like I do Sophie*. The reminder resounded through him like a thunderclap. Why hadn't he told her sooner?

For a moment Chester Dean Wyatt stared into his empty glass. "I'm a fool, aren't I? I should have been here for you then, Gabe. I

should have done *something*. But you're right.
Different times, and this is one heck of a night
to get—" He was out of his chair, the glass
clinking down on an end table. "What time is
it for real?"

Gabe glanced at his watch, not quite sure
what was happening.

"After midnight."

"She'll still be awake—sits up reading half
the night."

He stalked from the room, then up the stairs,
and Gabe heard the heavy door close to his father's suite as it had earlier for Jilly. The faint,
far-off rumble of voices reached him, one low,
the other sweet and calm.

Gabe smiled to himself. It seemed his father,
Mr. Brynne CEO, had a human side Gabe had
never seen before. His dad might be about to
propose marriage. An excellent idea. Would
Gabe get the same chance with Sophie?

ON SUNDAY MORNING the final sesquicentennial
celebrations were underway, which Sophie had
lived for all summer. But as she'd expected,
she had come in last during the Fun Run yesterday, although it had been a great event. Last
night, she'd gone to the carnival with Max,
bought cotton candy, which she loved, but

never finished because it had tasted to her like spun cardboard. Neither of them had felt able to enjoy themselves.

"You try Gabe in Texas again?" Max had asked as they strolled the midway.

"My call went straight to voice mail. I've been ghosted," she said.

So had Max. He'd phoned Averill, who'd told him to forget about her. She hadn't answered her phone since.

This morning, unable to let it go at that, and with apologies for missing the last celebrations, he'd taken off for Farrier. Sophie didn't see that as neglect. He wouldn't be here when the award winner was announced, or be able to cheer her on, but Max would try for another chance with Averill. Sophie had no idea how she was going to get through the day herself.

The carnival rides were running, the happy cries of children and adults carrying through the fairgrounds. The aromas of cotton candy and hot dogs permeated the air. For company Sophie had brought Rembrandt with her. The dog sniffed at a nearby bush, tail quivering in excitement. Handling him still required her full attention.

"Good job," she said as Remi moved on to the next clump of weeds.

He'd certainly made a lot of friends but kept tugging at his leash, and Sophie made a mental note to sign him up for a beginners' obedience class. Having finally conquered the potty problem at home, Remi needed to learn some manners.

"Hey, Sophie." One of their teenage helpers rushed up to her. "We can't get the apple dunking thing to work. The mechanism's stuck."

Sophie followed the boy to see what she could do, and even she—not being mechanically inclined—realized that the creaking mechanism simply needed oil, which Earl, the owner of the hardware store, supplied. Then she stopped by the booths where local crafts and food were being sold, to see how that was going.

Clara gave her a thumbs-up. "We've made a nice profit today. Smile, Sophie."

The women's library committee had also done well with their book sale, and the general fund should end up with a surplus, too. Maybe she could twist Finn's arm to let her have part of that for the library to give Rachel, who was crossing the fairgrounds arm in arm with Nell Ransom, a small raise. The two had formed a friendship at the Girls' Night Out meeting. Nell's husband, Cooper, was in the rodeo arena scheduled to ride a bucking bronc, but Nell had told Sophie she couldn't watch.

Later, she ran into Annabelle who melted as she bent down to pat Remi. "Is this guy a prince, or what? You've done great with him, Sophie."

Remi tried to pull the leash from her hands. "Are you seeing the same dog I am?"

"You've given him a second chance. Don't blame him for taking advantage of it."

Sophie grinned. "He knows I'm a pushover. He takes up more of the bed than I do."

She had no regrets there. Annabelle was right: she had saved the goofy, lovable border collie. He'd gone from being a ranch dog living outdoors to an indoor pet, and at his age Remi still had tons of energy.

In the next few hours, aided by her dog's sociability, and as one of the chief organizers, Sophie put out a few more sesquicentennial fires. She talked to everyone in town, it seemed, but her thoughts kept returning to Gabe. Where was he? Why wouldn't he answer his phone? Sophie had become a news junkie, repeatedly checking for TV updates that might put Gabe's father in a more favorable light, but Brynne stock—she checked that, too—had plummeted again. Maybe Gabe was being interrogated by the feds or had gone back into hiding in Texas rather than Barren.

If only she could talk to him...

The last events seemed to pass in a blur. The rodeo ended with an eruption of cheers— Zach Bodine, who'd taken over Noah's duties for the event while he was on his honeymoon, had come in second in the bull riding, which Lizzie's husband Dallas, a former pro, had won—and for perhaps the tenth time in as many years Ned Sutherland was the champion of the chili cook-off.

Still, she continued to worry about Gabe, and by the time the award announcement came, Sophie was tied in knots.

This was what she'd waited for, craved with every fiber of her being.

Yet during her campaign she'd discovered that her perceived lack of acceptance in town was more a matter of Sophie not trusting in herself than of other people thinking of her as an outsider. Her speeches, her new image, had obviously helped, but had she misjudged her situation before? Even Bernice had wished her well earlier, and while Claudia had eyed Sophie's pink print sundress, which buttoned down the front and had big patch pockets, she hadn't said a word. Feeling more comfortable within herself rather than bowing to anyone else's tastes and expectations, Sophie had dressed to please herself.

The day had turned hot, and she was glad the dress had a flowy skirt. She'd seen a similar style on, of all people, Lauren, who was now hovering by the bandstand as Sophie approached, dragged by Remi.

"Sit. Stay," she commanded him. He nailed the sitting part, but there was no telling how long he would remain in one place. She hoped he could until the award was announced.

"Front-row view." Lauren didn't meet Sophie's eyes.

"This is it. Best of luck."

"I won't need it." Despite her recent failure to publish the scoop about Gabe before it hit the national media, she hadn't lost all her confidence. And Lauren hadn't left town. Sadly, maybe she had nowhere else to go, and Sophie knew all about losing what you wanted twice over.

Absently petting Remi, she turned her gaze to the podium where Finn had taken the microphone. "Everybody, listen up. Gather in, we're about to announce the winner of this year's Citizen of the Year award. Thanks to you all for voting. We had a record turnout."

Finn made a big production of opening the envelope that contained the winner's name. He pretended to study the card, milking the moment while people in the crowd groaned, one man yelling for him to hurry up.

"Settle down, Earl. Patience."

Everyone laughed but Sophie stood at the foot of the bandstand, hands clenched at her waist. Lauren had moved even closer beside her, tilting her head to look up at the mayor. Sophie had to admit Lauren had been a strong campaigner. It wouldn't be a shock if she'd won.

As Finn cleared his throat and read the list of nominees, Sophie's fingernails dug into her palm. *I did want this so badly.* Maybe, unlike Lauren, she hadn't been the best candidate...

But if I don't win, does it really matter now? She'd changed her image, not for others but for Sophie, done everything she could to sway people while handling half a dozen committees, yet did she really need an award to feel she belonged in Barren?

If she didn't win, she'd still be head librarian, Max's sister, a friend to all the people she cared about and who loved her. Except for Gabe who was gone, not answering his phone.

Maybe he *had* left for good. Because she'd called him a liar.

What she should have done was not only trust him but let him know she loved him.

She was still lost in regret when Finn made the announcement.

"And the winner is—Sophie Crane! Come on up, Sophie." Finn held out a plaque that would soon have her name on it. Barren couldn't afford a plaque for each nominee, ready for whomever won. "The engraving will be done ASAP. You can hold onto this today."

Remi let out a sharp bark, but Sophie was barely aware of having moved. She climbed the few steps to the podium, walked across the stage, then clasped the plaque to her chest without feeling a thing. The way she'd felt ever since she'd confronted Gabe.

What was wrong with her? She should be ecstatic. She'd actually won just when she'd decided she didn't need to.

"Thank you, Finn. Thank you all, everyone here in Barren who voted for me. This is a dream come true, and I promise it will have a prominent place in my house. I've already got the right spot picked out."

"I'm sure you do." Lauren gazed at her for a moment from the foot of the bandstand, then strode off into the crowd. Sophie felt sorry for her. Lauren hadn't won the award, and she'd had a troubled past, but she didn't seem to have a bright future in Barren, either. After Gabe left, she'd scrapped the feature article on him, Sophie had heard. At best, she'd be stuck writing her Who's Who column for the *Journal* on someone else.

Sophie wouldn't be uncharitable, and she had no one to celebrate her victory with, but goodness, the plaque felt solid, real, in her hand. At least she had Rembrandt waiting patiently at the bottom of the steps.

As she turned to make her way down the stairs, Sophie gasped. A tall figure was suddenly there, blocking her way. Broad-shouldered, wearing a Stetson, a tan plaid shirt with pearl buttons, dark jeans and boots. Gabe. He swept her off her feet, swung her around, hesitated for a second as if unsure of his welcome, then kissed her soundly right in front of everyone. Men whistled, women clapped, kids hooted. Remi jumped up and down, tail wagging, body wriggling with happiness.

Sophie felt breathless. "Where did you come from?"

"Midland. My hometown." An arm around her waist, he walked her toward the carnival rides, which had started up again. All around them was chaos, the townspeople of Barren enjoying this sesquicentennial celebration that she'd helped to spearhead. "Sophie, I—"

"Gabe, I called. You didn't answer."

"I was tied up night and day with lawyers, the media, sick of phones. I finally turned mine off, and it was in flight mode today. I was on my way back. I wanted to talk to you in person. Can you forgive me?"

"I already have. I was wrong, Gabe. I should have trusted you."

She couldn't believe he was here, taking her hand, leading her and Remi around the corner of the nearby bleachers to a quieter spot.

Gabe good-naturedly told the dog to sit—which, to her further amazement, Remi did. Then he took Sophie in his arms. "Okay, Miss Barren Citizen of the Year, let me tell you everything. No more lies," he promised, nuzzling her neck before he pulled back, his gaze serious. "Do you understand? I had to go, for my father's sake. Things still aren't completely okay with us, but I believe he did at least propose to Jilly."

"They're getting married?"

"If he did what I suggested, yeah."

"I've been following the news," Sophie admitted. "Were you able to help his case with Brynne?"

Gabe told her about Rowena Bixby's email. "It's more that it helps him not to feel as awful as he did. The fines will still be big, and the cleanup ongoing, but there hasn't been as much environmental damage as was first thought—and the spill is slowing to a trickle. More or less. He did try, Sophie, to do something about that oil rig. He just trusted the wrong person. And should have followed through himself, not left that to Bixby. He'll bear that responsibility for the rest of his life." He shifted his stance, clearly intending to change the topic. "So, with the award in hand, you ready for tonight's banquet, some fireworks?"

For Sophie right now the rockets and starbursts were inside her.

She looked around at the crowds. People were having such a good time, and Sophie would be sad after all to see that end.

"The sesquicentennial's a success, isn't it? Thanks to our anonymous donor, we didn't have to eliminate a single event." She noticed the color that suddenly stained Gabe's cheeks. And, with a burst of insight, gaped at him. "The donor. I thought so. That was you, wasn't it?"

"If that's what you want to believe." But he was smiling. "My way," he admitted, "of being part of this town. Why not? Of course, I won't ever hold a candle to you."

Sophie doubted that, but she had another question. "Do you know who nominated me for the award?"

"Not a clue." Sophie didn't quite believe him, and for another second she wondered if he was fibbing. They couldn't base a relationship, though, on a lack of trust. Someday she'd find out about the nomination. For now, she wouldn't let it matter.

"Millionaire cowboy. What about your job as CEO? When your dad retires."

"I told you that wasn't a done deal, and he won't hand over the reins for a while anyway. First, there's all the court stuff to get through. Probably some company reorganization to prevent the same thing ever happening again. New maintenance and safety protocols. I've also suggested setting up a foundation for the families that were directly affected by the spill, plus a wildlife rehabilitation group, and he wants me as chairman—"

She didn't even bother to suppress the disappointment in her voice. "Which means you living in Texas?"

"No, attending a few meetings a year there. Probably lots of phone stuff." He took Sophie's face in his hands. "The important thing is, I love you, Sophie Crane," Gabe murmured, his mouth close to hers. "I love you so much it hurts—nearly killed me while I was gone—and I have the perfect solution. I want to marry you."

"But—"

"That was a proposal, but don't answer yet. First, here's what I'll do. I'm staying in Barren—my adopted hometown—and at Sweetheart for now. I'd like to buy land here, start a ranch before I find Kate a new foreman, then build a house…for you and me, the family we can have." His lips whispered over hers. "I missed the Fun Run yesterday, didn't I? And the rodeo today." He smiled. "I won't miss anything again."

Sophie's eyes filled with tears. "Are you sure? About us?"

"More than sure. Cowgirl, I've probably loved you since the second I laid eyes on you."

"Well," she said, "me, too." He was Sophie's impossible crush made real. It seemed a long while, not a few months, since she'd hidden her dreams of Gabe, never believing they might come true.

"Is that a fact?" She felt him smile against her mouth.

"No lie," she said. "I love you, Gabriel Morgan—" the biggest truth of all "—I mean, Wyatt." Then Sophie answered him, "Yes."

"Yes, what?" He drew back. For a second longer, he looked uncertain. Remi leaned against his leg, staring up at Gabe with adoration. Sophie felt much the same. She knew he would never lie to her again. She trusted him with her whole heart.

"I don't care if you're a hotshot CEO or a cowboy. I'll marry you."

"Ah, Soph," he said, then went back for another kiss. "The sooner the better."

EPILOGUE

The next spring...

THE HOUSEWARMING PARTY, or rather pre-party, was winding down. As the sun began to sink in the west, many of Gabe and Sophie's guests—most of the townspeople—had started to head for home. There were horses and pets to be fed, and children to bathe then tuck into bed. And on ranches the long days ended early for adults, too. Tomorrow there was work to be done as soon as that same sun crested the horizon again.

"Only the hardcore left now," Gabe said, meaning family members.

Sophie leaned her head against his shoulder. "I think everyone had a great time."

"Yep." He gazed at the fields where black Angus cattle grazed on lush, green grass. Last winter Gabe had bought a nice chunk of land from Kate along her western boundary. Like the herd he was building—she had helped him pick the right breeding stock—the fences were new, and Sophie had said the other day that she couldn't believe the ranch was theirs.

He couldn't believe how lucky he was to have her. And he was hers.

"Glad you married me, Mrs. Wyatt?"

Sophie nestled closer to fit perfectly against him. "Best decision ever." She held her hand in front of his face, the diamond on her ring finger sparkling in the late sun. The edge of Gabe's world at the horizon was turning a soft, rosy pink tinged with lavender. "My man even bought me a horse of my own."

He laughed. "If the house doesn't get finished soon, we can always bunk in the barn." Which was new as well. "You already spend half your time there fussing over that mare."

"Precious and I understand each other."

He and Sophie had also purchased the little chestnut, along with his roan horse, Critter, from Kate. The pair were a start, but Gabe needed to add more horses to their fledgling string of cow ponies.

With no need any longer to hide at Sweetheart, he did a lot of thinking, planning these days about the future with Sophie, not the past.

"Look," he said, pointing toward the tables where the last of the food was laid out. Sophie had produced a real feast and Gabe laughed again. Remi was sitting there, looking up, obviously hoping something good would magically fall his way. Gabe saw his father toss the dog a burger.

And smiled. "Just look at him—Dad, I mean. He's always been all about Brynne Energy. Now he's actually playing with a dog."

"About the company," Sophie began. "I've been wondering. Why is it Brynne?"

"He named it for my mother. Brynne Morgan Wyatt."

Sophie slipped her hand into his. "Oh, Gabe."

"Yeah. I don't think I fully appreciated what that meant until now." He hesitated. "He *really* loved her. She was the center of his life. Even at work."

"But so are you. He loves you too."

For a moment Gabe couldn't speak. Then he didn't have to as his dad and Jilly began to walk toward him and Sophie.

Uh-oh. What now? but he didn't say that aloud. He didn't need to. Still, Gabe never knew what to expect from his dad.

Finally, he said, "I'm glad he's happy again—with Jilly."

And to Gabe's relief the agreement had finally been reached about the fines for Brynne. Chet had come off well, considering, and he certainly looked more relaxed, a benign smile on his face and with Jilly's arm tucked through his. They'd been inseparable the whole time they'd spent with Gabe and Sophie.

"Here's my girl." Jilly hugged Sophie. "You did a magnificent job with this housewarming, sweetie. And you've been the best hostess letting us stay with you this week."

"We love having you."

"Well, maybe not one of us," his father said, shooting a look at Gabe without seeming at all perturbed.

Jilly took her arm. "Come, Sophie. Let's leave these men to talk. I could use another slice of that fabulous crème cake you made."

"I'm afraid the credit goes to Jack Hancock."

Arm in arm Jilly and Sophie left them, chatting as if they'd been best friends all their lives. Soon Max, unsmiling, walked over to join the two women at their table.

Sophie's brother had had a rough year. Last summer, when he and Averill McCafferty broke up, she'd moved back to Farrier, but eventually Max had convinced her they needed to try again. Then Averill had moved a second time to a town farther from Barren where she'd found a good counselor. A bigger commute for Max. The two had maintained an off-again, on-again relationship until last month. Gabe felt sorry for him.

"Glad you took my advice, Dad," he said to Chet. "Put a ring on that woman's finger."

"You think I was following your example?"

Gabe and Sophie had married last fall after Thanksgiving. They were still living in town at Sophie's house while theirs was being— too slowly—built, a sprawling house with all the modern amenities. The framing was now done, and from here he could make out the layout of the rooms. That progress had been enough to inspire this party, but during their visit his parents had slept in Sophie's modest guest room on Cattle Track Lane. Neither of them seemed to mind that it was much smaller than their house in Midland.

"Jilly and Soph get along great, don't they?"

"Thick as thieves." Chet cast a look around, as if to make sure they were alone. "Gabe, I've been meaning to talk to you before we go home tomorrow. Not because Jilly says I should. I know I've never been the best father and I'd like to—"

"Don't worry about it." His father had been humiliated by the disaster at Brynne, but with his support as well Gabe's new foundation was already helping the people who'd been harmed. And the company—again at Gabe's urging—had plans to increase its focus on renewables like wind and solar. Why quarrel now? Gabe had Sophie and the ranch he'd always wanted. He didn't need to see his dad humbled all over again.

"But I do worry," Chet insisted. Both men gazed at the sunset. "Took me a long time to see where you really belong. This is going to be a magnificent spread and that view from the new house...wow." He clapped a hand on Gabe's shoulder. "What I'm trying to say is, I'm glad you're happy here. Jilly and I plan to visit often."

"I hope you will."

"That is, when she has time. Jilly will be busier than I ever was." He saw Gabe's blank look. "She hasn't told you?" At the end of last year Chet had announced his pending retirement and Gabe had made it clear he wouldn't take over. "The search for my replacement has ended. At last. Jilly will be our new CEO."

Gabe was speechless. No, Jilly hadn't said a word. Maybe she'd wanted his father to tell him.

"Remember, she worked for me once, has

the same degree as yours, rose through the ranks until she was in line to become chief of operations instead of Gerald Bixby. If she hadn't quit to care for your mother then, maybe the spill would never have happened. That woman can organize anything, which she's ready to do at Brynne—in my old office, no less. I'm so proud of her I could burst."

"That's terrific, Dad." Jilly would be perfect in the job. "But how—"

"I looked everywhere for the right person to succeed me. All the time she was there in front of me." He paused. "I never should have pushed for you to head Brynne. From the time you were a boy doing chores on that ranch near Midland, this has been where your passion lies." He swept a hand to indicate the ranch. "I kind of like the idea of having a retreat here myself."

"You're welcome anytime."

"Gabe, during the Brynne debacle, I did want your support. Now I understand you gave as much as you could without making things worse for me. I've given your friend Aaron a nice raise, by the way, a new title. He's going to head the changes on that rig. Jilly's idea. See what I mean?" Chet cleared his throat. "But what I want you to know is, it wasn't simply your support I needed. Or some pipe dream about you taking over Brynne. I just needed *you*. My son."

They exchanged awkward, one-armed hugs. "I need you, too, Dad."

Gabe also understood better now. His father's absences had been his way of providing for Gabe's future. His withdrawal after Gabe's mother died was because, as Jilly had said, he couldn't manage his own grief. He'd never be a demonstrative father, but he was basically a good man. If he went off track, Jilly would set him on the path again.

Sophie had been right. Gabe had always yearned to have his dad's love, not just his approval, and he'd had that all along. Having cleared up their relationship, or at least made a good start, together in a companionable silence they watched the last of the sunset as that beautiful golden orb finally slipped below the horizon, the sky a glorious display of color. No words were necessary—until Sophie and Jilly crossed the yard again. At the table they'd just left Max was clearing plates and glasses, keeping himself busy. Sophie slipped into Gabe's arms, and Jilly did the same with Chet.

"When are you two going to make us grandparents?" his stepmother asked.

Gabe looked down at Sophie. They both grinned. "We're working on it."

* * * * *

Get 4 FREE REWARDS!

We'll send you 2 FREE Books plus <u>2 FREE Mystery Gifts</u>.

FREE Value Over **$20**

Both the **Harlequin® Special Edition** and **Harlequin® Heartwarming™** series feature compelling novels filled with stories of love and strength where the bonds of friendship, family and community unite.

YES! Please send me 2 FREE novels from the Harlequin Special Edition or Harlequin Heartwarming series and my 2 FREE gifts (gifts are worth about $10 retail). After receiving them, if I don't wish to receive any more books, I can return the shipping statement marked "cancel." If I don't cancel, I will receive 6 brand-new Harlequin Special Edition books every month and be billed just $4.99 each in the U.S or $5.74 each in Canada, a savings of at least 17% off the cover price or 4 brand-new Harlequin Heartwarming Larger-Print books every month and be billed just $5.74 each in the U.S. or $6.24 each in Canada, a savings of at least 21% off the cover price. It's quite a bargain! Shipping and handling is just 50¢ per book in the U.S. and $1.25 per book in Canada.* I understand that accepting the 2 free books and gifts places me under no obligation to buy anything. I can always return a shipment and cancel at any time. The free books and gifts are mine to keep no matter what I decide.

Choose one: ☐ **Harlequin Special Edition**
(235/335 HDN GNMP)

☐ **Harlequin Heartwarming Larger-Print**
(161/361 HDN GNPZ)

Name (please print)

Address   Apt. #

City   State/Province   Zip/Postal Code

Email: Please check this box ☐ if you would like to receive newsletters and promotional emails from Harlequin Enterprises ULC and its affiliates. You can unsubscribe anytime.

Mail to the **Harlequin Reader Service:**
IN U.S.A.: P.O. Box 1341, Buffalo, NY 14240-8531
IN CANADA: P.O. Box 603, Fort Erie, Ontario L2A 5X3

Want to try 2 free books from another series! Call 1-800-873-8635 or visit www.ReaderService.com.

HSEHW22

COMING NEXT MONTH FROM

(H) HARLEQUIN
HEARTWARMING

#431 WYOMING PROMISE
The Blackwells of Eagle Springs
by Anna J. Stewart

Horse trainer Corliss Blackwell needs a loan to save her grandmother's ranch. Firefighter Ryder Talbot can help. He's back in Wyoming with his young daughter and is shifting Corliss's focus from the Flying Spur to thoughts of a forever family—with him!

#432 A COWBOY IN AMISH COUNTRY
Amish Country Haven • by Patricia Johns

Wilder Westhouse needs a ranch hand—and Sue Schmidt is the best person for the job. The only problem? His ranch neighbors the farm of Sue's family—the Amish family she ran away from years ago.

#433 THE BULL RIDER'S SECRET SON
by Susan Breeden

When bull rider Cody Sayers attempts to surprise a young fan, the surprise is on him! The boy's mother is Cody's ex-wife. He still loves Becca Haring, but she has a secret that could tear them apart...or bring them together.

#434 WINNING THE VETERAN'S HEART
Veterans' Road • by Cheryl Harper

Peter Kim needs the best attorney in Florida for his nephew's case—that's Lauren Duncan, his college rival. But she's tired of the grind. He'll help show her work-life balance...and that old rivals can be so much more.

YOU CAN FIND MORE INFORMATION ON UPCOMING HARLEQUIN TITLES,
FREE EXCERPTS AND MORE AT HARLEQUIN.COM.

HWCNM0622

Visit ReaderService.com Today!

As a valued member of the Harlequin Reader Service, you'll find these benefits and more at ReaderService.com:

- Try 2 free books from any series
- Access risk-free special offers
- View your account history & manage payments
- Browse the latest Bonus Bucks catalog

Don't miss out!

If you want to stay up-to-date on the latest at the Harlequin Reader Service and enjoy more content, make sure you've signed up for our monthly News & Notes email newsletter. Sign up online at ReaderService.com or by calling Customer Service at 1-800-873-8635.